"I'm happy you could come to the party tonight."

"Thank you for inviting me."

He maneuvered a turn toward a quiet hallway. "I want to talk to you about a problem that's causing me a lot of trouble. I think you can help me. Seeing that I gave you a little leverage to advance at the studio, maybe you can do something for me."

Addy felt her face burn. What did he want? Surely he couldn't be going to make advances toward her, too. It would be so awkward, with him being Muriel's father-in-law, but she would fight him just as she had Mr. Abrams and John. "What is it?"

"The master ledger for the studio has been missing for a while." He tightened his grip on her. "I think you know where it is."

Silver Screen Heroes

Dangerous Times, Book One

by

Ilona Fridl

Silver Screen Heroes: Dangerous Times, Book One

Cover Art by *Rae Monet*

The Wild Rose Press
PO Box 706
Adams Basin, NY 14410-0706
Visit us at www.thewildrosepress.com

Publishing History
First Vintage Rose Edition, 2009
Print ISBN 1-60154-509-6

Published in the United States of America

Dedication

To my family:
Mom, my mate, Mark, Micki, Briana and Brian.
Also, to my Wednesday Afternoon Workshop,
especially Kathie.

Prologue: Part I

San Francisco, California
1906

Adeline Garcia didn't know what woke her from
a sound sleep. She heard movement in the room next
to hers and knew it must be her papa getting ready
to go to work, even though it was still dark outside
her window. He had to be downstairs early to let in
the food vendors who delivered to the restaurant.

She snuggled her face into her pillow. *Maybe*
he'll let me help in the kitchen later this morning,
when he's cooking. Her carefree days of childhood
would be over when she started school in the fall,
but she was looking forward to that. Mama had her
hands full with two-year-old Joey and didn't have
much time to play with her anymore.

Suddenly Addy heard a horrible rumbling noise
as a violent jolt brought her upright in bed. Her
mama screamed and her papa's anguished voice
called out, "Abigail!"

Before Addy could take another breath, the
whole building shook as if a giant were trying to pull
it from its foundation. She was thrown to the floor
and bounced around wildly as the planks bucked and
heaved beneath her. She screamed as one of her
bedroom walls disappeared and she clawed the floor
to keep from being jostled out of the building.
Somehow she managed to work her way to her bed
and hold on to one of its legs for dear life.

When the shaking finally stopped, there was a
loud groan from the walls. Addy's hands were still

1

clamped to the iron bed and she was panting hard and saying, "Help!" with every breath. In her fear, her bladder had released, and her nightclothes were soaked. She was shivering violently. Dust was everywhere as she stared into the street through the gaping maw where her bedroom wall with the window used to be. "Mama! Papa! Where are you? Help me!" she called out hoarsely, but there was only silence.

She lay there for what felt like forever, until the gray light of dawn streaked the sky. She heard things falling off the building. There were cries and moans from a distance. *Where are Mama and Papa? Didn't they hear me?* With the light, Addy rose from the floor and picked her way through the debris to the door of the small hallway that separated the two bedrooms, and the sight that met her as she opened it brought a gasp of dismay. The brick chimney that had run up the side of the building from the restaurant kitchen was now collapsed through the outer wall into the other bedroom, the room where her parents and Joey had slept.

Addy looked around desperately for her family. What she saw was a huge pile of bricks in and around Joey's crib, with blood flowing from beneath it. She found her papa's arm extended from beneath another pile of bricks and wall boards, his hand only inches from the twisted, motionless body of her mama. Addy crawled over to touch their hands. Both were ice cold. That was when Addy began to shake and scream hysterically.

She didn't know how long she sat there crying, her screams becoming sobs and eventually whimpers, but the hazy sun was creeping into the room through the open gaps of the building. It might have been several hours, since her nightclothes were nearly dry. *I've got to find someone to help my family. I can't do anything, but maybe someone older can help,* she realized, just before she smelled smoke in the air. *Fire!* She heard the sound of the fire bells and the pounding of horses' hoofs on the streets around the buildings. *Where is it?*

Intent on finding both help and the source of the smoke, Addy climbed over a large wooden beam to the door of the apartment and was able to open the door wide enough to squeeze through. Dim light helped her find the top of the stairs, where she grabbed the banister to go down and stopped herself just in time. The stairs had fallen into the hallway below. There was a gaping hole to the ground floor. The banister was still intact along the wall, though, so she sat on it and inched herself down. By the time she reached the bottom, thick smoke choked her.

As she ran out the door, her bare feet crunched on all manner of things, but she kept going in spite of the pain. In the street a policeman was directing dazed people along and Addy ran up to him. "Please, sir, my family is hurt. Can you help them?"

When he picked her up, the blood from her feet smeared his uniform. "You poor little thing! Where is your family?"

Addy pointed back to the building and let out a cry. Where her family had lived was engulfed in flames.

While she sobbed and hiccuped in his arms, the policeman quickly carried her away to a white truck with a red cross on its side. A woman in a nurse's uniform was helping the injured into the back, and he handed Addy to the woman, saying, "I think her family is dead—the place is in flames—and she's got badly cut feet."

The truck was full, but the nurse wrapped Addy in a blanket and put her on her lap for the ride to a hospital tent in one of the parks away from the fires. Addy was settled on one of the cots and the nurse gently tended to her feet. A harried doctor saw her a

3

while later and put alcohol on her wounds, which made her scream with pain, and then her feet were bandaged tightly.

Lapsing in and out of consciousness, Addy wasn't aware of time passing, except when the nurses came to give her soup. Every time there was an aftershock, she cried out.

It was raining hard when Addy finally awoke completely. She could hear the hard raindrops pelting the hospital tent as she ate some bread crust a nurse had salvaged for her. Addy was ravenous, but the nurse was telling her how scarce food had gotten in the four days since the big earthquake. Besides that, a heavy rain was making things even more miserable for everyone. Just then the doctor came in with two men, all looking soaked to the skin.

The doctor pointed at Addy. "Is this the girl?"

The man with dark hair and a well-trimmed mustache checked a picture he had in hand. "It looks like the child. Tell me, miss, are you Adeline Garcia?"

Addy nodded slowly, not knowing what to make of these men.

"I'm your Uncle Henry Carter, and this is your grandfather, Lorenzo Applegate, your mother's father. Do you know if the rest of your family is still alive?"

Addy felt a lump in her throat. "No, sir. They were in the apartment. It burned."

There were tears in the older man's eyes as he took her hand. "We're here to take you home with us."

A cold wind blew in through the tent flap, and Addy shivered. *What will become of me?*

Prologue: Part II

Evanston, Indiana
1919

"Zeke Shafer, what have you done?" His mother looked at him in horror. Zeke's father was out cold on the floor of the enclosed back porch, blood pouring from his nose.

"I couldn't take it anymore! I won't be hit again!" Zeke shook as adrenaline coursed through his body.

"Go up to your room. I'll take care of him."

"But, Mother..."

"Now, Zeke!" She grabbed a towel as his father moaned and started to come to.

Zeke nursed his aching hand as he charged upstairs. *I have to leave now. I wish he didn't make me do that.* He slammed the door to the bedroom with a bang. "That's it! I've had enough of him. I'm leaving and not coming back!" He grabbed a case from the wardrobe and threw it down on the bed.

His brother, Josh, looked at him in shock. "What happened this time?"

Zeke gingerly pulled his shirt out of his pants and showed Josh the angry red welt from the razor strop. "He's done that for the last time. Damn it! This time, when he hit me with the strop, I hit him back. I'm going to be twenty-one next month. I don't deserve to be treated like this. It's time I find my own way in the world."

Josh took a deep breath. "What about all your family and friends?"

"I'm going with Nathan Hayes to California to

find work in the motion pictures. We've been planning this for weeks now. Since Helen two-timed me, I have no reason to stay here. Because Father wouldn't let me join the army, everyone in Evanston has been calling me a coward for not going to war in '17. In a way, they were right. I was so conditioned to getting beat, I actually feared what he would do if I enlisted. I'm sick of it, and I'm sick of him."

Josh, on the chair by the window, quietly studied his hands. "Keep in touch with me. I'll miss you something terrible."

Zeke stopped packing for a moment and went over to put his hands on his brother's shoulders. "Josh, this will make you the oldest son. I advise you to get out as soon as you can. Until then, look out for our younger brothers and sisters. He'll take out his righteous wrath on them all. I'm leaving a note for Mother, so she won't worry." Zeke finished packing his case and headed for the window. He embraced his brother and felt the tears burn his eyes.

When Josh pulled back, he looked distressed. "Take care of yourself."

Zeke handed him the case. "Throw it to me when I get to the ground." He grabbed the large limb of the old oak tree that grew beside the house and shinnied to the yard. The dark shadows were a perfect cover for a fugitive. When Zeke looked up, Josh tossed him the case, and he waved to Josh as he hurried to the street. There was just time to make the journey to the train station where Nathan waited with two tickets to Los Angeles.

Finally, he was free of his father's grasp. Zeke had never felt so happy in his life. A new beginning!

Chapter 1

Hollywood, California
1920

Addy Garcia flinched as the wind-driven water blinded her. She clutched frantically at the small tree, trying to hold herself up against the wind that threatened to blow her over. Her hand slipped on the rough bark and she felt it skin her wrist, but she grasped a branch, regardless, and rubbed her eyes with her good hand. When she saw a dark figure coming toward her, Addy held out her free hand as if pleading with the phantom. Suddenly there was a bang and she jumped.

"Stop the camera! Damn it, girl, you ruined the shot. Turn off that water!" The last order was barked at the crew.

Addy had never felt so wet and miserable in her life. She slumped to the ground under the tree. "I'm sorry, Mr. Hanson, the noise startled me."

Mr. Dan Hanson, the director, stalked to Addy and cast a giant shadow over her in the suddenly cloudless sky. His sandy hair blew about in the breeze as he glared down. "You are Miss Steele's double, and I expect you to conduct yourself like an actress while the cameras are rolling. Do you understand? You are to ignore anything you hear from the other sets."

The motion picture photographer ran over and put his hand on Hanson's shoulder. "Sir, the film is still good. We can cut the last part out where the shot was fired."

"Swell. Tell Miss Steele we're ready for her."

One of the director's gofers hurried to the big spacious tent a few yards away. Hanson turned back to Addy. "Get out of the shot, girl, and mind your business or you will be fired."

"Yes, Mr. Hanson." But the man was already walking away. Addy's foot slipped in the mud and she fell, catching herself on her sore hand. Another of the gofers, Zeke, who had befriended her from the first day she started here, offered her his hand. "Thank you, Zeke," she said, smiling as he helped her up.

"You're welcome, mi'lady." The words were accompanied by a sweeping bow.

With a wafting of heavy perfume, Nora Steele walked past Addy, her perfect nose in the air. Nora looked at everyone with disdain. Her majesty wanted everything at her beck and call, and her entourage seemed like a gaggle of geese honking behind her. Her sable-colored hair, flowing like rich milk chocolate, was unfettered and she wore a brown print farm dress like Addy's. The perfect nose wrinkled as she glanced at Addy. "Do I have to look that bedraggled?" She sniffed.

Addy narrowed her eyes. *Would you like some help?*

"We will have to wet you down a bit for the shot, Miss Steele, but it won't take long." Mr. Hanson waited in his director's chair while the crew gently wet Nora's hair and clothes with water from a bucket. "Now turn on the fans and the rain, but not so hard this time." The crew started the hoses in front of the fans again, and the fair maiden was rescued from the storm by the handsome hero.

Addy sat shivering on a hay bale, still soaked to the skin. *I wanted so bad to be in the moving pictures, but now I don't know. Mr. Hanson doesn't even know my name, and I've been on this picture for*

8

a week. I've seen the pictures at the Bijou and dreamed to be the heroine on the silver screen, but.... She sighed as she gazed at John Payton, the movie's hero. *John's so handsome, but he's as snobbish as Nora. Maybe Uncle Henry is right, and I should give up this silly idea.*

The crew wrapped up the shot, and Hanson bellowed, "Get Miss Steele some warm towels—*now!*"

As Zeke passed by Addy with his arms full of towels and a bathrobe, he flipped a small towel to her. "Don't let Hanson see you," he mouthed as he slid by.

Addy ran to the crew tent and buried her face in the fresh warm towel. *Oh, that feels wonderful! Zeke seems to be the only one who'll give me the time of day. Not bad-looking, either.*

"Careful, girl. Don't sit on any of the chairs! You're dripping wet." The large woman in the stained white apron glared at her from behind the lunch counter.

Addy pretended not to hear and walked to the back of the tent, where she watched the western scene that had made her jump when the gun was fired. A group of outlaws robbed the fake bank on the outdoor set as the director shouted at them. She chuckled to herself. The motion picture was silent, but the process itself was very noisy. Several other sets were sending up a similar hubbub.

She climbed to the top rail on the fence to watch the filming. The steady breeze soon dried her clothes and hair, helped by the warm California sun, which felt so good on her skin. *I remember those cold damp days in San Francisco when I was a child.* Addy shuddered involuntarily at the thought of her hometown. *No, I don't want to think about that.*

"Addy, I need the towel back. They always count to make sure none were taken." Zeke climbed onto the rail fence beside her. "Oh, and they called a halt to the session again. Nora is in one of her tizzies."

"Too wet for her delicate constitution, right?" Addy laughed as she handed him the towel.

He added it to the stack of used towels on his lap. "We all know she's spoiled to the core. She has the director jumping at her heels like a puppydog. Say, do you need a way to get home? I go by the young ladies' dormitories."

"No, thank you. Muriel, my cousin, and I take the streetcar to the Beverly and Western stop. I live with my aunt and uncle. But thank you for your offer." Addy felt her cheeks warm in spite of herself. "I would like to get into one of the dormitories, though."

"Your cousin works here?"

"Yes, she's a clerk in the shipping department. She was the one who suggested I try for a job here. I was very active in our local theater and vaudeville, but it was a dream to be immortalized on film." Addy giggled. She looked into Zeke's boyish face and deep brown eyes. He seemed to be around her age. She flipped back her waist-length brown hair, now drying into long ringlets. "Would it be too forward to walk with you back to the crew quarters?"

Zeke grinned and his eyes crinkled at the corners. "I think we won't cause a scandal." Jumping off the fence, he offered her his hand, and she had no warning for the tingling that danced up her arm as she grasped it. She ignored the reaction as well as she could and slid from the fence, and they started the half-mile walk to the building the crew used, a large structure set away from the administration area and the star buildings.

"What's your full name, Addy? Mine is Ezekiel Shafer."

"Mine's Adeline Garcia." She paused and watched his eyes, waiting for a reaction to her name.

He didn't seem repulsed. "You're Mexican?"

"My father was. My mother was American."

"Was? Are you an orphan?"

Addy nodded. "I live with my mother's family."

"I'm sorry, I guess I shouldn't have brought that up."

She glanced at him. "That's all right. Where are you from?"

"Indiana. My family is still back there."

"I was born in San Francisco."

As they walked by the administration building, an expensive automobile pulled up to the entrance and several sinister-looking men in long dark coats with telltale bulges near the sleeves got out and headed for the entrance.

"That's Tony Giovanni!" Addy stopped in surprise.

Zeke gaped at her. "You know one of them?"

"He's courting Muriel. Why? Is there something wrong?"

He gritted his teeth. "Come on, keep walking. I heard the Giovannis ran a syndicate out east and are searching for a legitimate business for their front out here. I'd hate to think your family was mixed up with them. They're known for their ruthlessness."

"Tony's always been nice and polite when he's been to my uncle's house. He doesn't seem like a mobster." Addy's chest tightened with a sudden anxiety. *What is Muriel getting into? Tony doesn't act dangerous.*

Zeke shook his head. "Maybe I heard wrong."

As they continued toward the crew building, Addy pushed the fear into a far corner of her mind. *Tony would never do anything to hurt Muriel.* And she put aside the small pebble of doubt that still remained.

At the door, Zeke stopped and took her hand. "Got to go over to Laundry with these towels. I'll see you tomorrow?"

"Yes, I'll be here. I hope Nora comes out of her tizzy by then." They laughed together at that, and Zeke held her hand for a moment longer, as though he wanted to say something. Then he let it go and, with a wave, left Addy giddy and lightheaded as she went through the door.

****

Zeke pondered their conversation as he headed for the laundry. He hoped he hadn't reacted badly when she told him she was Mexican. He could picture his father preaching about "those soulless racial inferiors." Is that why he was drawn to her the first day he saw her? This would be another way to defy his father, at least in his own mind. He held no desire to see his father again.

As for Addy herself, he was afraid for her, if her cousin was getting involved with the Giovannis. He knew he hadn't heard wrong about them. There was no question that they were sent from out east to start a front in Los Angeles for their bootleg business. His roommate, Nathan Hayes, had overheard a conversation at the studio where he worked, a discussion about the financial problems at Majestic and how it was what the Giovannis were looking for. Now they were here.

He had wanted to ask Addy if he could visit her, but he wanted to sort out his feelings first. It would be better to sleep on it. He delivered the towels to the laundry, then headed to his auto.

****

In the women's area of the crew building, Addy changed into her street clothes. In the mirror, as she pinned up her thick curly hair, she evaluated. She didn't look completely Mexican, but she did have darker skin and almost black eyes. *Zeke didn't seem to mind that I'm part Mexican. He's better than some men I've known, who turn away when they find out my parentage.* Her mind drifted back to her cousin Muriel, who seemed to have found, in Tony, someone who truly admired her. *I wonder about his family. Maybe I should say something to Muriel.*

With a last pat to her already perfect hairdo, Addy picked up her satchel and walked the three blocks to the structure that housed the shipping department. Boxes and barrels littered the building on the outside, and she wound her way between them to the big double doors. Her nose wrinkled at the strong smell of packing straw, excelsior and wood as she carefully stepped to the office area. She waved at Muriel, then sat down to wait on a wooden chair off to the side of the busy warehouse. Muriel's head bowed again over her shipping labels, her fingers carefully typing them on her Underwood.

Muriel, with lighter brown hair than Addy and a couple of inches more height, was considered the prettier of the two by most people. Addy remembered comments about herself like, "She's a dusky little thing," by well-meaning people such as the family of the boy she'd loved in school. They'd put a stop to that romance. She couldn't shake the stigma of looking Mexican. But Muriel had another beau besides Tony vying for her attention. So, at eighteen Muriel would probably be married first. Addy, according to her uncle, was too plain to attract a man.

Muriel broke into her reverie, leaning on a crate nearby. "Hi, Addy, are you ready to go? Mr. Hanson seems to have finished early."

"Nora was showing her temper again, so he closed the set for the day." Addy rose from her chair and winced as her wrist brushed against her rough wool suit.

"Honey, you're hurt!"

"Just a skinned wrist. I washed it off. Let's go." The girls headed out the big double doors toward the entrance of the studio. "Muriel, you know a few of the girls that live in the ladies' dormitories, don't you?"

"Yes, some of them that work in shipping do. Why?"

"I've been thinking I'd like to move there. Your father makes me feel like I'm a burden to him. Ask around, will you?"

"I hate to think about you moving out, but I do understand about Father. I'll see what I can find out."

Addy wondered if she should mention what she'd heard about Tony's family, but she dismissed it for now. It wasn't a subject to discuss with other people around, after all.

They waited for the streetcar and paid their tokens when it picked them up. As they rode the seven miles to their stop, Addy watched out the window. Automobiles lined most of the route, but here and there were horse-drawn farm wagons bringing in produce from the outskirts of the city. Workers busily harvested oranges in the few groves that were left within the city limits. Addy remembered when there were many farms along the way; now blocks of businesses and homes had sprung up where food was raised earlier. Los Angeles was stretching and growing.

When they reached their stop, they had a short walk down a palm-tree-lined street in a quiet neighborhood. Most of the houses were only twenty years old or so. There were a few steps up to a green lawn where Addy and Muriel had played when they were children. Their pretty white two-story house had a large brick porch in front, with a terracotta urn, filled with ivy that flowed down like lace, on each of the brick shelves on either side of the steps up to the house. The dark wood front door held an etched glass oval that showed a distorted view of the hallway inside.

Muriel reached the door first, and as she opened it the warm cinnamon smell of baking wafted out. "Mother, Addy and I are home," she called from the hallway.

"Go up and get dressed for dinner," Aunt Jen's voice came from the kitchen. "Your father will be home soon."

Addy and Muriel tiredly pulled themselves up the staircase to the large second-floor hallway, off which opened the four bedrooms for the children. Uncle Henry and Aunt Jen had their room on the ground floor. Muriel and Addy shared a bedroom in the back southern corner, overlooking the yard with the fruit trees and the small apartment where Grandpa and Grandma lived.

Muriel used the bathroom first, and then Addy went in to freshen up while Muriel changed for dinner. Muriel was already downstairs by the time Addy came back into the bedroom to put on a clean cotton dress. As she brushed her hair, she gazed out the window next to the vanity. It was nearly dark, that November day, but she could see the shadows of the fruit trees in the yard and the old plum tree with its low forking trunk. It was the perfect tree to climb on a warm summer day when the plums were ripe. She remembered how it was when she and Muriel were children, after she came to live with them. They used to climb that tree and pick the black fruit near the bottom of the branches. The sweet liquid would run down their chins and arms and stain their clothes.

She glanced at the alarm clock and gasped. It was five after six! She bound up her hair quickly and rushed down the steps and into the big dining room where everyone, including her grandparents, already sat around the table. Uncle Henry, who ruled his house in the Victorian manner, glared at her. He was impeccably dressed in his black business suit, his hair freshly combed and oiled. And now his hazel eyes sparked under his dark eyebrows. "Adeline Rose, you're late for supper. Sit down so we can eat. Just for that, you will do the dinner dishes tonight. Is that understood?"

"I'm sorry, Uncle Henry." Addy pulled back her chair and sat down. *My goodness, I'm being treated like a child again.* Muriel's three brothers tried to hide their glee by looking at their plates, and the baby of five years giggled.

"Maggie, hush." Aunt Jen glanced sharply at the little girl.

Uncle Henry looked stern. "You'd think a girl of your age would work harder trying to find a husband instead of these frivolous theatrical pursuits. I haven't said much, because you were making money for yourself, but you're twenty now and should be married."

Addy picked at the food on her plate. "Yes, Uncle Henry." *Hold the temper.*

He turned his attention to Muriel. "That goes for you, too. Don't follow Adeline's example."

Muriel looked at him. "Father, I have two beaus to decide between."

"Two? You will choose Thomas Martin over that Anthony Giovanni. I will not have you marrying a foreigner, like Adeline's mother did."

Aunt Jen looked up. "Henry, Mr. Garcia was from one of California's oldest families."

"Yes, while it was still a foreign country. Remember, California was still part of Mexico when the Garcias arrived here. I will not have an argument from you at the dinner table, Jenette." Everyone was quiet for the rest of the meal.

Addy glanced at her grandparents, who hadn't said anything. They were Aunt Jen's parents, and Uncle Henry let them stay in the apartment. Her grandpa gave her a smile and a wink.

After they were excused from the table, Addy took the dinner dishes into the kitchen. She was scraping the leftovers into the garbage can outside the back door when Grandpa came out, on his way to the apartment, and put his arm around her shoulders. "Don't let your uncle intimidate you."

"Thank you, Grandpa." She smiled at him, and he went on to his own door while she took the dishes back inside and started the water running in the sink. As she washed the dishes, she let her thoughts go.

I must get out of this house. Uncle Henry is like a ruling sheik. Grandpa can't say anything, because he's Aunt Jen's father. Uncle Henry seems to think I can't find a young man because of the attitude in this city against Mexicans.

Her thoughts turned to Zeke. *He's nice to me, but does he just want to be friends? The boy I wanted to marry broke it off because his family thought I was too dark-skinned.* Addy sighed, then finished up the last of the dishes and headed for her room.

Pausing by the parlor door, she looked in. Uncle Henry was reading the *Times* and Aunt Jen was tatting. "Uncle Henry, I've finished the dishes and I'm going upstairs now."

"I hope, Adeline, you've learned the importance of being on time," he said, looking up from his newspaper.

"Yes, Uncle, I have."

"Good. You may go."

Addy went up the stairs and stopped at the french doors to the balcony. The half-moon glowed in the night sky. She quietly opened the door and felt the sweet night breeze ripple through her hair. There were low voices below her and she couldn't make out what they were saying, but one sounded like Muriel. She backed inside and closed the door.

Maggie was in bed and the boys were playing Parcheesi in their room as Addy went into her bedroom and closed the door. She pushed the white button and the electric light winked on. She had just finished getting ready for bed when Muriel came in, dancing the length of the room in her excitement.

"Addy, I've got something to tell you," she said, finally perched on the foot of Addy's bed.

"What is it?"

"You have to promise you won't tell Father." She grabbed both of Addy's hands.

"Okay, I promise. What is it?"

"I'm going to elope with Tony next week." Muriel's eyes sparkled with excitement.

"Muriel, what a crazy thing to do!" *Should I tell her what Zeke said?*

"I asked to go outside for a while after dinner, and Tony met me in the backyard. We've been planning this for a week now."

The terror she felt for Muriel welled up inside of her. "Are you sure Tony is right for you? What do you know of his background?"

"I know his family owns many businesses, and they moved out here a year ago to tap into the California market. They have plenty of money, so we won't have to scrape to begin with, like so many do."

Addy bit her lower lip. "Dear, I've heard some things about his family that worry me. I've heard the Giovannis are caught up in the syndicate. I'm afraid for you."

Muriel's eyes grew wide. "Who's been spreading those lies? I'm sure they're on the up and up."

"It doesn't matter. If it's true, you could be in danger. I have to agree with your father."

The tears started to flow. "I love him! You've met Tony—he's always been a gentleman."

Addy unclasped her hands and gripped Muriel by the shoulders. "Promise me you'll reconsider."

"Addy, I know Tony would never hurt me. He's not like that."

Addy was shaken. "You know I'll have to tell if Uncle asks me where you are."

"Don't worry. The night it happens, I'm leaving him a note. I won't tell him you knew about it."

A hundred emotions went through Addy at once, including fear of what Uncle Henry would do. Would he blame her for this? After all, she did know about the elopement, now. She worried too about what kind of family Muriel would be marrying into. And she felt some sadness for herself, because her cousin, who was as close as a sister, was leaving. That pebble in her gut was turning into a stone.

"Addy, he is so good to me. We're going to be very, very happy." They hugged, but Addy remained scared for her cousin.

Addy broke off and looked Muriel in the eye. "Don't tell me which day you will leave, because I don't want to know. Just remember, I love you as a sister. If you ever need me, I'll be there."

"I'll keep in touch with you, I promise."

****

The next day at the studio, in between her stand-in takes for Nora Steele, Addy was distracted by her fear of Muriel's coming elopement. Even Mr. Hanson's temper tantrums didn't bother her.

At lunch, she had seated herself alone at one of the tables in the tent when Zeke brought his lunch tray over. "May I sit here with you?"

Addy was startled out of her reverie and didn't answer for a moment. "Uh...yes, you may."

"Is something wrong?" He sat down on the folding chair.

She looked into his honest brown eyes and wanted to tell him everything. "Just a problem at home. Nothing to be concerned about."

"Addy, are you seeing anyone?" The question

seemed to have dropped out of nowhere.

She drew a breath and held it for a moment. "No, I'm not." she said, her eyes on his fingers as they fidgeted with his pocket watch chain.

"May I come to visit you?"

She looked back up to find his intent gaze on her. Maybe she would have a chance with Zeke, if he didn't have family who would judge her. "Do you live with your family?"

"No, I share an apartment with my friend, Nathan. We came here to Hollywood together to work. But you didn't answer my question." His eyes held hers.

She smiled. "I'll talk to Uncle Henry, and I'll let you know."

On the way home that evening, Addy told Muriel about Zeke. "He wants to come over to visit me. I hope Uncle Henry says yes."

"Just don't tell Father he's a gofer. Call him an assistant to the director. That sounds better."

"I like Zeke, and he doesn't live with his family here. Maybe I can have a beau who'll like me for myself."

"I hope you find someone like my Tony. Maybe someday we can live next door to each other, just like we planned when we were small."

Addy's fears about Tony's family surfaced again and she only half-heard Muriel's happy chatter.

At dinner that evening, Addy looked up from her plate. "Uncle Henry, may I ask you something?"

He glanced suspiciously at her. "Yes, Adeline, what is it?"

She took a deep breath. "There's a man at work, Zeke Shafer, who would like to come visit me. May I have him over sometime?"

He looked steadily at Addy. "Does the boy seem of good character?"

"Yes, he's very nice and polite."

"What does he do at the studio?"

"He's a g-, an assistant to the director," she stumbled, and Muriel hid a smile behind her hand.

Uncle Henry turned to Aunt Jen. "Shall we invite him to dinner Saturday?"

Her aunt smiled at her. "I think we can manage that."

"All right, Adeline. Tell him to be here no later than five-thirty."

Addy whooped on the inside. "Yes, sir. Thank you, Uncle." She exchanged a grin with Muriel.

****

Saturday at five, Addy had finished buttoning her dark pink dinner dress with the white lace trim. Muriel was helping to pin up her hair.

"Addy, this color really brings out the rich brown of your eyes." She was silent for a moment. "Oh, I almost forgot. A room has come available at one of the dormitories today. You'd better be quick or it will be gone."

Addy's smile brightened. "Thank you for telling me. I'll ask Uncle about it tomorrow." She bit her lower lip as the last pins were put in place in her hair. *Am I pushing my luck too far with Uncle? Here I'm starting to court, then asking to move to the dormitory. But I can't help the timing. I have to take the chance.*

With butterflies playing tag in Addy's stomach, the girls hurried down the stairs just as Zeke's Model T pulled into their driveway.

Addy waited inside for him to walk up the steps to the porch. At the sound of the two-tone chime of the doorbell she opened the door. *My goodness, he looks handsome.* He was dressed in a suit, with a clean starched collar on his shirt and a conservative necktie neatly fastened with a tiepin. He swept off his hat and bowed to her.

She stifled a giggle. "Zeke, come in. You look

wonderful."

"You look swell, Addy. That dress is a pretty pink. I never saw you in a fancy dress before."

She felt her cheeks warm. "Come in and meet my family." She took his hand and walked him into the parlor where everyone was gathered. "Zeke, this is my Uncle Henry and Aunt Jen Carter. These are my grandparents on my mother's and Aunt Jen's side, Lorenzo and Sarah Applegate. And these are my cousins, Muriel, James, Casey, Buster, and Maggie. Everyone, this is Ezekiel Shafer."

Uncle Henry stood, came over to Zeke, and shook his hand. "I understand you want to start seeing Adeline. She is my ward, and I treat her like my own. I expect you to treat her like a lady. Is that understood?"

Zeke stood straight, his hat in one hand. "Yes, sir."

"Good. Let's go in to supper. Adeline, see to Mr. Shafer's hat and coat."

"Yes, Uncle Henry." She put them in the wardrobe at the other side of the hall, then turned to Zeke, who smiled and offered her his arm. In the dining room, Zeke held Addy's chair for her, then sat down himself.

When everyone had taken a serving, Uncle Henry looked at Zeke. "Do you live with your family, Mr. Shafer?"

Zeke glanced up from his plate. "No, I don't, sir. I share an apartment with a friend of mine. He works in motion pictures, too."

"Where are you from?"

"Evanston, Indiana. My father is a preacher there."

"Why did you leave your family?"

"My father was pressing me to be a preacher, too, but I didn't have the calling. We had several arguments about it, so I moved here. I'd heard the studios needed workers."

"Do you make good money?" Uncle Henry gazed steadily at him.

"I make enough to live comfortably on, sir."

That seemed to satisfy her uncle for the moment. *Maybe I'll have a chance with this young man.*

After dinner, Addy asked her uncle if she and Zeke could talk outside on the porch swing. "You can see us from the front window."

"All right, Adeline, but be sure to stay there where I can see you."

Zeke put on his coat and Addy slipped on her sweater, for the November evening was getting chilly. They sat on the swing together and she heard the familiar squeak of the wicker and the springs as it swayed from the ceiling. Uncle Henry switched on the outside light, as she had known he would.

Zeke turned to her and smiled. "You have quite a family in there."

Addy giggled. "Yes, I have. Uncle Henry is old-fashioned and strict, but he was very generous to take me in."

"What happened to your family, Addy?"

"I don't really like to talk about that." He took her hand, and she gripped it tightly. Through the dark cloud that had descended over her mind, she heard herself saying, "They all died."

There was deep compassion in his eyes. "How did it happen?"

Addy squeezed Zeke's hand as tears ran down her cheeks. "We lived in San Francisco. The earthquake... in 1906... the building we lived in collapsed. My family... all... were killed."

Zeke put one arm around her as he handed her his handkerchief with his other hand. "Oh, Addy, I'm so sorry. Here, take this." His arm felt good, and she gratefully dried her face.

Suddenly the front door opened. "Adeline!" Uncle Henry said sharply.

"It's all right, Mr. Carter. I just asked Addy what happened to her parents, and I was comforting her." Zeke withdrew his arm.

Uncle Henry said, "Harrumph," and went back inside.

"I'm truly sorry, I didn't mean to upset you. I won't ask you anything else."

"It's hard to talk about that day without all those memories flooding back. It was so horrible. Tell me why you decided to leave Indiana."

" My friend, Nathan, convinced me to come with him to Hollywood and work in the motion pictures. I thought it meant being up on the screen. I guess I don't have that appeal."

Addy smiled. "I thought you were handsome when I first saw you."

Zeke turned serious. "I thought you were pretty from the start, too."

Addy felt genuine surprise. "Me? Uncle Henry says I look too Mexican to be pretty."

"You're just enough of both of your parents to be very attractive. I love the way your hair is thick and curly and your eyes are so dark brown they're almost black." She watched his face grow more intense. His fingers interlaced with hers.

Addy felt giddy and would have melted into his arms if she'd dared. *The boy from school made me feel that way, too. Oh, Zeke, if I fall in love with you, please don't leave me like he did.* She thought of the audience on the other side of the glass. "Zeke, I think we'd better go back inside."

As though coming out of a trance, he took a deep breath. "Yes, and I really should be going." They went indoors, where Zeke thanked the Carters for dinner and said goodbye. Addy retrieved his hat for him and then walked with him to his auto.

"Goodnight, Zeke. Thank you for coming to dinner. I like being with you."

He planted a chaste kiss on her cheek that left her tingling all over. "Good night, my Mexican Rose." Zeke held both of her hands tightly, and a warmth flowed through her until he let go and caressed her cheek. Then he went to the front of his Model T and gave the crank a few turns. As the engine exploded to life he stepped away and slid behind the steering wheel, where he jostled the shift into reverse and backed down the driveway. Addy waved in reply to the asthmatic horn he sounded as he drove off down the street.

"I'm going to visit Grandpa and Grandma," Addy called out to the pair of ears she knew was there. She walked on air to the backyard and saw the lights were still on in the apartment, just as she'd hoped. Dancing up the steps, she rapped on the door.

Her grandmother opened it, still holding in one hand the doily she was crocheting. "Why, Adeline, come in, child."

Her grandfather was at the table with his new crystal radio set. With the earphones on his head, he didn't notice Addy. "Dad-blamed thing doesn't work right. I don't know why I bother with these damned new-fangled contraptions." He turned to say more to his wife and saw his granddaughter. "Adeline, excuse me. I didn't hear you come in."

Addy stood there, her hand over her mouth, covering a smile. "That's all right, Grandpa. Maybe you can get James to help you. He's interested in anything electric."

"I'm seventy-seven years old. You'd think things would be getting easier to understand instead of more confounding." He grinned at Addy. "Sit down, Adeline. I know you didn't come in to hear me cuss at radios."

She sat across from him at the table and smelled

the warm mingled scent of Bay Rum cologne and pipe tobacco that was so much her grandpa. "Something has been bothering me for a while. Could I ask you a question about my parents?"

Grandpa exchanged a glance with Grandma on the couch. He looked back at Addy. "What's the question?"

She studied her hands. "Uncle Henry keeps talking about how bad it is to marry a foreigner. What happened when Mother married my father? I need to know."

Her grandfather picked up his pipe and started cleaning it. "Adeline, you have to remember it was a different time then, although these prejudices are still with us. No, I didn't give the marriage my blessing. You've never seen your father's side of the family because they disowned him for marrying a gringo. The Garcias are a family that has lived in California since the late 1700s and still consider the Americans invaders. There has been hatred on both sides. That's the reason your parents moved to San Francisco. We never saw you until you were six."

"How did you know to find me after the earthquake?"

He lit his pipe and leaned back in his chair. "Your mother wrote us letters about you and your brother, and sent pictures, but we were too hurt by the elopement to come and see you. We couldn't forgive either of them. When we heard about the disaster, it was too late. Uncle Henry and I traveled up there to see if any of you had survived. We went to the address of your apartment, and the building was ashes after the fire. The rosters of the dead were far from complete, so we went to the police to find out where the survivors were. Henry carried a family portrait your mother had sent the Christmas before. We finally found you in one of the camps that had a section for orphans. You'd told the police that the rest of your family was dead."

Addy nodded. "I remember that."

"We raised you for our daughter. I couldn't see a child being rejected because of a family split like that."

"Did the Garcia family ever try to find me?"

"No. We've never seen nor heard from them."

Grandma came over and put her arms around Addy. "We love you, Adeline. We're so sorry we couldn't see how terrible we were being to your family before that disaster happened."

Is it going to be the same for Muriel? Should I tell Uncle Henry what she's planning to do? "Thank you both. I needed to know. But I should go in now."

Grandma smiled and held Addy by the shoulders. "We like your young man. This should prove to Henry that you are not plain. I always thought you were lovely."

They exchanged their goodnights and Addy went back to the house. When she entered the parlor, Aunt Jen was the only one there. "Aunt Jen, I'm going up to bed now."

"Goodnight, Addy." Aunt Jen lifted her eyes from her knitting and smiled. "See you in the morning."

Muriel was already in bed when Addy came into their bedroom.

I wish she was still awake. I'd really like to talk to her. What Zeke said about Tony's family is still bothering me, and I just know I need to try to convince Muriel not to elope. I guess we'll have to talk tomorrow.

She changed into her nightclothes, pulled the covers down, and snuggled into the bed, switching her thoughts completely to Zeke. She felt so close to him already.

****

Nathan jumped up from the couch as Zeke came

into their apartment. His friend seemed always to be a perpetual motion machine.

"Zeke, are you sure you saw the Giovannis at Majestic yesterday?"

"Yes, Addy recognized Tony. Why?"

Nathan paced around the room, combing his fingers through his auburn hair, while Zeke relaxed into the armchair. "The latest gossip with the workers at our studio is that the Giovannis are now in as silent partners at Majestic. I think you should get out of there and find a new job. And a new girl, if Addy's family is mixed up with them."

Zeke bristled. "It's not her fault if her cousin is seeing Tony Giovanni. I like Addy a lot. I won't stand by and see her get into danger."

"Okay, okay! But you should lie low and get out at the first sign of trouble. And tell Addy to do the same." Nathan's green eyes registered his concern.

"Yes, but wouldn't they want any illegal activity to remain quiet? So why stir up the workers? I think if we just keep working, they'll leave us alone." Zeke stood up and stretched. "I'm ready to turn in. Don't worry, Nathan, I can take care of myself."

Despite his brave words to Nathan, Zeke's inner voice nagged him as he got between the sheets.

Can I just go on working like nothing's happened? I have a feeling things might turn out for the worst. And Addy... I haven't known her long, but I can't leave her out for the wolves. I want to protect her. She's been through a lot in her life.

Just the thought of her aroused him. *Is that love I feel, or lust? All I know is, she's always in my thoughts.* He slowly drifted off to sleep, to dream of Addy.

Chapter 2

"Adeline! Is Muriel in there?"

Addy was stunned from a sound sleep by her uncle's angry voice on the other side of the bedroom door. As she struggled to get her mind clear; she heard the door open with a bang, and she sat up, holding the covers in front of her. Uncle Henry stormed in, with Aunt Jen right behind him. "She's not here," he said to Aunt Jen, who turned pale and started to cry. "Adeline, what do you know about this?" He thrust a paper into her hand.

Addy looked at the note:

Dear Father,

When you read this, I will be far away, getting married to Tony Giovanni. I'm sorry you feel the way you do about his family, but I love him very much. Tell everyone I will pray for them every day. I hope that someday you will find it in your heart to forgive me. No one knows what I am going to do, so there is no one to blame but me.

Muriel

Addy did some quick thinking. "Uncle Henry, I didn't know she was planning to run away last night." That was the only truth she could tell him, and she hoped he wouldn't question her further. *Oh, Muriel, why did you have to do this now?*

Her uncle looked at her like he didn't believe her, but he didn't say anything more. "Come on, Jen. We'll figure out some way to find her." He put his arm around her aunt, guiding her out of the bedroom and closing the door behind them. It was the first time Addy had ever seen any real evidence of compassion from her uncle.

She glanced at the alarm clock; there was still a half hour before it would go off, but she reached over and pushed the lever to the off position. *I won't get back to sleep now.*

When Addy went to the wardrobe, she found that all Muriel's clothes were gone. Muriel had been already in bed when Addy got to their bedroom the evening before, so she must have packed while Addy was with Zeke. Moving to Muriel's unmade bed, Addy started to straighten it up. *I'm going to miss her so much.* Suddenly the tears flowed, and she sat in the middle of Muriel's bed and hugged the pillow while she mourned her missing cousin.

The family went to church as usual that morning, but they didn't stay for the fellowship after service like they usually did. It was a quiet ride home in Uncle Henry's Packard. When they sat down to Sunday dinner, even the boys were subdued.

Sixteen-year-old James glanced up. "Father, is there anything you can do to get Muriel back?"

Uncle Henry looked sadly at his son. "I don't know if there's anything we can do legally, since she is eighteen. I will hire a detective to find out where she is. I don't want to deal with those Giovannis. I've heard rumors about them that I pray aren't true. Working around the newspaper editors, I know they have information they can't print because they have no proof."

A shadow passed over Aunt Jen's face. "What have you heard?"

"They might be mixed up in the syndicate."

"Do you think Muriel could be in danger?"

He gritted his teeth. "That's what I want to find out."

That evening, everyone was in the parlor. James was tinkering with a radio, the children were playing a picture lotto game, and Uncle Henry was reading, while Aunt Jen and Addy did needlework. Addy took a deep breath. *I have to say something or I'll lose my chance to go to the dormitory.* "Uncle Henry, Aunt Jen, I hate to bring this up now, but I think it's time I move out. I've been thinking about this for a week or so, and I want to move into the young ladies' dormitory near the studio. A room has just become available, and I must apply quickly if I'm going to be able to get it. They have housemothers who look after the girls in their sections and see that they live by strict rules. I promise I will take care of myself."

Uncle Henry surprised her by not getting angry. "I'd like to see the place for myself, but I do agree you are old enough to be on your own. Will you arrange an appointment for us?"

She hid her excitement. "Yes, of course, I will."

Aunt Jen put her hand on his. "Do you think that's wise?"

He pursed his lips. "Don't question me. Adeline is twenty and too old to be under care. Our commitment to her is over. That's all I'm going to say."

Later, Aunt Jen took Addy aside. "Do you really think you should be on your own?"

"Oh, Aunt Jen, many girls my age are on their own now. This is the twentieth century, after all. Women have the vote and can own property. Anyway, I think Uncle Henry looks at me as an obligation and not as a member of his family."

Aunt Jen held Addy in her arms. "Oh, Addy, we feel about you as we do Muriel. Remember, it was your uncle who went with your grandfather to find you in San Francisco." She caressed Addy's cheek. "I know your parents would be very proud of how you turned out. My dear sister loved you very much."

"Thank you, Auntie. I'm glad you took me in, even if Uncle is very hard to live with." They both smiled, as though at a shared secret. "And I won't be that far away. I'll visit as much as I can."

Suddenly, Aunt Jen broke down. "I need to know I won't lose both you and Muriel. I don't see how we'll get Muriel back."

"I'm sad about Muriel, too, but don't let what happened to my family happen to yours," Addy warned, thinking of how her parents had been outside the family circle because of their marriage.

The next day, on her way to work, Addy made an appointment to see the dormitory the following evening. It took longer than she had expected. She hurried with her costume, took down her hair, and ran out to the set, where they were already filming.

Mr. Hanson was furious. He waved his megaphone at her. "Girl, you're late! Get in this wagon. We're going to bolt the horses and you need to drive them."

Addy felt faint. "But, Mr. Hanson, I..." *Careful, saying you never handled horses before could get you fired.* "Yes, Mr. Hanson. Could you have someone give me a boost up into the wagon?" She almost fell into Zeke's arms when he was waved over. "What do I do?" she said under her breath. "I never drove horses before."

Zeke looked concerned. "Hold the reins, then pull back on them when you're out of camera range."

Addy was sweating, despite the chill of the morning. Steam seemed to be rising from the horses as they stood hitched to the buckboard. At a waving signal from Mr. Hanson, the two wranglers holding the horses slapped the rumps of the nervous animals—hard. The steeds took off with Addy in the wagon hanging on for dear life. The wheels jumped over rocks and ruts until she thought her insides were going to be thrown out, at least. After she went over the rise, she pulled back hard on the reins, and the two beasts reared, then kicked the wagon with their back hooves, and Addy flew out onto the hard ground.

A shadow stood over her by the time she had cleared her head and checked to see if anything was broken. "Thanks to you, we almost lost that wagon! Now get back over to the crew, because we have to film the rescue scene." Addy had landed on her left side, and her elbow, hip and knee were bruised and scratched. A scrape on the side of her leg was bleeding slightly.

Zeke came running down the rise. "Addy, are you all right?"

She took the hand he held out to help her up, wincing a little as she put weight on her left leg.

Mr. Hanson glared at Zeke. "Boy, help Miss Steele!"

The pampered princess, Nora, was driven to the wagon in an automobile. She had an entourage with her: the wranglers held the horses, the handsome hero was on his mount near the wagon, and one helper had already boosted her into the seat.

Zeke set his jaw. "Miss Steele has plenty of help. Now, I'm going to walk Miss Garcia back to the crew station to make sure she's all right."

Mr. Hanson looked at him with a shocked expression, then turned on his heel toward the wagon.

Zeke looked at Addy. "Can you walk?"

"I'm a little battered and bruised, but I can make it." *I have a handsome hero all my own.* Zeke put his arm around her, and they went slowly and carefully over the rise. His closeness was raising havoc with her feelings. She was tingling all over, and her quickened breath wasn't all from the fall she had taken.

As they were going to the tent, Zeke said with a laugh, "I know I'm going to get the 'Miss Steele is important to this studio' lecture from Mr. Hanson, but everyone kowtows to her every wish. They can replace us, but not her. She brings in money, but I won't let him treat you like you don't matter."

"I hope we don't lose our jobs. I need the money right now. I'm moving into the ladies' dormitory." She fingered a rip in the skirt. "And I hope they don't expect me to pay for the costume." Addy sat on a folding chair in the tent while Zeke poured some water into a basin and picked up soap and a towel. She continued, "I was thinking it was time for me to move out from under Uncle Henry's thumb, even before Muriel eloped the other night."

"And did he agree to let you move?" Zeke's delighted expression, as he retrieved the first aid kit from a cabinet, had Addy's heart double-timing all over again.

"Since I'm twenty, I don't think he feels obligated to house me anymore. He's been grumbling ever since I was sixteen that I'll be a spinster."

Zeke set all the items down at her feet and grabbed her hand. "Spinsters don't look like you. I think you're beautiful." She felt her cheeks burn. "And you blush prettily, too." They both laughed.

He washed her scrapes and put salve on them. She was very aware of the heat of those hands. When he had finished, she put her fingers lightly on his shoulder and they looked at each other, unspoken words flying between them. Their silent communication forged a bond of understanding before Addy glanced away. "Thank you."

Zeke grinned. "Anything for my Mexican Rose."

****

The next evening, Addy, Uncle Henry and Aunt Jen showed up at Dormitory Number Three. It was a large plain clapboard building. A woman came to the door and welcomed them, introducing herself as Mrs. Cora Hutton. She was a woman of around fifty, with a ready smile and reading glasses perched on her sharp nose.

Addy introduced her aunt and uncle.

After greeting them, Mrs. Hutton turned to Addy. "I was widowed two years ago, so I took this job as housemother. We have some strict rules around here, Miss Garcia, and you are expected to abide by them. Are you being courted at this time?"

Addy nodded.

Uncle Henry turned to Mrs. Hutton. "I hope there's some supervision."

"We feel the girls are responsible enough for proper decorum." She glanced at Addy. "You are allowed to go out with him, but he is never to go any farther into the building than the lobby. You must be back by ten o'clock or you will be locked out. Is that understood?"

"Yes, ma'am. May we see the room?"

"Yes, come with me." She led them up a flight of stairs, plain but clean, as was the hallway at the top with a row of doors down either side. She stopped at number sixteen. "This will be your room," she announced, opening the door to a pleasant room that contained a bed, a wardrobe, a couch, a desk, a chest of drawers and a wash stand. There was a large window at the far end. "The bathroom is at the end of the hall. Six dollars is due promptly at the end of each month. Breakfast is served at six o'clock and dinner at seven, in the dining room downstairs. For twenty-five cents a week, you will be provided a laundry service."

Aunt Jen turned to Uncle Henry. "What do you think?"

He looked straight at Addy. "Are you going to abide by the rules here?"

"Yes, sir." She turned to Mrs. Hutton. "May I move in Saturday?"

Mrs. Hutton took out a contract. "I need three dollars and your signature here." Addy complied, and Mrs. Hutton held out her hand. "Welcome to the ladies' dormitory, Miss Garcia."

Addy felt like skipping back to the Packard. Finally, she was free of Uncle Henry!

At the house, Aunt Jen helped her pack. As she put Addy's toiletries into a box, she wiped away a tear. "Addy, I feel like I've lost two daughters at once. I really wish you wouldn't go."

Addy looked up from packing her clothes. "Aunt Jen, I've been planning this move for almost a month. I didn't know Muriel was going to elope. It's not that I'm not grateful to you and Uncle for taking me in when I needed you, but I feel like I've become a burden. I can take care of myself now. I make a good wage at the studio."

"I worry about you being courted by Zeke."

Addy smiled. "If you mean what I think you mean, don't worry. I know how babies are made."

"Adeline!" Aunt Jen turned red.

Addy stifled a giggle at her aunt's Victorian thinking and went back to her packing.

The night before Addy left found her with her grandparents in their apartment.

"Adeline, I worry about you being off on your own," Grandma said. "When I was your age, girls didn't leave home until they were married."

"You have to remember, Grandma, girls have more opportunities now. I'm making money I can live on, and I don't have to depend on my family to take care of me." Addy held the skein of yarn between her hands while her grandmother wound it into a ball.

"I was twenty-one when I left home, after I married your grandfather. We were to be married earlier, but war broke out between the states. Such a dark time for our country."

Grandpa mused at the table and chimed in, "I was hoping that would be the end of war, but that business with Spain, in Cuba, took our son, and then the Great War that ended two years ago seemed to be bad, as well. Let's pray things don't get worse. Well, that's enough of that. You and your young man can come with us to the GAR balls."

Addy smiled. "They probably will only play those old-fashioned waltzes and polkas. You've got to get a jazz band."

Grandpa chuckled. "I'd bring it up at the next meeting if I didn't think they'd turn the cannon memorial around and aim it at me. Some of my generation consider that music to be sinful and base. Of course, I personally don't." He took both her hands. "Really, Adeline, come and see us often."

"I will." Addy would miss them most of all. Grandpa and Grandma always had time to talk when the rest of the family was too busy.

The next morning, Zeke drove over to help Uncle Henry and James load Addy's boxes and suitcases into both his Ford and Uncle Henry's Packard. There were tearful goodbyes all around, as though she were moving across the continent rather than just across town. Even Casey and Buster, who enjoyed tormenting her, seemed sad.

Addy and Zeke climbed into the Model T. Uncle Henry, Aunt Jen and James followed in their auto. Fathers and brothers were allowed up to the rooms, and Uncle Henry and James would fit that category. Mrs. Hutton waved the rules temporarily and let Zeke help carry boxes up. Aunt Jen and Addy put things away as they opened the boxes.

By mid-afternoon, they had finished and all gathered outside by the Packard.

Uncle Henry cleared his throat. "Well, Adeline, you're on your own now. I expect you to remember everything you were taught."

"I will, Uncle. Thank you."

He awkwardly offered her his hand, and she

took it. Then he let go and slid into the driver's seat. "Jen, James, let's go home."

Aunt Jen held Addy in an embrace for a moment. "You and Zeke are invited to Thanksgiving dinner, and I won't take no for an answer."

Addy looked at Zeke questioningly, and he nodded. "We'll be there, Auntie."

Her cousin James looked so grown up, towering over her, but she could still put her hand on his shoulder.

He stared at the ground. "I'll miss you."

When she stood on tiptoe and gave him a kiss on the cheek, he blushed.

"I'll miss you, too. Thank you for your help," she said. He smiled at her as he got into the back seat, and Addy and Zeke waved as the auto went down the street.

Zeke, his arm around Addy, said, "Well, you're an independent woman now. Would you like to go to dinner and a moving picture tonight, to celebrate? I'll pick you up at five-thirty."

She gave him a big smile. "I'll be ready."

He started his Ford and waved as he drove away. Addy practically skipped back into the dormitory, where she found Mrs. Hutton in the sitting room mending a skirt. "I'm going out with my young man to dinner and a moving picture tonight."

Mrs. Hutton looked up from her sewing. "Remember to be back before ten o'clock, Adeline."

"Yes, ma'am." She took the stairs two at a time, intending to rearrange some of her things. Aunt Jen's way of doing things wasn't always Addy's preference, but she hadn't wanted to say anything, with Aunt Jen upset already at "losing" both her girls almost at the same time. Addy had barely started on her project when she heard a knock at the door and opened it to find two girls of about her own age standing there. One had light brown hair, and the other was a blonde. Both sported bobbed hair.

"Hello, I'm Anne Reynolds and this is Roxie Peterson. We're your neighbors on either side."

Addy smiled. "Come in. I'm Addy Garcia. Have a seat on the couch there. Are you new at the studio? I don't think I've seen you before."

Roxie laughed. "We've seen you several times before. We're the atmosphere people, in the crowd."

"You know, the last in the pecking order," Anne added.

"I don't know, being a double isn't very high, either." Addy sighed.

"Well at least you're something." Roxie looked her in the eye. "We're considered part of the scenery. I wanted to work in pictures, but I didn't think it would be this hard to get anywhere." Roxie was silent for a moment. "You're a Mexican, Addy?"

Addy was immediately on guard. "Part. Is there a problem with that?"

Roxie shook her head. "Not with us, but there are a few in this building who may be bothered."

Addy set her jaw. "Then I'll just avoid them." Then she changed the subject. "Do you both have a theater background, too?"

They nodded.

Addy snorted. "Well, we have that over the great Nora Steele."

"Have you ever talked to her, Addy?" Anne asked.

"She would never discuss anything with the hired help, but I heard her mention it to Mr. Hanson. He asked her to give a wider theatrical gesture, and Nora said she was never in theater."

Roxie sniffed. "Well, ain't that swell! She must have spent time on the casting couch for her job."

"What does that mean?"

"That means she was someone's hooker in the casting office."

Anne touched Addy's shoulder. "Have you ever talked to John Payton? He's enough to make a girl cry."

Addy shook her head. "He's as bad as Nora is. I wouldn't be surprised if they have a 'casting couch' of their own. I've seen them coming out of her dressing tent several times."

"By the way, I noticed Zeke Shafer helped you move in. Are you seeing him?" Roxie inquired.

Addy felt warm. "Yes, we have our first outing tonight."

Anne smiled. "Mm, he's the cat's meow. Lucky you! Well, it looks like you're busy getting settled, and I've got stockings to wash out, so I guess we'll see you at breakfast tomorrow." She and Roxie rose to leave, and Addy held out her hand.

"It was nice meeting both of you." *I'm going to like living here, but I'll still miss Muriel.*

After a bath, Addy dressed in her light blue pleated dress with the white lace on the elbow-length sleeves. As she pinned up her hair in front of the washstand mirror, she wondered about getting her hair bobbed. It might be nice. Uncle Henry would never have allowed it, but she could make her own decisions now. She felt pleased with herself even to consider being so modern, but then her thoughts moved on to Zeke.

How do I really feel about him? When we first met, I thought of him as a friend. Now I feel lightheaded and giddy. But I'm almost afraid to let myself care about him that way. I don't want him to leave me like my high school sweetheart, Tim, did, because his family didn't want him married to a Mexican.

She glanced at the clock—a quarter after five. She hooked a long strand of faux pearls around her neck and knotted them halfway down, slipped on a matching blue and white hat, and white gloves, and threw her fringed shawl across her back. Looking in the mirror once more, she flipped the corner of the shawl over her right shoulder. *Now you're a sophisticated lady!* Addy giggled as she grabbed her beaded drawstring purse, and with a spring in her step she went down the stairs.

She met Mrs. Hutton coming up. "Adeline, I was just going to tell you that your young man is here. You look very nice, dear."

Addy grinned. "Thank you, Mrs. Hutton. I'll be back in time, I promise."

At the bottom of the staircase stood Zeke, hat in hand, looking handsome in a suit, with his hair slicked back. *So well-groomed.* He beamed when he saw Addy. "You are beautiful tonight, my girl."

"Thank you, Mr. Shafer. Shall we go?" Addy offered one hand to him, then turned to wave to Mrs. Hutton with the other as they went out the door.

Zeke had put the top up on the Model T. "Just in case," he said, and like a true gentleman he opened the door for Addy, helping her in. Then he cranked the auto to life, climbed into the driver's seat, and reached to a toggle switch on the dashboard to turn on the headlights.

"Well, Miss Garcia, off we go to the supper club." And the auto took off with a backfire.

The Sunset Supper Club was crowded for a Saturday night, but Zeke had reservations, and the host, in his crisp tuxedo, seated them almost immediately.

"Would you like ginger ale with your supper?"

Zeke slipped him a tip. "Yes, my good man."

The host came back with the menu, which he gave to Zeke, then opened a chilled bottle of ginger ale and poured it into two wine glasses. After he left, Zeke studied the menu and asked, "Do you like Beef Wellington?"

Addy nodded. "That's the roast in pastry, isn't

it?"

"Yes, I've ordered it here before. They put on a very tasty gravy."

"All right. Sounds good."

Zeke smiled and raised his glass of ginger ale. "Here's to a wonderful evening." They clinked glasses and drank the fizzy liquid, chatting until the waiter came to take their order. Zeke requested two Beef Wellingtons with all the accompaniments; oysters and assorted breads, soup, new potatoes with parsley, steamed carrots, dessert and coffee.

Talking casually about their work filled the time until they were served. Addy paused between bites of the savory dinner. "How long have you been working at Majestic?"

"A little over a year. I started in the props department, then went to work for Mr. Hanson as an assistant." He looked at her with a twinkle in his eye. "I went from 'hey, you' to 'boy' in just a few months. How did you get to stand-in so quickly?"

Addy shook her head. "I happened to be the same size as Nora and the same type of hair. Seeing what I've been through, I don't know if that was lucky or not."

After their supper, they drove to the Hollywood Bijou, where *Mark of Zorro,* with Douglas Fairbanks, was playing. In the darkened theater, Addy thrilled to the picture show and studied Zeke's face. A very boyish, young face. She loved the way his brown eyes sparkled when he laughed. And she appreciated the way he'd stood up to Mr. Hanson on her behalf. *Zeke, let me trust you. Let me fall in love with you and not get hurt.*

It was just after nine-thirty that evening when the Ford pulled up in front of the dormitory. Zeke got out of the auto and went around to open the door for Addy. As he helped her out, his arms encircled her and he started dancing with her on the lawn, humming, "Sweet Adeline."

"You're the flower of my heart, Sweet Adeline," he sang in a rich baritone. They stopped and looked at each other, suddenly very quiet. "Addy, may I kiss you?"

She trembled, held steady only by his arms still around her. "Yes." And he lowered his face to hers. Their kiss was sweet and passionate. She felt his hardness pressed to her and her body responded. When he pulled away, he took her heart. She took a breath to steady herself and gazed at him. "Zeke, I have to go in now. Thank you for a wonderful evening."

He held her hand as they walked to the door of the dormitory, where he said simply, "Goodnight, sweetheart." With one more look into each other's eyes, they separated.

Inside, Addy passed Anne and Roxie with a smile as they tried to pretend they hadn't had their noses pressed to the doorway windows. Some things never changed. She was still being checked up on. "Goodnight, neighbors. Sweet dreams," Addy called over her shoulder as she climbed the stairs.

They hurried up behind her. "You're not getting away that fast." Anne stood at the door to Addy's room as Addy opened it.

"Addy, you have to tell us, how *was* your outing tonight?" Roxie's eyes danced.

"Absolutely wonderful. Zeke is so sweet. We went to the Sunset Supper Club, and then to the Bijou to see *Mark of Zorro*."

Anne looked at her. "Zeke is so handsome. What a catch! Well, see you tomorrow."

After church, Addy came into the dining room and found the two girls had saved her a spot next to them. Addy loaded her plate with Mrs. Hutton's chicken, mashed potatoes and gravy, as well as the peas and fresh biscuits with butter. "And there's apple pie for dessert," Anne informed her.

The girls had just started eating when a well-groomed blonde came over and politely extended her hand to Addy. "Hello, I'm Georgia Banes. I hear you just moved in yesterday. And you are?"

Addy clasped her hand. "I'm Adeline Garcia, but you can call me Addy. How do you do?"

Georgia stiffened visibly, and the smile froze on her face.

"Well, I didn't know they let your kind of people stay here. Isn't that nice of them." With that, Georgia withdrew coldly to another table.

Anne gave Addy a level look. "Don't let Georgia bother you. She's a super snob. We don't all feel that way."

Addy asked a little harshly, "Even though my father was Mexican?"

Roxie put her hand on Addy's shoulder. "We don't care. We like you."

Addy gave her a half-smile. "Thank you. Uncle Henry taught me there would be people who dislike me because of what my family was, not for who I am. There are probably a lot of Georgias around, but I won't let any of them get to me. I'm happy about who I am, not ashamed. I remember having to fight a few like that in school." She hid a smile. "I got the best of them, too, although Uncle said it wasn't ladylike to knock someone out."

Anne laughed. "Then Georgia Banes and everybody like her had better look out."

****

Monday, as Addy was on her way to the crew tent on the set, she caught a glimpse of Zeke, and her heart raced. Their eyes met and held. The unspoken understanding between them gave her more confidence than she'd ever known before. *I must get to work, but I do love him.*

They worked a long day, because Mr. Hanson

wanted to get some dusk shooting in for the story, so it was nearly dark when Zeke and Addy walked together to the crew quarters after the filming was completed. As they strolled hand in hand, an automobile whizzed in front of them on a cross street. By the yellow glow of a corner streetlight, Addy caught a glimpse of a woman in the back seat. She squeezed Zeke's hand in excitement. "That looked like Muriel in that car!"

Zeke glanced at the retreating auto. "I didn't notice. Are you sure you saw her?"

"It looked just like her. I thought she would be miles away from here by now. I wonder if her boss, Mr. Leman, could tell me if she is still working here."

"Wouldn't Shipping be closed by now? It's seven o'clock." Zeke checked his pocket watch.

"Well, I remember Muriel saying he often works late in his office, because he's the chief accountant and responsible for so much." She looked at the large building. "The light is still on in there. I'm going to go ask him. I want to know where Muriel is."

"I'll go with you."

They carefully made their way to the double doors of the warehouse and found them unlocked. The building was cavernous in its darkness. The light from the office area seemed farther away than it did in the daytime, but they could hear a lot of noise coming from that end of the building, like things were being thrown around, and angry voices yelling. Addy couldn't make out what was being said.

Suddenly they heard what sounded like a gunshot.

Zeke pushed Addy down behind a crate and leaned toward her to whisper, "Stay there! I'm going to call the police." He slipped over to the shipping clerk's desk and jiggled the cradle on the tall thin telephone before he held the receiver to his ear and spoke in a low voice. "Operator, get me the police." After a pause, he continued, "This is Zeke Shafer. There is some sort of disturbance at the shipping department here at Majestic Motion Pictures. It sounded like a gun was fired in the office area. Hurry!"

There were sounds of running from the far end of the warehouse. "I heard a voice over there," a man called out. Another shot rang out, closer this time, and Zeke dove under the desk.

"It ain't here. Let's go!" said a voice, gruffer than the other. "If you know what's good for you, you'll stay down until we're gone," he called toward the clerk's desk where Zeke hid. Addy tried to get a look at them as they left by way of the dock door, but it was too dark.

"Zeke, I'm going to check on Mr. Leman!"

"Addy! Come back! Those guys might still be around." Zeke glanced around the warehouse. "I'm coming with you. The police should be here soon."

She gasped as she entered the office. It was strewn with the contents of all the drawers, cabinets and shelves. To her horror, she found Mr. Leman on the floor, a bloody pool growing beneath him. He moaned and both young people dropped down beside him, and at the same moment they heard several automobiles stop outside.

Zeke jumped up. "That must be the police! I'll go get them."

As Zeke ran out of the warehouse, several policemen came toward him with guns drawn. "Hands up!" Two of them grabbed him as a plainclothesman came running up and shone a flashlight in Zeke's face. "I'm Inspector Cannon. Who are you?"

Zeke scowled at him. "I'm the one who called. I came out to get you. There's a badly wounded man in there. My girlfriend, Addy Garcia, is with him. I'm Zeke Shafer."

Cannon waved his hand at the two officers. "You can let him go. Now tell me what happened."

Zeke angrily pulled out of their grasp and told what little he knew. He had just finished when the ambulance pulled up and they all hurried into the building.

Meanwhile, Addy had propped Mr. Leman's head up, and his eyes slowly opened. "Are you...one of them?" he asked weakly.

"One of who?"

"No, you're not. They wanted...my master ledger. I put it...in a safe deposit box...at the Hollywood First National Bank...this morning. You... only one...knows this. Tear...lining of coat...right side."

"What?"

"Just...do it. Not...much time." His voice was getting weaker, and it seemed very hard for him to breathe.

She ripped the silk of the lining, and a key with a card tag fell out.

"Don't tell...where...ledger is. Give...key to—" He coughed and something let go inside him. As the police and ambulance crew ran in, blood poured from his mouth and his body trembled violently. Addy stood with Zeke, watching while the ambulance crew worked on him. She had slipped the key into her shoe before stepping back out of the way. *Now what do I do? Who are 'they'? And who am I supposed to give the key to? Are the police the ones I'm not supposed to tell about the ledger? Are they corrupted?*

Mr. Leman gave a great sigh and was still. One of the men in a suit came over to Addy, "Miss Garcia? I'm Inspector Reese Cannon, with the Los Angeles Police." He showed her his badge.

She looked at him, still dazed. "How did you

know my name?"

"Mr. Shafer told us. I'm sorry, Mr. Leman is dead. Did he happen to say who shot him?"

"I—um, no. All he said was it was 'them.' He didn't say who they were."

"How many men were there?"

"All I saw were two, but it was too dark to see their faces."

"Where were you?"

"We were both on the other side of the warehouse, by the double doors, just coming in. I was behind a crate, and Zeke called the police from the shipping clerk's desk."

"What were you doing here?"

"I was going to ask Mr. Leman if my cousin still worked here. We saw the light on in his office and decided to stop in."

"Thank you, Miss Garcia. Your story and Mr. Shafer's match. I'll be in touch if I need more information." He touched his hat and turned to go.

I wonder if I should tell him about the key? I'd hate to see it get into the wrong hands. I have to do the right thing. Addy thought about telling Zeke, but she knew he would take it from her. No, she needed to do this on her own. Anyway, how well did she know Zeke?

Suddenly, as the shock of what had happened wore off, Addy trembled, lightheaded and nauseous at the sight of the corpse and the metallic smell of blood, and then everything went black. When she came to, they were outside. Zeke was holding her while one of the ambulance crew waved a foul-smelling bottle under her nose.

"Looks like she's come around." The man stepped back.

"I'll take you home, Addy." Zeke helped her to her feet, and she gratefully accepted his strong arm around her as they walked to his automobile.

At the dormitory she turned to him as he helped her from the auto. "I'm sorry I got you into this."

"You didn't know that was going to happen. I'm just glad I was there with you."

She studied his face in the soft glow of the street lamp as they went hand in hand to the door of the dormitory. Addy's eyes teared up. "They shot at you. You could have been killed."

He put his hand on her cheek. "Sweetheart, if you'd gone in there by yourself, you could be dead." Zeke looked down. "I needed to protect you."

As if drawn together by some unseen force, they melded together in a kiss. As Addy reluctantly left his arms, she moved her hand to the stray lock of hair that was forever falling in his eyes. "Goodnight, Zeke, my hero."

Addy was more than tired as she went up the stairs. She sat on the edge of her bed and slipped her shoe off, then studied the key in her hand. *What should I do to find out who gets the key? Maybe I should've given it to the police, but I remember Uncle Henry talking to Grandpa about the government officials being paid off by the mob. How do I know who's honest? I'll have to hide it until I find out.*

She went to the window at the far end of the room, where she had put a small block of wood under the corner of the sash, so she would always have fresh air. She lifted up the sash and put the key under the block, then set the sash down on it again. *There, that should keep it safe.*

Then, taking off her bloodstained work dress, she rinsed it out in cold water at the washstand and hung the dress on one of the hooks on the wall. When it was dry, she would put it in the laundry bag she was provided.

She didn't sleep well that night, with guns, corpses and blood permeating her dreams, so it was a good thing she didn't have a whole lot to do the next day. They were filming busy crowd scenes, which meant that Anne and Roxie were there. Addy made a point of taking a few breaks with them. They sat on the wooden sidewalk of the western town set when Mr. Hanson gave everyone a ten-minute break.

Anne spoke up first, her eyes large as she asked, "Addy, is it true that Mr. Leman was killed last night and you were there?"

Addy took a long breath and gave them the story.

Roxie shuddered. "I've never seen somebody shot. It must have been horrible."

Anne put her hand on Addy's arm. "I've heard they have a woman taking over Mr. Leman's job as bookkeeper and shipping head."

Addy was surprised. "Do you know who she is?"

"No, but I hear she's very young."

Could that be Muriel?

The set shut down fairly early that afternoon, and it was around four-thirty when Zeke and Addy were walking back to the crew quarters. Addy happened to glance toward the shipping department, where a very elegant automobile was parked. Several people emerged from the building, and she squinted at them. Suddenly, she grabbed Zeke's arm. "That's Muriel getting into that auto!"

Zeke looked over. "Are you sure?"

The vehicle took off towards the entrance. "I'm sure. I wonder what she's doing here."

He gave a low whistle. "The Giovannis must be really loaded. That was a Harley Earl Cadillac Limo. Only the wealthiest people have those. Fatty Arbuckle has one that was made just for him."

Addy shook her head. "If she's still working here, I wonder why. She surely doesn't need the money."

Questions buzzed in her head as they continued

their journey to the crew quarters. *Why is Muriel still at the studio? Is she aware of Mr. Leman's death? Did she set him up for those gangsters who killed him? How much have Tony and his family corrupted her already? How much danger is she in?* The knot in Addy's stomach was growing.

Chapter 3

"Good morning, Muriel. I thought you'd be long gone from here by now." Addy stood at the door of the temporary bookkeeper's office. The room where Mr. Leman had died was being cleaned and refurnished.

"Addy! How did you know I was here?" The shocked expression on Muriel's face quickly changed to one of pleasure, and the two cousins embraced. As Muriel pulled back, tears stood in her eyes. "Addy, I've missed you so much."

Addy firmly held her emotions in check. "I've missed you, too. I saw you once on Monday, and then again on Tuesday. Yesterday, someone told me a young woman had taken over Mr. Leman's job, so I was hoping... But I thought it was against company policy to be married and work here."

"Addy, come in and sit down." Muriel motioned to one of the two chairs in front of the desk. As Addy sat down, Muriel closed the door and leaned against the corner of the desk. "My husband's family bought into the studio. When the unfortunate thing happened to Mr. Leman, Tony's father asked me to take over the bookkeeping, since I know the system."

Addy was surprised. "But Mr. Abrams is still president, isn't he?"

"The studio was in financial trouble and the Giovannis came in as a silent partner. Everyone in the administration staff is still here, except Mr. Leman, of course."

"Are you going to get in touch with your family and let them know where you are? I think you should give them at least that. They can't make you come home."

Muriel's eyes were troubled. "They won't forgive me for what I did. You heard my father. Maybe in time, but not now."

"From my own experience, you don't always get that time. Neither of my parents ever saw their loved ones again."

Muriel shook her head. "Disasters like that may not happen. We just need time. So tell me how you are? Have you seen that nice young man again, what was his name, Zeb or Zane or..."

"You mean Zeke?" Addy laughed. Yes, I've seen him. I not only work with him every day on the set, but we're going on outings now." She filled Muriel in on details, and the girls chatted a few minutes more before Addy stood up. "I'd better get to the set. Zeke and I are invited to Thanksgiving dinner at your family's home, tomorrow. Think about what we discussed. Remember what happened to my parents."

Addy ate lunch with Zeke in the crew tent. "Zeke, remember we are invited to my aunt and uncle's house for Thanksgiving tomorrow."

He looked up at her. "What time should I pick you up?"

"We usually eat about two in the afternoon on holidays, but I'll be ready at eleven o'clock. I want to help with the dinner." She was quiet for a moment. "I wonder if I should tell them about Muriel." She had already filled Zeke in on her morning's visit to the bookkeeping department.

"I think you should. I know if I had a daughter missing, I would want to be told if someone knew her whereabouts."

"Have you ever told your parents where you are?"

He stopped in mid-bite of his sandwich. "No, I

left my mother a note when I moved out. I was so angry with my father, I didn't care if I ever saw him again. I guess I didn't think about what it was like on their end."

"I'll tell you the same thing I told Muriel. You don't know if you'll ever see your parents again. Mine died before they could patch things up."

Zeke nodded. "I guess you never think about the heartaches you cause in the heat of an argument."

Addy smiled. "I love you."

Zeke gave her a sideways glance. "I love you, too, but put away the nightstick you're hitting me with."

****

Zeke brooded as they walked back to the set after lunch. Would it hurt to write a letter to his mother? She suffered from his father's self-importance as much as any of them. He hated to think he had hurt his mother, but for the first time he realized that's probably what he'd done.

Later that day, he came to a decision. Zeke watched the door of the crew quarters, waiting for Addy to come out. When she did, he felt that warmth and joy that overcame him every time he saw her. It was getting harder to tell her goodbye, even for a few hours. He wanted to be with her all the time.

As soon as she had bounced into the passenger seat, he closed the door and started the auto. Almost immediately Zeke spoke what was on his mind. "Remember what we were talking about at lunch? Well, I'm going to sit down tonight and write my mother a letter. I don't think it crossed my mind before that I've really hurt her because of my father. All of this wasn't her fault. She protected her children as best she could."

Addy put her hand on his arm as they pulled into the parking lot of the dormitory. He pulled the brake on and looked into her shining dark eyes. "I'm glad you decided to do that. If you can't come to terms with your father, at least your mother won't suffer, too."

Zeke gazed into the face he adored and then gave her a kiss he felt from head to toe. "I love you so much. Sometimes I need to be reminded there are others involved."

Addy cupped his face in her hands. "I'm proud of you. Goodnight, my love." She hopped out of the vehicle, and he watched her all the way to the door, not daring to take his eyes off her.

****

Addy was ready when Zeke arrived at eleven the following morning. He smiled as she walked down the stairs. "You're wearing that pretty pink dress again. I love you in that."

"Thank you. You look pretty great yourself. Shall we go?"

The Model T took off with a few backfires that shook the auto and made them laugh, in their holiday mood. Fifteen minutes later, Zeke pulled into the driveway at Uncle Henry's home. There was a welcoming committee on the porch—all the male members of the family, plus Maggie. After greetings for all of them, Addy left Zeke in their company and went to the kitchen to help Grandma and Aunt Jen.

The odors of fresh-baked bread, pumpkin pies with warm spices and the succulent turkey wafted around the kitchen while Aunt Jen and Grandma greeted her warmly.

Addy laughed. "I've only been away for five days." *Although it seems like years.* She put on an apron and busied herself in the preparations for dinner, setting the table in the dining room and doing all the things she'd done every Thanksgiving as she grew up in this household. Finally, the large bird was pulled from the oven, baked to a golden brown.

After Aunt Jen had put the turkey onto a huge platter, she set the roasting pan on the stovetop. "Here, Addy, make the gravy for me, please."

Addy took some of the cream and dissolved flour in it. With the clear fat already poured off, she started stirring the mixture into the hot pan. As it bubbled from the heat, Addy put in some salt, pepper and sage. When it had thickened, Grandma brought over the gravy boat.

"Addy, you'll do very well as a wife," Grandma said, as she ladled gravy into the dish.

"I've been taught by the best," Addy replied with a kiss on Grandma's cheek.

The three of them took the feast to the table and set the large bird in front of Uncle Henry's chair with his special ivory-handled carving knives. Addy went around to Zeke, who held her chair for her. Everyone sat down except Uncle Henry, who bowed his head, and everyone around the table did the same. "Dear Lord, we thank you for the many blessings given to our family throughout the year. We gather here to celebrate with the bounty you have provided us." He took a deep breath. "May we remember absent family and friends as we partake of your goodness. Amen." There was silence around the table for a moment. Addy was sure everyone was thinking of Muriel.

As the many dishes were passed around, Uncle Henry turned his gaze to Addy. "Mr. Shafer tells me you've seen Muriel."

She shot Zeke a withering glance. "Yes, I have. She's the head of bookkeeping and shipping now."

Aunt Jen's expression was a mixture of sorrow, concern and joy. "How is she?" her aunt managed to say.

"She seems to be fine, but there's something strange about her getting such a high position after working there for only a year."

Uncle Henry looked up. "The detective I hired found out she lives in the hills north of Hollywood. The Giovanni family is quite wealthy, and that may have given her more influence."

"She said the family is now the silent partner of the studio."

"It seems on record that they made their wealth investing in businesses, but the detective said the records were vague."

Concern tinged Addy's voice as she considered the situation. "I wonder what they want with a movie studio, if it was in trouble. There are plenty of studios doing very well."

Her uncle shook his head. "Sometimes it's an interesting diversion for the rich to see if they can pull a business out of trouble. Or it could be a front for something illegal."

Addy went into worry again. *What has Muriel gotten into?*

Addy pulled Zeke into the garden after dinner. "How dare you bring up Muriel to my uncle when I wasn't there," she lashed out at him.

"Addy, I'm sorry, but he asked me pointblank. He'd read a story in the newspaper about the murder and had seen that we were there. He didn't want to tell your aunt or the rest of the family. The detective he hired told your uncle about Muriel's position, and so your uncle asked me if you had seen her yet."

Her anger gave way to her overwhelming concern for her cousin. "I'm sorry, Zeke. I shouldn't have accused you like that without knowing the whole story, but I'm really worried about Muriel. Something about this whole thing doesn't sit right with me."

When they came in the back door, Buster started up with, "Zeke and Addy sitting in a tree, k-i-s-s-i-n-g!"

Addy sighed. "Oh, hush," was her only reply to the sing-song chant as Buster went running outside with Casey and Maggie after him. While Addy went to help with the cleanup in the kitchen, Zeke joined Uncle Henry, Grandpa and James in the parlor.

It was a good afternoon, but around seven o'clock Zeke asked Addy if it was perhaps time for them to go. After hugs and good wishes all around, Uncle Henry drew her aside. "Adeline, stay out of trouble. I purposely didn't tell the rest of the family about your unfortunate adventure, because I didn't want to worry them."

"Uncle, I really didn't mean to be caught up in that. I'll try to stay out of any problems in the future."

"Good. Rely on Mr. Shafer. He's a fine man."

Addy smiled. "I know. Goodnight, Uncle." She pecked him on the cheek.

Zeke helped her into the auto, then started the engine and slid into the driver's seat. Addy turned to him as they drove off. "I'm sorry I got upset with you earlier. I've been worried about what happened to Mr. Leman." Her thoughts turned again to whether she should tell Zeke about the ledger.

His words invaded her inner turmoil. "I know. I wish I could change what happened, but we didn't know what we were walking into, remember." He took his hand off the shift and squeezed her fingers.

Parked by the dormitory, they sat in the auto, holding hands and simply looking at each other, until he put his arm around her and drew her to him. When Zeke lifted her chin and kissed her deeply, it set her body tingling all over. She ran her fingers through his hair and let her hand rest on his neck.

"Oh, Addy, I want you bad." His voice quivered. When he kissed her again, she felt the heat from his body. Her own temperature rose as his lips moved down to her neck and kissed her below her ear.

Addy caught a movement out of the corner of her eye. The outdoor light was snapped on. Mrs. Hutton opened the door of the building and stood on the threshold, tapping her foot, her arms crossed, a disapproving look on her face. Addy pulled back. "Zeke, we've got an audience." She nodded toward Mrs. Hutton.

"Damn," he said under his breath. "Sorry, Addy, I didn't mean to swear."

"Well, I do mean to. Damn!" They both laughed as they rested forehead to forehead.

"How shocking! Goodnight, sweetheart. See you tomorrow. I love you." He put on his hat as he got out the driver's side and went around help her out of the auto and walk her up to the door. "And a happy Thanksgiving to you, too, Mrs. Hutton." He tipped his hat and went back to the Ford.

"Miss Garcia, may I remind you to act with some discretion when you are at the dormitory?" The housemother's eyes flashed in the light.

"Sorry, Mrs. Hutton. I'll remember next time." Addy walked past her, grinning, skipped up the stairs and went to bed, dreaming of Zeke.

Roxie sat next to Addy at breakfast. "Addy, can you sing and dance?"

Addy looked at her, slightly puzzled. "I have when I've been in theater. Why?"

"There's a night club looking for singers and dancers in the evenings. They pay quite handsomely, too. I'm going to see if I can get a job there to make extra money."

"I didn't see any notice on the work board about it."

"The owner came and asked us when we were at the crew quarters. The auditions will be held at seven o'clock Wednesday evening." She took out a piece of paper from her pocket. "Here's the address.

We can go together if you'd like." Roxie hesitated for a moment. "The only thing is, you would have to bob your hair."

Addy spread butter on her toast. "That will give me a good excuse. I've been thinking about doing that. Nora did, and she wears wigs when needed. I can do that, too. But where can I go?"

"There's a barber shop down the street that bobs hair for women. I need a trim, and you can go with me."

"When?"

"This afternoon, after work."

Addy felt a surge of excitement. *Well, I've been wanting to do this. It's now or never.*

She didn't tell anyone at work what she planned to do, and after they were done for the day and back at the dorm, she and Roxie walked the mile to the barber. The shop was small, in the middle of a row of businesses. The pole outside rotated its red and white stripes next to an awning that echoed the colors.

They went up the two steps to the door and inside, where smells of cigar smoke, soap, Bay Rum cologne and hair tonic enveloped them. The cologne made her think of her grandpa, a moment of homesickness. It was a decidedly masculine establishment, with two barbers working on customers.

The older of the two turned. "Hi, Roxie. Here for a trim?"

"Yes. And my friend, Addy, would like a bob."

"Ray, you take Roxie next and I'll do her friend."

"Thank you, Butch." Roxie smiled. The girls sat on the caned wood waiting chairs, trying not to see the racy covers of the *Police Gazette* magazines strewn on the table in front of them.

When the occupants of the two chairs were finished, the girls took their places. As Butch laid out his tools on the tray by the chair, Addy watched in the mahogany vanity's fancy mirror set between the small shelves holding ornate shaving mugs and matching brushes.

Butch had her take out all her hairpins, and he put a piece of tissue paper around her blouse collar. Then he put a huge cloth around her shoulders and tied it in the back.

"Butch." Addy hesitated for a moment and sighed. "Could you please turn the chair around so I can't watch this?"

"Your first time, right?" He laughed, and Ray snorted.

Addy ignored them. She screwed her eyes tight and felt the first cut. The cold steel of the scissors rested against her neck, and she was sure she felt every hair that was sheared and heard the soft plop of each lock as it hit the floor. By the time Butch reached the other side, she was in tears.

Roxie, already finished, stood next to Addy, handing her a handkerchief. Butch finished up. "Would you like to see your hair now?"

Addy nodded, and he turned the chair around. The being who looked back at her was a stranger. Her dark hair curled slightly at the nape of her neck and the sides curled to a point along her jawline. Butch took off the cloth and the tissue and then used a little brush to clean off any hair on her clothes. When Addy got out of the chair, there was no weight on her neck. She steadied herself for a moment.

Roxie laughed. "Yes, I felt the same way the first time, too."

Addy shook her head and the hair fell perfectly back into place. "I love it!" she gushed. She threw the hairpins away in the trash can and scooped up a lock of her hair off the floor to save, before paying Butch. She generously included a ten-cent tip. Butch and Ray had a new customer.

On their walk back to the dormitory, Roxie dragged Addy into a garment shop. "One more thing you need—a Symington Side Lacer."

Addy looked at her, puzzled. "A what?"

"Dear, you have bosoms. This will bind you in."

Addy felt her cheeks burn. "How much will this cost? I only have a dollar left."

"They're twelve cents apiece. Here, take four of them. I'll show you how to put them on when we get back."

"How do you know they're my size?"

Roxie held one up. "They're adjustable. See?" Both sides of the garment had laces for tightening.

Addy shrugged and paid the woman at the counter.

Anne joined them in Addy's room and made over her new bob. "Your hair's so thick, and it waves beautifully. I don't think you'll need to crimp it."

Roxie took out the sidelacers. Addy thought the one she held looked almost like a brassiere except for being a flat piece of material with lacing on both sides. She took off her blouse and pulled her slip out of her skirt and stepped out of it. Then she removed her brassiere. Roxie slipped the lacer over her head, and then she and Anne tightened the laces on both sides. Addy watched as her womanly shape disappeared. When she put her blouse back on, she was flat.

"Now you're modern!" Roxie declared.

Now I look like a stick. Anything for fashion, I guess. Addy was aware of definite pressure where she was flattened. "That really feels tight around my chest. Should it be that uncomfortable?"

"You'll get used to it. Just ignore it."

Addy looked at herself in the mirror. *I waited so long for my body to change, and now I look like a ten-year-old again!*

****

Addy dropped in to see Muriel the next morning before she went to the set.

Muriel looked at her in shock. "Oh, my, you bobbed your hair! It's nice on you, dear. And you don't have curves—you're straight up and down."

"Do you like the changes?"

"Uh-huh. It looks good on you. Say, Addy, I want to invite you and Zeke to dinner on Friday. Could you ask him, and let me know?"

"Sure, I will. And right now I'd better get to the set before Mr. Hanson sends the dogs to find me." She laughed.

Mr. Hanson was livid. "How dare you cut your hair! Now we'll have to find you a wig, too, as well as Miss Steele. You must check with me before you do something so impulsive again. Do you understand?"

While Mr. Hanson had his tirade, Zeke was in the background, grinning. He mouthed the word, "Beautiful!"

"Yes, Mr. Hanson." Addy was quickly fitted with an extra wig from the costume department.

After work, Zeke walked back with her to the crew quarters. "I like your hair like that."

Addy smiled. "Thank you. Oh, I almost forgot. Muriel invited us to dinner on Friday. Are you free?"

He put his arm around her. "Do you think we should associate with the Giovannis?"

"I want to find out more about the situation she's gotten herself into. I'd like to find out more about them before I start condemning them based on the gossip. I owe Muriel that much."

Zeke sighed. "All right, I'll go with you, but if there's any sign of trouble, we're leaving."

Addy ducked into the shipping building and found Muriel. "I asked Zeke, and he said he was free on Friday for dinner."

Muriel clapped. "Wonderful! I'll have our driver pick you two up at the dormitory at six o'clock on

Friday."

"You don't need to do that. Zeke can drive there."

"But, dear, the place is not easy to find. I insist."

Addy got a funny feeling in the pit of her stomach. "We'll be ready at six."

When Zeke picked Addy up at the door of the crew quarters, to drive her back to the dormitory, she looked at him uneasily. "Muriel is having their driver pick us up at the dormitory at six on Friday."

He ground his back teeth. "Addy, I don't like any of this, but I won't let you go alone." They finished the trip in silence, but he kissed her before she got out to go to the dormitory.

****

Nathan looked thunderstruck. "You're going to do what? Where do you want the flowers sent?"

Zeke shook his head. "I can't let Addy walk into that den of lions without me."

"Just don't do anything to make them angry. Revenge is their specialty."

"I'll be the perfect gentleman. After all, maybe Addy is right, and we should see what we're up against." Zeke sat brooding most of the evening, however. All his instincts, as well as his roommate, were telling him to get out of the commitment. *Are my feelings for Addy strong enough to go ahead even though I know it means trouble? If it wasn't for her cousin, she wouldn't be in this situation, and we could lay low at the studio and not attract the attention of these hoodlums. Damn! I feel like getting out, but I want to protect her. I'd never forgive myself if anything happened to her.*

Zeke's worry had him tossing and turning all night.

****

Meanwhile, Addy sat with Anne and Roxie at dinner that evening. Roxie was excited about the

64

auditions for the club the next day. "Addy, you're still coming with me, aren't you?"

"Why else did I get my hair bobbed? But I'm still thinking about it. Anne, are you going?"

"No, I can't carry a tune in a bucket. Anyway, something that Mr. Rudd said bothers me."

Addy stopped in mid-bite. "What exactly did he say?"

"Well, the location of the auditions is not being posted. He said he was only asking special talented groups for this job. It's supposed to be a very exclusive club with rich customers. A question came up about whether we could get back to the dormitories before ten o'clock, and he said they had rooms with beds upstairs, if the show went late."

A big red danger flag started waving in Addy's head. "That sure sounds suspicious. Roxie, please don't go—I'm not going to. I have a very bad feeling about this. It could be a speakeasy, with a house of ill repute included."

Roxie's look of frustration and determination was withering. "He also said we could make fifty dollars a week. I don't make that in a month at the studio."

"The money isn't worth you being in danger. I've heard that hookers are no better than slaves. What if they want you to stay there?"

Anne nodded. "I agree with Addy. The whole thing smells foul."

"If anything bad happens, I'll turn around and come back, okay?"

Anne and Addy looked at each other. Addy couldn't shake off the dread she felt for her friend. Beth, one of the new girls who had just moved in, came over to the table. "Roxie, are you still going to the audition tomorrow for the night club? I'll come with you, if you are."

Anne put a hand on Beth's arm. "We were trying

to talk her out of it. Something sounds wrong about this. They may be looking for hookers. It sounds like a speakeasy connected with prostitutes."

Beth looked puzzled. "What's a speakeasy?"

"It's a hidden place that sells illegal liquor, usually connected to a syndicate, and this one apparently has hookers, too."

"I told them I would come back if anything happens. It'll be good to have someone with me." Roxie smiled.

The next evening found Addy and Anne nervously playing gin rummy on the table downstairs. Mrs. Hutton checked the pendulum clock on the wall. "Quarter to ten. It's about time to lock up."

Addy slammed the card deck on the table. "I should have stopped them. I should have *made* them not go."

"How?" Anne looked at her. "By handcuffing them to a chair?"

"Who isn't in yet?" Mrs. Hutton glanced over at them.

"Roxie and Beth. They went to a so-called audition for a night club, but Addy and I thought it sounded like a recruitment for hookers."

Addy filled in, "Roxie said she could make more money at that job, so she went to try out. She said she'd come back if it was a shady deal."

"They knew the risk and still they went anyway. Sometimes girls are very naïve when it comes to money." Mrs. Hutton shook her head.

"Roxie comes from a very poor family and probably thought any way of making more money is worth it. I just pray that she and Beth—and any of the other girls that went—are all right." Anne stood up. "Come on, Addy. We have to go to work tomorrow."

Addy went to bed, but she didn't sleep well. *I*

wanted to go off on my own, and so far I've seen a murder, and now what I think is a trap swallowing up one of my friends. Well, I learned early this is a harsh world to live in.

In the morning, Anne and Addy knocked on Roxie's door. There was no response. They looked at each other, and Anne turned the knob. Roxie's bed hadn't been slept in. The girls went downstairs.

At breakfast Addy asked, "Do you think we should report missing persons to the police?"

"I think they have to be missing at least forty-eight hours before you can report it."

"Then do you know the address of the place where the auditions were held?"

Anne looked at her plate. "No, I don't. I didn't pay attention, because I decided not to go. I think I'll ask one of the other girls who were there when Mr. Rudd spoke to us about it. Maybe they'll remember, so we can find Roxie and Beth."

Anne came into the lunch tent while Addy and Zeke were on their break. Addy had already discussed the disappearance of Roxie and Beth with him. Anne picked up a lunch tray and joined the line at the counter. When Anne paid for her sandwich and tea, Addy waved her over to their table. Zeke had finished his lunch, but Addy's half-eaten sandwich lay on her plate.

Anne sat down and leaned in so they could hear over the hubbub in the tent. "I didn't have too much luck with the address. One of the girls remembered it was on La Brea Boulevard. Maybe we can find a night club around there."

Zeke shook his head. "From what Addy told me, I don't think you're going to find this place open to the street. If it's what I think it is, it will be well hidden. It definitely sounds like they were auditioning for a speakeasy."

"What should we do?" Addy gritted her teeth

and absentmindedly tapped on the table top.

"Let me ask some of the men I know. Some of them have gone to speakeasies, and they may know of one on La Brea." From the troubled look on Zeke's face, Addy knew there was something he wasn't telling them.

After Anne left, Addy spoke up. "What are you keeping to yourself?"

He sat back in his chair. "Addy, I hate to say this, but if Roxie didn't come back, she may have gotten into a house of ill repute. Procurers don't give up their girls very easily. Especially if the owners of the place belong to the syndicate."

She felt faint. "What can we do?"

"I don't know, sweetheart, but thank God you didn't go." Zeke reached to squeeze Addy's hand. "I'm glad you trust your instincts."

"I feel like I should have stopped her from going." Addy shook her head and went back to nibbling her sandwich.

Another evening went by, and still Roxie and Beth didn't come back. Addy hoped they could find them from what little information they had. When she checked her date book the next morning, she realized she'd almost forgotten the dinner date she and Zeke had with Muriel that night.

She reminded him of it at work. "You have to be at the dormitory before six o'clock this evening. Muriel said they were going to send the driver for us."

Zeke frowned. "I still don't like this. Something keeps telling me we're going into danger."

Nevertheless, Addy and Zeke were sitting on the low wall next to the lawn of the building complex by five minutes to six that evening. She wore her best blue dress, and he was dressed up in his good suit. A large automobile, the like of which they had only seen the very wealthy ride in, pulled into the drive.

It had an open-air section in front for the chauffeur and was completely enclosed in the back, with a window between the driver and passenger sections.

"Isn't that the auto we saw Muriel get into, over by the shipping department?" Addy asked.

"Yes, I remember it."

The chauffeur who got out of the auto was a very large man in a black uniform. Addy immediately didn't feel comfortable around him. "Mr. Shafer, Miss Garcia?"

They nodded.

"I'm here to take you to the Giovanni home." He opened the door to the back. "Please be seated."

Zeke helped Addy inside, then slid in beside her. The chauffeur closed the door and climbed into the front and started the engine.

"There's something about that man that bothers me," Addy said in a low voice, her head bent toward Zeke.

Zeke put a protective arm around her and leaned in close. "He's carrying a gun in a shoulder holster. I saw the bulge under his coat."

Their tension on the ride gave them a strong awareness of their route as they headed north toward the hills on the other side of Hollywood Boulevard. They saw the Hollywoodland sign in the distance. Once up the winding road several miles, they looked back and could see the lights of the city spread out across the basin below.

As they arrived at a large ornate iron gate, the man standing behind it swung it open and rang an iron bell hanging by the gatepost. The drive wound around some woodland, and then all at once Addy gasped. A building the size of a large hotel stretched out in front of them, constructed of white stone, with decorative iron on the lower part of each window. There was a carport with a grand entrance next to it, where Muriel and Tony stood waiting to greet them.

The chauffeur got out and opened the passenger door of the car. Zeke climbed out first, then turned to help Addy. With Muriel in a satin dinner gown and Tony wearing an expensive serge suit, Addy felt suddenly very shabby. She took Muriel's hand. "Why did the gatekeeper ring a bell when we came in the gate?"

Muriel smiled. "That let us know you'd arrived." She introduced Zeke to Tony, and the two men shook hands. Zeke looked as uncomfortable as Addy felt, shifting his feet as he glanced at her.

Tony took Muriel by the arm and led the way into the building. In the foyer, Addy stood in awe. It was big enough to hold both Uncle Henry's house and the dormitory. It went up two floors and was solid white marble, with gilded mirrors around the walls. A huge crystal chandelier lorded over the entire room. Everything sparkled, and there was a scent of roses everywhere.

A servant girl came and took Zeke's coat and hat and Addy's wrap before they followed Muriel and Tony to the grand parlor. There, waiting for them, was Tony's family. Tony introduced them to his brothers and their families, his sisters and their husbands. Finally, there was his mother, Sofia, a warm friendly woman with her iron-gray hair pulled back into a tight bun, and his father, Joe. Joe was a very large man in a tailored silk suit. But what took Addy aback were the patch over his left eye and the ugly scar snaking out of it over the bridge of his nose.

Joe shook Zeke's hand and kissed Addy on the cheek. "Since you are a cousin of my daughter-in-law, you will be treated like family here, eh?" He turned to a couple of men standing by the door. "Is that understood?"

They both nodded and stepped into the shadows. Addy felt a chill go down her spine. These people seemed very warm, but there was an undercurrent of tension in the air. She glanced at Zeke, and he nodded like he knew what she was thinking.

When the butler announced that dinner was being served, Addy and Zeke were given the place of honor in the parade following Tony's parents to the dining room, with Muriel and Tony behind them, trailed by everyone else.

The dining room was another huge hall, with a table that could seat forty people easily. There were two chandeliers in this room, which was also two stories high. Halfway up were large wooden beams spanning the walls. Deep blue velvet drapes flowed down the floor-length windows.

The table was set with elegant white china rimmed with gold and cut crystal goblets that shimmered in the light of the candelabras. Joe Giovanni took his place at the head of the table and indicated that Addy and Zeke were to sit on the right hand side, next to him, with Muriel and Tony across from them. Sofia took her place at the foot, and the rest of the family found their places down the long table.

After Mr. Giovanni said grace, the servants brought in the first course, a cream of potato soup. When they got to the main course of beef rib roast, the servants poured a liquid into the crystal goblets, and Joe Giovanni stood up with his glass and said, "I welcome Muriel's cousin, Addy, and her gentleman, Zeke, into our home. May we always have a cordial relationship." The rest of the family raised their glasses. Then everyone drank. Addy was shocked. This was real wine, but Addy was not going to ask where Joe had gotten this, since it was outlawed by the Volstead Act. After all, he could have argued that merely possessing liquor was not against the law. *I guess rich people can get away with this.* She was also frustrated at the seating arrangements.

They were sitting in the traditional man-woman-man pattern, and she couldn't talk confidentially to Muriel very easily across the table, with both Tony and his father right there.

During the main course, Joe Giovanni turned to Addy and Zeke. "What do you two do at Majestic?"

Zeke glanced at Addy. "I'm a director's assistant, and Addy is Nora Steele's double."

Mr. Giovanni seemed interested, and they told him in detail about their jobs. When the dinner was over, everyone retired to the grand parlor. By this time it was nearing nine o'clock, and Addy and Zeke begged off because she had to get back to the dormitory. Mr. Giovanni called for the chauffeur and in just a few minutes the auto was ready at the front door. They made their goodbyes to Tony's parents, expressing their thanks for dinner, before Tony and Muriel walked them out to the auto.

Addy couldn't shake the dread she felt for Muriel. When she hugged her, Addy said in a low voice, "If you ever need me, you know where to find me."

Muriel smiled. "I'm all right. You take care of yourself."

"I really wish I had more time to talk to you."

"We'll get together at work. Goodnight, Addy."

Addy took hold of Zeke's hand when they were well on their way back. "I don't know what it was, but—"

Zeke touched her lips with his fingers. "Not now." And he nodded toward the chauffeur.

They were silent for the rest of the way, for fear the chauffeur would hear them. *Muriel, what have you gotten yourself into? Yes, Tony has money, but how did his family get it? Are you in danger now?*

When the chauffeur let them off, Zeke offered a tip, but the man waved him away. The auto disappeared down the street while Addy walked with Zeke to his Model T.

"I was going to say I didn't feel comfortable with Tony's family. They were kind to us, but something about Joe Giovanni was menacing. I don't mean his eye patch, although it looks like he got that in a fight."

Zeke nodded. "I got that impression, too. They've bought into the studio. I wonder whether that's going to be a good thing. I don't trust that man."

They held each other in a brief embrace. Addy felt so safe in his arms that she didn't want it to end. All the bad things of the world seemed to go away when she was with Zeke. She put her face next to his shirt and breathed in the warm scent of him, a scent that was becoming very familiar to her.

He pulled back and kissed her. "Let me walk you to the door."

She put her hand on his cheek. "That's all right. I can find my way."

"Goodnight, Addy. I love you."

She smiled. "I love you, too."

Zeke set off in his auto, and Addy had started toward the building when she heard a scuffling sound coming from the wall. "Addy!" she heard a voice call in a harsh whisper she thought she recognized.

"Roxie? Is that you?" She saw two crouched figures. "Beth, is that you, too?"

"Yes! We've run away from Mr. Rudd. He and one of his goons—" Roxie got no farther before an auto came squealing up the drive.

"Stop, you!" yelled a man from the auto.

Addy grabbed both girls by the arm. "We've got to run inside!" She dragged the exhausted girls as she flew along the walkway. They had gotten to the corner of the building when she heard a bullet whiz past her head. Another hit Beth, who cried out, and then Mrs. Hutton was at the door, pulling them all in and locking the door behind them.

"Roxie, Beth, go into the parlor! Addy, call the police. I'll be right back!" Mrs. Hutton charged to the back room.

Addy jiggled the cradle of the phone in the lobby. "Operator! Get me the police!" When the station answered, she said, "I'm Adeline Garcia at Dormitory Number Three at Majestic Studios. There are two men with guns trying..." Suddenly, the line went dead.

Mrs. Hutton came back with a shotgun. Addy looked at her, shocked to the core. This didn't look like the sweet woman she had come to know. One of the men was at the locked door, trying to get in. Addy forgot how to breathe. Mrs. Hutton hissed, "Get back!" Addy slipped into the parlor doorway and Mrs. Hutton shouldered the gun.

The man blasted his revolver at the lock and slowly opened the door.

It was at that point Mrs. Hutton spoke, in a voice Addy barely recognized, it was so gruff and demanding: "I'm only going to warn you once. Get out of this building!"

The man kept coming, raised the revolver in hand. There was a loud report from the shotgun, and the man was blown out the door and down the steps.

There was a shout from out in the yard. "Jake, did you get them?"

Mrs. Hutton went out, stepping quickly and deftly over the body and into the shadows. Addy watched, peering around the front door. Mrs. Hutton cocked the shotgun. "Stop right there, mister. Drop the gun and freeze, or I'll drop you."

The man in the dark hesitated, then let go of his gun just as the police arrived.

Back inside, Addy went to find out how Roxie and Beth were. Practically the whole population of the dormitory was in the parlor by this time, wondering what was happening. Anne hugged Roxie while one of the other girls tried to stop the flow of blood from the wound in Beth's arm. Both of them looked like they'd been in a fight. Beth had swollen lips, and Roxie's left eye was bruised. Their clothes were tattered rags.

Addy looked out the door at the man with Mrs. Hutton. She recognized Inspector Reese Cannon from the night Mr. Leman was killed. He came in with Mrs. Hutton and the ambulance crew that would take Beth to the hospital. "Well, Miss Garcia, we meet again. I hear that you and Mrs. Hutton took care of things tonight."

Addy shook her head. "Mrs. Hutton rescued us all. I just happened to be outside when Roxie and Beth got here."

"It sounds like the girls wouldn't have made it if it hadn't been for you," he replied. "Mrs. Hutton filled me in on what happened. We've been searching for Mr. Rudd for some time now. Miss Garcia, may I speak to you in the lobby?" They walked out of the parlor door together, and he closed it behind her. "I've been investigating Mr. Leman's murder. The studio told me that the master ledger is missing. Did he happen to give it to you?"

Addy was in a quandary. *Should I tell him, or is he working for the Giovannis?* Addy knew some of the police force worked with the syndicate. She didn't know if the Inspector was on their payroll. She decided to wait. "No, he didn't give me the ledger."

He looked at her like he didn't quite believe her. "If you find out anything, let me know."

Addy nodded. As she returned to the parlor, Beth was being taken to the ambulance for the ride to the hospital, where the bullet would be removed from her arm. Roxie saw her friend off, then turned and hugged Addy. "Thank you. You saved our lives!"

Addy felt a little embarrassed by all the attention. "It was really Mrs. Hutton who saved us." She turned to the older woman. "Where did you learn to shoot like that?"

Mrs. Hutton smiled. "I lived on a ranch for many years, over in the Arizona Territory. We had to protect ourselves from all sorts of vermin. Both four-legged and two-legged."

Addy and Roxie sat on one of the couches in the parlor, with the others gathered around. "What happened to you?" Addy asked.

Roxie looked at her. "When we went to the place for the auditions, we found that the night club wasn't on La Brea at all. There was a private bus that took us to a large building on Olympic. It was a warehouse of some kind. We got off the bus and went through a door in the back of the building. It opened to some sort of office, and then behind a large crate was another door. We saw it was a speakeasy, not a legal night club.

"We did our auditions. There were seven of us. Then Mr. Rudd told us we were all hired, but we were to stay there. One of the girls said she couldn't stay, and she tried to leave. She was taken out and shot. They made us all watch—oh, it was horrible!" At this point, Roxie nearly broke down, but she gulped and continued, "He said that would happen to any of us that tried to escape. Mr. Rudd is a pimp, and that's his brothel." Roxie started to cry. "I don't want to think about what happened next, but this evening he wanted Beth and me to work the streets. We were taken to Hollywood Boulevard, and that's when we put up a fight and managed to escape, after getting hit a few times, so we got back here. And, well, you know the rest."

Everyone sat quietly, trying to absorb this information, while Mrs. Hutton got an ice pack and put it on Roxie's eye. Finally the other girls started to drift up to their rooms. Addy gave Roxie a hug and said her goodnights to them all. There weren't many people she could trust, she realized, and that made it harder to know what to do about that key. She had trouble sleeping that night.

****

Zeke had just put the water on to boil for the coffee when Nathan came in with the morning paper under his arm. He slapped it down on the table, along with a bag from the bakery down the street. The smell of hot cinnamon rolls made Zeke's mouth water.

Nathan sat down at the table. "Well, how did it go with Addy last night? It looks like the Giovannis didn't do you in."

Zeke turned around. "No, they didn't, but it was damned uncomfortable. Joe Giovanni is a person you don't want to meet on a dark night. How was your outing with Babs?"

Nathan grinned. "I asked her to marry me, and she said yes. I talked to her father last week."

Zeke clapped him on the shoulder. "You old dog, you. Congratulations!" He turned back to the coffee, and Nathan opened the newspaper. As Zeke put the coffee in the boiled water to steep, Nathan whistled.

"There was some sort of disturbance at the dormitories at Majestic last night."

The coffee cup dropped from Zeke's hand and shattered on the floor. "What happened?"

"Here, read it yourself."

Zeke took the paper and read about the arrest of Mr. Barney Rudd. He sucked in a gasp when he found that Addy was involved. *Hell, why didn't I see her to the door? She could have gotten killed.* He sat heavily on the chair.

"Buddy, you look like you've seen a ghost. Are you all right?"

Zeke slammed *The Times* on the table. "No, I'm

not. I'm going to go over there after breakfast to make sure she's okay." They stared at each other. "Nathan, this is getting to be a very dangerous town." Zeke got the dustpan to clean up the broken cup.

****

Addy, dressed in her navy blue skirt and white linen middy blouse, spent the morning after breakfast in the parlor, quietly reading "Little Women." It was a pleasant day for early December, so the windows in the room were open and the warm California breeze billowed the white lace curtains. Addy sighed. It was the calm after a stormy night.

Relaxed, she let the wind play in her hair and over her body like a gentle massage. Then she heard an auto come up the drive and stop. After a glance to see who was visiting, she ran to meet Zeke in the lobby.

"Oh, Addy!" He eyed her with concern as he drew her into an embrace. "I read what happened; it was in the newspaper this morning. Are you all right?"

She felt fine now. "Just shaken up a bit."

"If only I would have stayed a little longer..."

"You might have gotten hurt," she finished for him. "I'm glad you didn't."

Mrs. Hutton came into the parlor. "Hello, Mr. Shafer. I thought I heard someone come in."

He let go of Addy. "I stopped by to see if you were all right." He looked at Mrs. Hutton. "I wanted to take Addy to Westlake Park for the afternoon." He turned to Addy. "If that's something you would like to do."

She smiled. "That sounds swell."

Mrs. Hutton agreed wholeheartedly. "That's just what this girl needs. Addy, there's a picnic basket in the cabinet under the sink in the kitchen. Help yourself to anything in the icebox."

"Thank you, Mrs. Hutton." Addy hurried through the kitchen door. She found the basket and filled it with cold chicken, bread, apples and two slices of Mrs. Hutton's orange cake. She found a clean Mason jar and poured some lemonade into it, screwing the cap down tight. She added two plates, cups, napkins and utensils. When she returned, Zeke was holding an old blanket Mrs. Hutton had given him for sitting on the ground. Addy ran upstairs to get her broad-brimmed hat, and then they loaded the things into the auto and took off to the park.

Westlake was a city park on Wilshire Boulevard. It was a carpet of green lawn, with trees, around a small lake with rowboats to rent in a little wooden boathouse on the shore.

They found a place on the grassy green carpet to spread the blanket, amongst the many other people taking advantage of this pleasant Saturday afternoon. Addy took off her hat, since they were under a shade tree, and let the breeze go through her hair while Zeke opened the picnic basket. Together they shared the lunch.

After they'd finished eating, Zeke took Addy's hand and gazed into her eyes. "You look especially beautiful today. I hate to think I almost lost you."

She moved over and leaned back against his chest. He put his arms around her and cradled her, nuzzling the back of her neck, and the tingling ran throughout her body, settling in her private parts. Turning her head to the side, Addy ran her hand up his neck until her fingers stroked his hair. Their temperatures rose and their breathing became ragged as they kissed passionately.

"Sweetheart, I'd take you here, if there wasn't anyone around." Zeke's voice was hoarse with lust.

She too was nearly at the point of being ready to rip their clothes off, but her upbringing won out. "We really mustn't do this out in public." Addy caressed his face. They separated and collected themselves.

"Would you like to go out on the lake?" Zeke looked hopefully at Addy as she put the plates, cups, napkins and utensils back into the basket.

"That would be wonderful." She secured the basket top. "Why don't you go to the boathouse to see about it, and I'll take these things back to the auto." She put her hat back on as he folded the blanket.

Addy met Zeke at the lake just as he was paying a young man the rent for one of the boats. They stepped off the small pier and into the rowboat, where she sat in front while Zeke manned the oars and rowed to the center of the lake. He stopped, and for a moment they listened to the slapping sound of the waves against the side of the boat.

"Addy, are you all right? You've been through a lot these past few weeks. I worry about you."

"I'm still shaken from last night, but whatever happens, I seem to survive. It's been that way all my life. I guess God really has a purpose for all of us and when that's finished, we go." She shook her head. "I keep telling myself that, but I don't know if I believe it."

He reached out and held her hand. "You're one of the bravest girls I know. I think that's why I love you so much." They stayed that way for a few minutes until they felt a gentle bump. The boat had drifted to the shore, so Zeke took up the oars again.

Addy adjusted her hat when a breeze caught it, changing the subject as she did so. "Did you ever contact your family?"

"I sent my mother a letter telling her where I am and what I'm doing, but I haven't heard back from any of them yet."

"You've never told me about your family, except to say your father is a preacher."

Zeke rowed toward a willow at the edge of the

lake, and set the boat so the waves kept it near the shore. "I'm the oldest child of ten brothers and sisters. We lived at the edge of town next to the little Baptist church where my father was and still is the preacher. You think your uncle is strict? He's a lamb next to my father. He takes the Ten Commandments literally. Any minor mishap by me or my brothers or sisters was...well, he didn't spare the rod. Finally, he insisted I go into the ministry, and when I said I didn't want that, he beat me, saying I hadn't honored my father. That's when I left."

Addy reached out and took his hand in hers. "Oh, Zeke, I'm so sorry. That must have been terrible for you."

"It wasn't all bad, but having fun was almost against the church's teaching. I just didn't fit in there. Being with you and your family has shown me how good life with people who care about you can be. You're a very lucky girl to have a family that would take you in after your parents were killed."

She squeezed his hand. "Thank you for making me see that. I love you, Zeke."

"What happened up in San Francisco? How did you manage to survive?"

Addy took a deep breath and tears came to her eyes. "It was an early April morning, and we lived in one of the apartments above the restaurant where Papa worked. I slept in the front bedroom above the street and my parents and little brother, Joseph, were in the back bedroom. A mighty jolt woke me up, and the smell of dust came billowing up from the ground. There was dead silence from outside, and then the shaking started. I was thrown from my bed, but I hung on to it and watched as the whole side of the building disappeared.

"I heard a scream and a cry from the other room. When the shaking stopped, I picked my way through the debris and saw that where my family was, the wall had collapsed on them. They were all dead." Addy's voice broke and she started to cry.

Zeke held tightly to her hands. "How did your uncle find you?"

"I got out of the building, and a kind policeman took me to a wagon bound for one of the camps of survivors. Somehow, my uncle and grandpa found me with a picture they had that Mama sent them."

"Oh, Addy, I'm so, so sorry."

He handed her his handkerchief, then reached across and caressed her cheek, and the warmth of his touch traveled through her. "We both seem to have come out of terrible circumstances. It can't get anything but better."

Addy's heart twisted.

Say you'll be there with me. She looked deep in his brown eyes, trying to find the answer she sought, without asking out loud. Would he be there for her always?

Unaware of her question, Zeke picked up the oars and rowed a couple of times around the lake before heading back to the boathouse and helping her out onto the pier as the young man waited to take the boat back inside.

The late afternoon sun was nearing the horizon as they drove back to the dormitory. They enjoyed a kiss before they got out of the auto, and then Zeke carried the basket and blanket to the door, where he handed them to her.

"Thank Mrs. Hutton for me." He gave her a quick kiss. "See you at work. And please stay out of trouble."

Addy laughed. "I promise." She waved to him as he took off down the road.

Chapter 4

Back at work on Monday, Addy felt refreshed. She sat on a hay bale, enjoying the warm sunshine. As she waited to be called for her part in the filming, she read a letter that had arrived in the mail that morning from Aunt Jen. As well as reminding Addy that Christmas was only a few weeks away, the letter urged her to be sure to come for dinner and to bring Zeke. When Mr. Hanson gave a ten-minute break, Zeke joined her.

"Hey, beautiful, how are you doing?" Zeke plopped down beside her.

Addy smiled. "Swell. Do you have any plans for Christmas? This letter is from Aunt Jen, inviting us over for dinner. Are you going home to your family?"

"No, I don't have the money to go to Indiana. Anyway, I've never heard from them, and I'm not anxious to see my father. Your plans sound perfect. Tell your Aunt Jen I'll be delighted to escort you."

"How about your roommate, Nathan? He won't be alone, will he?"

"He's going to be with his girlfriend. He just got engaged. I suppose, after June, I'll be living by myself."

They watched as the studio limo pulled up to Mr. Hanson. The driver got out and talked with the director, who pointed in their direction. Almost immediately the driver came over to them. "Excuse me, are you Miss Garcia?"

Addy was startled. "Yes, I am."

"Mr. Abrams wants to see you."

She gasped. *Why does the head of the studio*

want to see me? She looked wide-eyed at Zeke, who shrugged.

"Come on, Miss Garcia. I'm here to take you to the main office building."

Addy followed him to the limousine, where he held open the door to the back seat. Addy got in and was whisked away to the large three-story building in the center of the studio grounds. She felt dowdy in the work dress costume she wore.

As the driver let her out, she stared in awe at the large glass entry before walking bravely into the lobby, where she said to the young woman at the front desk, "I'm Adeline Garcia. I was told that Mr. Abrams wants to see me."

The woman looked her up and down. "Take that elevator to the third floor. You will stop right in front of his office."

Addy went to the black iron cage in front of the elevator door. A man in a gray uniform opened the door for her. "Third floor, please." He closed the door behind her and switched on the lever controls. The machine whirred to life.

When the cables had tugged the box up far enough, the elevator attendant turned the lever to let her out. The iron door of the cage squeaked back and she stepped out right in front of a massive, polished oak door that bore a gold sign with the name 'Irving Abrams' in fine script.

Addy was shaking with nerves as she turned the knob and walked into the outer office. A beautiful young woman sat at a large desk, typing. The office was paneled in oak and hung with paintings. A huge Persian rug covered most of the floor, with expensive-looking chairs and couches here and there, intermingled with potted palms that stood like sentinels. The woman looked up from her typewriter. "Are you Miss Garcia?"

Addy nodded.

The secretary took a hornlike instrument off the hook on the wall behind her. It apparently had a tube snaking its way through to the inner office, because she said, "Miss Garcia to see you, sir," into the bell end, and a muffled reply came back. "Send her in."

The secretary rose from her seat and crossed the room to open a second oak door, motioning for Addy to follow and enter an office grander than the outer one. A dazzling crystal chandelier hung in the middle of the room, casting rainbows on the gilded angels near the ceiling. Deep mahogany paneling, which included a wall of built-in shelves, was set off by a dark green carpet that filled the room. Rich velvet couches and overstuffed chairs lined two walls. Behind Mr. Abrams, a large glass window looked out over the studio.

As she came in, he stood up from behind an elaborately carved desk with four leather chairs before it. "Please be seated, Miss Garcia."

Addy settled into one of the leather chairs and glanced around nervously, wondering what she had done to be called into the inner sanctum.

"Miss Garcia, we have been going over the screen tests you did when you arrived here, and I want to talk to you about them." As he spoke, he opened a cabinet by the shelves. Addy saw it contained bottles of various sizes and shapes. "Would you like a drink?"

Addy again wondered how wealthy people got away with having liquor so readily available when it was against the law for everyone else, but she kept her opinions to herself. "No, thank you, Mr. Abrams."

He poured one for himself and sat behind his desk again. "Miss Nora Steele is going to another studio. She was in her last year on her contract. The board had a meeting, and we decided that we would offer you a contract."

Addy gasped. "Why me? I haven't been here as long as some of the other girls." She was completely floored.

"You have worked closely with Miss Steele and Mr. Hanson. I heard you have been quite fearless in some of the things you were asked to do as a double. You also translate beautifully on film. You have a very expressive face. Are you theatrically trained?"

"Yes, I've done stage and vaudeville locally." She was in a daze. *This can't be happening. People try for years to get into the top roles. Something is wrong here. I wonder if Muriel said something to the Giovannis?*

"Good. I'll have our lawyer draw up a contract." He stood up and held out his hand to her. "I'll let you know when it's ready to be signed. Good day, Miss Garcia."

Addy arose and shook it. "Thank you, Mr. Abrams."

He didn't let go. "By the way, Miss Garcia, I heard you were the last to see Mr. Leman alive. Did he happen to say where the master ledger is?"

She felt a shock to her spine and hoped her "expressive" face didn't give her away. "He couldn't say much before he died."

"Pity. Well, you can go, Miss Garcia. The auto will be waiting to take you back to the set."

As she rode back, she pondered. *Am I supposed to give the key to Mr. Abrams? I don't know if I should trust him, if he's in with the Giovannis. If only Mr. Leman had been more clear. If only I knew who he meant wanted the ledger.*

When the auto deposited her back at the set, she nearly fell into Zeke's arms. "Mr. Abrams said Nora was leaving for another studio, and he offered me a contract!" She managed to get all the words out in less than two seconds.

Zeke laughed and whirled her around. "I won't complain about attending on the star anymore." Then he kissed her.

Mr. Hanson growled. "Shafer! Garcia! Get back to work!"

Addy smiled. *Just you wait, Mr. Hanson, until I'm the pampered princess. I'll demand some respect from you.*

A few days later, the limousine again came to take Addy to Mr. Abrams' office. When she walked in, Mr. Abrams was seated behind his desk, and a very thin, nervous man with a pack of papers sat in one of the chairs.

"Ah, Miss Garcia, please sit down. We are just waiting for our promotional director, Mr. McNeal, and his assistant. This is Mr. Hamilton, our lawyer."

Hamilton gave Addy a quick nod as she settled herself on another of the leather chairs. After a few minutes, Abrams' secretary appeared at the door. "Mr. McNeal and Miss Hathaway are here."

"Good. Send them in."

Introductions were made and Mr. Abrams took the papers from Mr. Hamilton. He began paging through them. "Since you don't have an agent, Miss Garcia, I will have Miss Hathaway serve as one. Is that satisfactory?"

Addy glanced at the attractive redhead who was concentrating on her chewing gum. "I suppose so."

"Now, Miss Garcia, for this contract, we require a few things in return. First, your entire loyalty will be to this studio. You cannot accept any work from anyone else or even mention any other studio in public. Next, any publicity appearances, charity or events that you are invited to because of your celebrity will be dictated by us. Any publicity photos will be put out only by our promotional department. No outside photographers will be allowed to take formal portraits. All your work will be assigned by us. You will be expected to work in roles in the motion pictures that we assign you. The contract is for two years. You will start at five hundred dollars a month. Then, if sales of your pictures warrant it, you will get raises at my discretion. If at any time you violate the rules of this contract or we find that your pictures are not profitable, we have the right to terminate this contract. Do you have any questions?"

Thoughts chased each other through Addy's head. *This is more money than I ever dreamed of, but is it worth having all the say-so of my life dictated by the studio? I wonder if I should ask Uncle Henry and Zeke what they think? No, if I want to take charge of my own life, I've got to do this myself.*

Addy looked at Miss Hathaway. She was hanging all over Mr. McNeal, practically sitting on his lap. Addy dismissed any thought of getting help from this woman. "Mr. Abrams, what if I want out of the contract before the end of the two years?"

He looked stunned. "No one ever asked that before. Well, sweetie, if you want out of the contract after it's signed, you have to pay the studio what we deem we're losing on you."

Mr. McNeal spoke up. "As head of the promotional department, I think she should change her name before she signs."

"And what's wrong with my name?"

"Too ethnic. Nora's last name was Burcowitz, if you remember. People like their stars to have American-sounding names."

"What do you suggest?" Mr. Abrams demanded.

"Adeline is fine, but we need another last name. What's your middle name, honey?"

"It's Rose."

Mr. McNeal gave it some thought. "Rose—Adeline Rose. Flows off the tongue real easy."

Mr. Abrams nodded. "I like it. Hamilton, have my secretary type that name on the contract as an 'also known as.'"

"Yes, sir." He exited the office.

"Now, McNeal, I want you to come up with a promotional campaign for our new featured actress, Adeline Rose."

Mr. Hamilton came back in and put the packet of papers in front of Addy. "Please sign here." He pointed to a dotted line that had the name 'Miss Adeline Rose' printed below her full one.

Addy, caught up in a whirlwind, found her old self-doubts surfacing under the pressure. *This is what I wanted, but why do I feel like there's something I should do first?* She pushed her feelings aside, dipped the pen into the ink and signed. Part of her was sad at cutting off the Garcia name. Was she being disloyal to her father?

Mr. McNeal and Miss Hathaway signed as witnesses, and then Mr. Hamilton signed, as well.

"Well, Miss Rose, you will now have your own dressing room at the star players' building," said Mr. Abrams with a smile. "Welcome to the big time." He put out his hand, and she shook it.

"Thank you, Mr. Abrams."

"Now, Mr. McNeal, I want you to arrange promotional appearances, charity events and press for Miss Rose. Let me see a list as soon as you have it."

"Yes, sir." He and Miss Hathaway hurried out the door.

"Mr. Hamilton, file the contract. I want you to give me a copy and have a copy for Miss Rose in her dressing room tomorrow."

"Yes, Mr. Abrams." He left the office with his stack of papers.

"Now, Miss Rose, we will have a drink to celebrate." Abrams walked over to his bar.

Addy realized she was trembling. "I don't drink, sir."

"You will have one with me." A slow smile spread across his face. "Please sit over there on the couch." He indicated an overstuffed tasseled couch by the wall.

"Oh, I'm fine here."

"Over to the couch, Miss Rose!" he shouted.

Addy jumped. What was wrong? She moved to the couch and sat on the dark purple velvet. Mr. Abrams brought two glasses with amber liquid over and handed her one.

"Here's to a successful career for you." He raised his glass, then took a sip, indicating with his other hand that she should do the same.

She gasped as the fiery substance burned down her throat, coughing as he settled next to her.

"Adeline, you can be more successful than you ever dreamed. I'll put your name all over this country." His arm came around her. "You can have any role you want." Before she realized what he was doing, his face nuzzled her neck and his other hand moved on her thigh, and then he raised himself up and came face to face with her. She looked at him in shock. *This man must be somewhere near the same age as Uncle Henry!* She shuddered with revulsion. "Mr. Abrams, please don't do this."

He pulled back and rubbed his crotch. "You have to understand, my dear. Everything has a price. You do me favors, I'll do you favors. That's how it works."

She leaped from the couch. "I didn't sign a contract to become a prostitute. I'm still virtuous, and I have a suitor."

He scowled. "Then you will have no say in the roles assigned to you until you get, let's say, more cooperative. You're lucky you have friends in high places, or you would be out of here." He stood also and put a hand on her shoulder. "You'll come around to my way of thinking. How do you think actresses get to where they are? Just make sure you're at the star players' building at six o'clock sharp tomorrow morning."

Addy set her drink on the end table by the couch and practically ran out of the office. This was worse than she could have imagined, and now she was stuck for two years. Maybe her refusal to be his trollop would get her fired. That would end the contract. She wondered whether the Giovanni family had anything to do with this, since Mr. Abrams had referred to friends in high places. Well, she had to finish up Nora Steele's final moving picture, and then she would find out, she vowed.

When Zeke greeted her as she returned to the set, Addy looked at him, ready to cry. "Just hold me." He wrapped his arms around her, and she stayed there for a few moments. *I need someone I feel safe with, someone like Zeke.*

"What happened at the signing? Didn't things go well?" he asked.

"I'm finding you can't get anywhere without people expecting favors in return. What we suspected about Nora may be true."

He pulled back and looked at her. "You didn't...?"

"No, but he tried." *Don't you trust me?*

"Who was it...Abrams?" His eyes flashed angrily. "He may be the boss, but he has no right trying to get favors from you. I have a good mind to go down there—"

"Zeke, please, nothing happened, because I didn't let it. They have to understand that not every girl is as loose as Nora. I'll just take what roles they give me and do my best. I won't sacrifice my virtue for better roles."

He held her in his arms. "I'm going to keep an eye on you to make sure you're safe."

"My hero." She sighed as she kissed him.

Just then Zeke was called to take some props

back to the truck, and Mr. Hanson walked over to Addy. "Miss Garcia, I've just been given the news that you're taking Miss Steele's place when she leaves. May I congratulate you on your promotion. I hope we can become...friends." He offered his hand.

"As a working relationship, yes." Addy shook his hand. *And are you after the same thing, too?* she wondered. *I'd better hold onto my virtue tight. At least Mr. Hanson knows my name now.*

****

Zeke glanced at the set where Addy was working. He hadn't stopped brooding since Addy told him about Abrams. He'd worked at this studio for over a year now, and he'd seen a number of young girls ruined because of the manipulations of the men over them. He knew Nora had bedded John Payton and Hanson, among others. Maybe even Abrams.

Was Addy ambitious enough to fall into that trap? She did tell Abrams 'No.' Or did she? Zeke gritted his teeth. *I want to believe her. But can I?*

Such thoughts swirled in his brain the rest of the afternoon, building into a very black mood as he sat in the Model T outside the crew quarters and waited for Addy to come out. It had become standard practice for him to take her back to the dormitory every day.

When Addy bounded out and plopped into the seat next to him it took only one glance at him and a shadow crossed her face. "Something wrong?"

He shifted the idling auto into gear and drove toward the gate. "I don't like this, at all. Every girl I've seen get a contract may as well have had a 'fresh meat' sign posted on her. I've seen a number of them ruined in the year I've been here. I don't want that to happen to you, but I can't be with you every minute." He turned onto the street toward the dormitory.

"Zeke, I didn't let Mr. Abrams touch me, and I'm

not going to let any other man, either. I love *you,* and I'm not going to trade my honor for a job. If it comes to that, I'll quit." Addy's eyes gave him a determined flash.

As Zeke pulled up in the driveway, he put on the brake, then caressed her face and ran his hand through the silky brown curls peeking out below her hat. He felt a swell of love for her and wanted to protect her from everything.

She took his hand in hers and tenderly kissed his palm. She squeezed his fingers and he could feel her trembling. "Nothing's changed between us." Addy traced his lips.

He gathered her in his arms, and with their deep kiss he felt a surge through his loins. God, he wanted her. "Goodnight, my love." Zeke reluctantly watched her all the way to the door before he took off toward home.

Nathan jumped when Zeke opened the door with a bang and then slammed his hand on the table.

"What's wrong with you?" Nathan retrieved a cup that had bounced to the floor.

"Addy is a contract player now." Zeke slumped in one of the chairs, feeling the darkness settle in his soul.

Nathan whistled. "That means she's bait for every stiff cock in the studio."

"Abrams already made a play for her. She told me she didn't give in to him."

"I hope, for her sake, she can hold the wolves at bay. You'd better keep a careful eye on her."

Zeke glowered. "Believe me, I will." He went back to brooding.

Chapter 5

In the morning, Addy arrived at the star players' building at five minutes to six and was met by the entourage of Mr. McNeal and Miss Hathaway.

"Ah, Miss Rose, welcome to your new job. I'll take you on a tour and give you the list of things you have to do this week." Mr. McNeal offered her his arm.

She walked with them into the building that was as large as the crew quarters but not nearly as plain and utilitarian. The lobby looked like a huge parlor, with carpeting and deep wood paneling. A few star players were seated on the fine furniture, reading scripts and newspapers.

"This lobby is where you can relax before the limousines come to take you to your set." McNeal motioned for her to follow him. They stopped by an elevator cage and the attendant opened the door. "Second floor, please." The iron door creaked shut and the cables sang out as they were hoisted up.

Stepping from the elevator, the small party turned to the left down the hall to room two-twenty. Addy ran her hand over a brass nameplate with the words 'Miss Adeline Rose' in fancy script.

"This is your main dressing room. You will report here each day at six o'clock for dressing, hair and makeup." He opened the door, and Addy gasped. Inside, it was furnished like a luxurious parlor, plus a wardrobe, a chaise lounge and several chairs. The chaise and chairs were elegant with gold paint and rich red velvet upholstery. The white walls held a few landscape paintings and gilded mirrors. Some potted ferns and palms gave accent to the room. Right in front of Addy was a huge vanity with a lighted mirror. Next to it, a young woman in a uniform stood smiling at her.

"Miss Rose, this is your personal attendant, Edwina. She will help you get dressed in the morning, do your hair or wig, as the case may be, and put on your makeup as required that day. She will be responsible for taking any needed change of clothing to the set as will be specified for the day's shooting."

Addy was completely speechless. *I don't seem to have to do anything for myself. I see why Nora was so spoiled. Well, I won't be like Nora. She didn't have someone like Zeke.* The glow at the thought of him warmed her.

"Miss Hathaway and I have to go, Miss Rose." Mr. McNeal turned to the door. "I'll send an auto for you at three this afternoon. You have an appointment with the publicity photographer for your stills."

"Thank you, Mr. McNeal, Miss Hathaway." Addy saw them to the door.

Edwina nodded to her. "Please sit in the chair so I can get you ready. Would you like me to bring you anything?"

"No, I'm too nervous."

"Here's your script for today. You can study it while I do your hair."

Addy looked at it. It was a modern day cops-and-robbers story. Addy almost snorted. *This will be a cinch. I'm living one now.*

After makeup, Edwina helped Addy into a white summer dress. Addy had never felt so helpless in her life. At crew quarters, she'd had to do everything for herself. When the telephone rang a few minutes later, Edwina answered it. "This is Miss Rose's room...Yes, we're ready." She hung up. "Miss Rose, the automobile is ready to take us to the set." She picked up a case and a garment bag.

Addy turned to her. "May I help you with that?"

Edwina looked at her incredulously. "This is my job, not yours."

"I'm sorry." Addy followed her out of the room and down to the auto. *My, she's snippy.*

When they both were in the back seat of the auto, Addy cleared her throat. "Edwina, I was just trying to help you. I didn't mean to usurp your job."

Edwina sighed. "Everyone starts out nice, but then you all turn into mean and spiteful women. I've worked here three years as a lead players' assistant, and it happens every time."

Addy's mouth went into a tight line. "Well, that won't happen to me."

Edwina snuck a glance at her. "We'll see."

Addy arrived on the set in grand style. Mr. Hanson helped her out of the auto and ushered her into the main tent for the briefing on the new film, walking her up to the front of the assembled cast and crew. "Let me introduce you to our new female lead. This is Miss Adeline Rose. Of course, most of you know her as Miss Steele's double, but with Miss Steele's departure Miss Rose has now moved up to take her place." There was polite applause. Addy smiled and looked at Zeke, who sat in the back with an unreadable look on his face. "Anne Reynolds will be her double."

With a glance at Anne, Addy mouthed, "Wonderful!"

At that moment the handsome hero, John Payton, entered the tent with a flourish. Mr. Hanson turned to him. "Of course, we still have Mr. Payton playing the lead." John, smiling his famous smile at the crowd, placed himself next to Addy and put his arm around her.

Addy thought he was getting awfully familiar for someone who, yesterday, wouldn't give her the time of day. She shrugged off his arm and went to sit in the chair next to Mr. Hanson.

The crew broke at midday, and Addy went over to Zeke, meaning to walk with him to the crew tent. Mr. Hanson cleared his throat. "Miss Rose, may I see you?" He sidled her over to the empty area of the assembly. "You don't eat with the crew anymore. You now are served in your own tent."

John Payton walked over to them. "Miss Rose, may I escort you to lunch? I was planning to get to know you better."

You had plenty of opportunities to get to know me before now. I wasn't good enough then. She looked at him. "Since you invited yourself, I guess you may come, but if you try anything, you're out." Addy walked by and saw John exchange a glance with Mr. Hanson. The director shrugged. She ignored the offered arm from John.

He followed her. "I'll be the soul of propriety."

In her tent, Edwina set up the lunch table for two. Included on the menu were poached eggs on toast, watercress sandwiches, sliced ham and assorted cakes and chocolates. Hot tea brewed in a pot next to a small bowl of lemon wedges. This wasn't like the fare at the crew's tent.

Edwina turned to Addy. "If it's all right with you, I'll go eat now."

Addy nodded. "Go ahead. And thank you for setting up." Edwina disappeared.

John held the chair for her. "Please sit."

"Do you always eat like this?"

He sat across from her. "The food varies, but the studio caterer comes in with excellent meals."

"Would you like some tea, Mr. Payton?" She poured some for herself.

"Yes, thank you. But you must call me John.

May I call you Addy? I've heard others refer to you by that name."

"All right…John. Lemon?"

He shook his head and she handed him his cup. "Addy, Mr. Hanson wanted me to school you on conduct, now that you're a lead player. It doesn't look good to associate with the crew."

"What?" Addy pursed her lips.

"Everyone knows about your dalliance with Mr. Hanson's gofer. Now that you're a star, that has to stop."

Addy threw down her napkin. "That's not a dalliance! Zeke is my suitor and is courting me!"

"Tsk, tsk, Addy. You should set your sights higher than a mere gofer. Like someone who makes more money. Also, you have to move out of the dormitory. Stars can afford their own homes or apartments."

"I don't like what you're saying. I have friends at the dormitory. I can't see any reason for moving away from them and living by myself."

"You'll find that your so-called friends will be very jealous of you. Leaving will be a relief. Believe me, I know." He stood up and came around behind her. He put his hands on her shoulders. "We could be very good friends if you give me a chance."

She shrugged off his hands, then stood up and turned to him. "I thought you were 'very good friends' with Miss Steele."

"Miss Steele was very good friends with a lot of people. She knew what she wanted and used men to get it." He put his hand on her waist. "You could get far, too."

"Mr. Payton, I want you to leave." She moved away from his hand and stood by the tent entrance.

"You'll find I'm right and you'll be coming back, begging me to help you." He gave a leer as he walked out the door.

Well, he has a nerve. I'm not going to abandon Zeke or my friends. John's no friend of mine. She finished her meal by herself.

Later, as Zeke dropped her off at the dormitory, she stayed in his arms a few moments. "Zeke, I don't know if I really want this. My freedom seems to be cut off. I could do more things as a lowly crew member than I can as a featured player. And I feel like a rabbit in a cage full of wolves."

He set his mouth in a tense line. "There's not much you can do about it, now that the contract has been signed. If it's any help, I'll always be around if you need me."

His kiss reassured her, and she got out and waved as he pulled out of the driveway. Addy was in deep thought as she went upstairs to her room. *I guess I'm stuck for two years. If it doesn't get any better than this, I don't know what I'll do.*

She was about ready to go down to dinner when a knock came on the door. Anne and Roxie were there when she opened it. "Come on, it's dinnertime," Anne said.

Before they got all the way downstairs, Roxie said, "Close your eyes." Both the girls guided her to the dining room. "Now open them."

Just as she did so, everyone there yelled, "Surprise!"

A colorful banner stretched across the back wall with 'Congratulations, Addy' in big black letters. Not only the girls from the building but their boyfriends, too, stood before her. She felt hands on her shoulders and, turning, found it was Zeke. She was too astonished to say a word.

Mrs. Hutton came over and gave her a hug. "I thought we would give you a party to celebrate your contract." She led Addy to a table, and Zeke held the chair for her. Anne and Roxie and their boyfriends sat with them, and they soon became engaged in dinner conversation. It wasn't long, however, before Addy noticed Georgia Banes glaring at her from a table across the room. As their eyes locked, Georgia got up and came toward her. She remembered Georgia was the one who had snubbed her right after she moved in.

"Well, Miss Garcia, I can see who the new pet is at the studio." She turned to anyone who would listen. "Isn't it interesting she has been at the studio less than a year and she gets a contract, while those of us who have been here longer were passed over?"

Addy bit her tongue and thought about punching Georgia in her face.

Georgia turned back to Addy, and in a voice dripping honey, said, "I guess it takes a Mexican whore to get anywhere in this studio."

It took only a moment for Addy to stand and, fists instinctively balled, to step around the table to where Georgia stood. "You take that back."

Georgia grabbed a glass of water from the table and dashed it in Addy's face, and Addy snatched a napkin and wrapped it quickly around her hand before, without a word, she slugged Georgia on the jaw. Georgia went to the floor with a scream of anger. As Addy was turning to go back to her seat, Georgia jumped up and grabbed her by the hair, toppling Addy into the table.

Mrs. Hutton took Georgia by the arms while Zeke held onto Addy as the girls tried to get to each other. "Stop it, both of you!" Mrs. Hutton shouted.

Georgia flashed her hatred. "Just like Nora, she's giving favors to the bosses!" And she spit at Addy.

"Miss Banes, I want you to pack your bags and be out of here in twenty-four hours. Is that understood?"

Georgia shook off Mrs. Hutton's grip and, with a look of sheer malice at Addy, she stalked out of the room. Mrs. Hutton glanced at Addy. "That temper of yours is going to get you in a lot of trouble one of these days."

Addy snorted. "Sorry, Mrs. Hutton." *How long do I have to endure such hateful people?* Zeke, his arm around Addy, walked her back to the table, where Anne put her hand on Addy's.

"Georgia is a troublemaker. We don't all feel that way."

Roxie agreed. "We know you better than that. She's just jealous."

Addy sighed. "John Payton warned me that I should move out of the dormitory. I see why. He said there would be people like that."

Zeke frowned and pointed his finger at her nose. "John also has designs on you. To get you out of the dormitory is his fondest wish. You'll want to be careful around him."

Mrs. Hutton raised her glass of ginger ale and clinked it with her knife. "Let's all drink a toast to Addy's success and hope that it comes to all of my girls."

Everyone clapped. "Hear, hear!"

Before Zeke left, he and Addy stood by the Model T. "Where did you learn to fight like that? I've never seen a girl wrap a napkin around her hand before a fight."

She felt her cheeks burn. " My father took me to see John L. Sullivan bare-knuckle box, before the earthquake. I remember asking why Mr. Sullivan put the cloth around his hand, and my dad told me it would cushion the blows. I haven't lost my temper like that since school. I didn't have many friends, because..." She gave a shuddering sigh. "Looking Mexican, I was a target for every bully there, and I always was the one in the principal's office. I've tried to keep calm, but tonight, I couldn't. I know relations between Mexicans and Americans have always been strained. That's the reason my parents had to move to San Francisco after they were married. Both families objected to the union. I've never seen my father's family."

Zeke buried his face in her hair. "I'm so sad you grew up like that. We didn't have many Mexicans in Indiana, so there wasn't a problem there. I guess nobody understands what it's like until they experience it." He kissed her.

She smoothed back the errant lock of hair on his forehead. "I love you, you know."

"Goodnight, my Mexican Rose."

As he drove away, Addy blew him a kiss, her heart swelling with love for the man who adored her.

A few days later, Addy invited Muriel to have lunch with her. Muriel came into the tent, looking good in her expensive gray business suit. She sat down across from Addy and took some of the roast turkey and wheat bread to make a sandwich.

"Who are those musicians out there?" Muriel asked.

Addy laughed. "Looks silly for a motion picture without any sound, doesn't it? It's something new Mr. Hanson is trying. Some of the studios are playing the music they will send to the theaters with the film, so we can get a sense of how the scene will sound, and we can play off it. It's quite nice to listen to."

"Well, how do you like your new position?"

Addy took a sip of her tea and sighed. "It's interesting, being pampered, but it can be irritating, too. I can't talk to my friends like I used to. And the handsome hero just wants to use me for recreation."

Muriel smiled as she buttered her bread. "You're making more money, though. I heard Mr. Abrams is pleased with your work. I'm glad I talked to Tony's father...oops!"

"What? You talked to Tony's father about me?"

Addy glared at her. *I thought Muriel was behind this. What was it Mr. Abrams said? You do me favors, I'll do favors for you. What kind of favors will I have to do for the Giovannis?*

"I'm sorry, Addy. I didn't mean to tell you. I thought since Nora Steele was leaving the studio, I would put in a good word about you."

"That's probably what Mr. Abrams meant when he said I had friends in high places. I refused to be his trollop, though." Addy gritted her teeth. "I want to get a contract for my work, not because I have a connection with the Giovannis. Because of my talent. Now I'll never know if I could do it myself, thanks to you."

Muriel lowered her voice. "I'm sorry. I only meant to help. Most women who get a contract are used for favors. I heard Nora had trysts with several men on a regular basis, with Mr. Abrams, Mr. Hanson and Mr. Payton among them. I wanted to save you from that."

"That explains why John Payton made a pass at me. I'm thinking less and less of this industry. They all seem to be users of one kind or another. Please don't do any more for me unless you check with me first."

Muriel flushed and nodded.

Addy plucked an apple from a bowl and took a bite. "Next week is Christmas. Won't you and Tony come to your parents' home? They do miss you very much, and I know it would be a wonderful gift to have the whole family together again."

Muriel shifted in her chair. "I think of them often, but Father may never accept Tony."

"You'll never know until you try." She put her hand on Muriel's. "Please come."

"I'll talk to Tony and see."

The following Saturday, Addy, Anne and Roxie took the streetcar to downtown Los Angeles to do their Christmas shopping in the middle of the bustling city. The smell of exhaust was everywhere from the number of autos in the street. The holiday mood was in full swing. They pressed their noses at the May Company windows to see the animated displays. There were scenes of families getting together in a setting such as it would have been before the turn of the century. A woodstove puffed smoke as the mechanical woman removed a huge fake turkey. Children laughed around an elaborately decorated tree with a train circling it. The section near the door was Santa's workshop, where elves worked with rhythmic movements on toys and the jolly old elf went over his long list.

The girls looked at each other and smiled, then headed into the department store. People crowded all the counters and the drone of voices was everywhere. The decorations sparkled with lights and the smell of evergreen and cologne filled the air.

Addy had made a list of things she wanted to buy. Now that she made more money, she could afford nicer presents—a humidor for Uncle Henry, some French bath salts for Aunt Jen, a magnifying glass for Grandma and a tin of pipe tobacco for Grandpa. Tony and Muriel were harder to buy for, because they could purchase just about anything in the world, so she got them a tin of assorted fancy chocolates. For James, she found some brand new radio crystals for his hobby. Casey and Buster would each receive a new baseball bat and glove, and for Maggie there was a doll that cried when you held her a certain way.

Zeke's gift was going to be special. He had an old pocket watch that was always losing time or stopping. Addy selected a fine silver wristwatch and had the engraver put 'To Zeke, Always, Addy' on the back.

The girls laughed and juggled their shopping

bags on the way home. Addy was truly in the Christmas spirit. She even sang Christmas carols while she wrapped the presents.

****

Whistling, Zeke opened the apartment door, put all his packages on the table and threw his key on the counter.

Nathan came out of the bathroom in his underwear. "Hey, pal, looks like you were shopping. What's for me?"

Zeke grinned at him. "Nothing, if you start snooping. Are you going out tonight?"

"Babs and I are going to a holiday dance." Nathan picked up a small box among Zeke's items. "Bud, that isn't what I think it is, is it?"

Zeke grabbed it back. "So what if it is?"

Nathan put his hand on Zeke's shoulder. "You haven't known her long enough. I've been seeing Babs for seven months now. You've only seen Addy a little over a month. What do you know about her?"

"Enough to know I don't want to be without her."

Nathan looked at his friend and narrowed his eyes. "You should plan on a long engagement. Whirlwinds never work out right."

"This will. Addy is the only girl for me. Now lay off!"

Nathan started toward the bedroom. "I don't want to see you hurt again. The way Helen used you, then flaunted—"

"I don't want to talk about Helen!" Zeke cut in, slamming his hand onto the table. "Addy's not like Helen."

Nathan turned around at the bedroom door and put his hands up. "Okay! I hope you're right, for your sake."

Teeth gritted, Zeke started to wrap presents, but he was no longer in the Christmas spirit.

****

Addy was ready when Zeke came to pick her up on Christmas morning. They were going to church with her family, and then she would help with the feast. Mrs. Hutton was adding some new ornaments to the tree in the parlor as Addy paused on her way out.

"Mrs. Hutton, you won't be alone for Christmas, will you?"

"No, dear, don't worry about me. A number of the girls can't go home for the holiday, so we are having a celebration right here. A Merry Christmas to you, and to you, too, Mr. Shafer."

With smiles, they both wished her the same.

Addy had put all her gifts into a satchel, and Zeke carried it out for her, setting it next to the gifts he had brought. He helped her into the Ford, and they headed for her aunt and uncle's home.

When they got there, Zeke carried more than one armful of gifts inside while Addy's family made much over her new hairstyle. Uncle Henry disapproved of it but said, "What's done is done." Aunt Jen thought it looked fine.

They followed Uncle Henry's Packard to church. Zeke seemed a little uncomfortable at the service. He kept clearing his throat and coughing. Addy attributed that to his problems with his father. She knew Zeke hadn't been to church since he left his family. Probably his father had ruined it for him.

When they returned home, there was a sleek roadster parked on the street. Addy's heart swelled with joy to see that Muriel and Tony had come and were waiting on the porch for them.

Aunt Jen tore from the auto and took Muriel into her arms while the rest of the family gathered around them. Uncle Henry approached Tony with a grim look on his face, and Addy nervously grasped Zeke's hand.

"Mr. Giovanni, I didn't like the way you stole my daughter away, and I still don't agree with this marriage, but the deed is done and Muriel is of age, so there is nothing I can do to end it." He glanced at Addy, then back at Tony. "Because I want this family to remain together, I have to accept it." He went inside the house without another word.

Aunt Jen hugged Tony. "Well, I welcome you. Please come in."

Tony looked uncomfortable as he gazed after Uncle Henry. "Thank you, ma'am." Tony and Muriel picked up the gifts they had brought and went in with the rest of the family.

Aunt Jen took Addy's arm and drew her aside. "I guess I have you to thank for this, since you were the one in contact with Muriel."

"I just suggested she should come for Christmas, to keep the family together. Muriel made the decision on her own."

Aunt Jen squeezed her arm. "Thank you, Addy."

In the kitchen, Muriel and Addy helped with the dinner preparations after Grandma gave Muriel a hug. "So glad to have you home again. Please don't stay away."

She smiled. "I'll come back to see all of you, don't worry."

Addy realized that this was the way it should be. The idea that all of them could be together again made Christmas perfect. Adding Tony and Zeke to the mix was wonderful. Tony certainly didn't seem as menacing as his father.

The smell of the Christmas ham filled the kitchen, and Addy put on one of the aprons and got to work snapping green beans. She knew Grandma and Aunt Jen would have gotten the breads and desserts ready yesterday, and the fruit cakes had been soaking in brandy-covered cheesecloth in tins since the day after Thanksgiving. They had bought a stock of brandy for that purpose before prohibition started.

As she worked on the beans, Addy glanced out the kitchen window into the backyard. Zeke and Tony were playing baseball with Casey and Buster, while Maggie sat on the back steps, giggling. Addy felt a warm glow as she watched Zeke. *He really seems like he belongs here. I do love him so much.*

Zeke took off his coat and rolled up his shirt sleeves. He stood there with the bat, waiting for Casey to throw the ball. His arms were taut and muscular from hauling scenery and props at the studio. Addy watched as his muscles tensed in anticipation. He was very trim, and as he leaned to hit the ball, she could see the rounded edge of his backside molded under his trousers. She started to breathe quicker and felt warmth creep under her skin.

Addy jumped as Aunt Jen put her arm around her. "Honey, those beans won't cook themselves."

Grandma chuckled. "Now, Jen, the girl is allowed some giddiness when she's in love. I remember how it was, don't you?"

Addy smiled as she put the pot next to the gas burner and took a kitchen match out of its holder on the wall. It was hard to imagine anyone getting giddy over Uncle Henry. Carefully, she scratched the match head on the sandpaper strip attached to the side of the tin holder and turned the gas jet on with the white enamel knob. The blue flame danced to life, and she adjusted the heat. She put the pot of beans and water on the burner, then put the lid on.

When dinner was ready, the women fixed the table with all the Christmas finery. The large haunch of ham with the clove-studded fat was set in front of Uncle Henry's place, along with the fancy carving knife.

As soon as all were at the table, Uncle Henry

offered a heartfelt prayer: "Bless this Christmas feast we share together, oh, Lord. Thank you for allowing us all to be at this table. And let us remember absent relatives and friends at the celebration of your birth. Amen."

Muriel took some of the ham and passed it. "Did Addy tell you she got a contract at the studio?"

Addy quickly jumped in. "No, I haven't told them yet."

Aunt Jen looked at her. "Does that mean you're a star now?"

"Yes. Nora Steele left to go to another studio, and they offered me a two-year contract."

Grandpa smiled. "Well, I guess you'll be making more money now. Congratulations!"

"Keep careful track of your finances, Adeline," Uncle Henry said. "Don't go spending on frivolous things."

Muriel snuck a glance at Uncle Henry. "I guess that proves that Addy isn't too plain."

Uncle Henry gave Muriel a withering look.

Addy shook her head. "I don't plan to go buying everything in sight. In fact, I'm still living at the dormitory." *Everything is a lecture with him.*

Every Christmas, it was the tradition that, while the ladies fixed the meal, Uncle Henry and Grandpa trimmed the Christmas tree and set the presents under it. They did this behind closed doors. After dinner, the doors were opened and the family crowded around the beautiful tree. This Christmas, Addy felt Zeke grasp her hand and squeeze it. She looked into his eyes and saw them glowing with happiness.

The tree was glorious with the new electric light strings woven through the branches. Glass ornaments that had been in the family for forty years seemed to have graced the tree forever, in the minds of the younger family members. Metallic silver icicles hung from the branches, reflecting the multi-colored lights. On the top, shining brightly, was a gilded star with an electric light in its heart.

Maggie jumped and clapped her hands in delight. Grandpa lifted her up and gave her the stocking that Santa had left for her the night before. When he put her down, she squealed and ran off with her treasures.

Zeke sat in one of the overstuffed chairs with Addy perched on the arm beside him. Her heart was so full, she almost cried with happiness.

Presents were handed out from under the tree, and Addy gasped when she opened the gift from Tony and Muriel. Diamond earbobs! She protested to Muriel that it was too extravagant, but Muriel laughed and said they could afford it.

As Zeke opened his gift from her, his eyes lit up. "Addy, what a nice watch. Thank you."

She leaned in and whispered in his ear, "Turn it over."

He read the inscription and gave her a kiss on the cheek. "That means a lot to me. I'll always cherish it." He put it on his wrist.

A moment later, Addy was perturbed at the realization that all the presents had been distributed and there was nothing for her from Zeke.

When the family gathered around the piano to sing Christmas carols, Zeke took Addy by the hand. "Let's go out into the garden for a while."

She hesitated, because singing carols was one of her favorite parts of the Christmas celebration, but she went with him out the back door, wanting to be near him, regardless.

The sun was getting low in the sky, casting long shadows on the grass. Everything around them looked golden. They settled on the wooden bench under the wisteria arbor, and as Zeke put his arm around her, she felt a warm loving glow that matched the sun. A light breeze rippled her hair, and she gazed deep into his brown eyes.

"Addy," he began, "I talked to your grandfather and uncle earlier. They agreed to what I'm going to ask you."

Her heart started thumping in her chest so hard the echo of it pounded in her temples. *I know! Oh, yes, yes, yes!*

"I wanted to give you your present in private." He took a small box out of his coat pocket. "Addy, I never loved anyone like I love you. I want you to have my children and grow old with me. Please say you'll marry me."

She opened the box, and inside was a ring with a lovely small diamond. She took it out and the sun rays hit it, making rainbow sparkles that glowed. The emotion in her heart swelled in her throat and tears spilled onto her cheeks. "I will!" was all she could say as she held him in her arms. "Let's tell the rest of the family." She pulled back and dried her eyes on her handkerchief.

He took the ring and put it on her finger. "There. Now we're officially engaged." He stood and gently lifted her to her feet, kissing her carefully before draping his arm around her as they walked back to the house.

Aunt Jen and Grandma cried and the rest of the family congratulated them at the announcement of their engagement.

Muriel hugged Addy. "I'm so happy for you."

"Have you set a date yet?" Aunt Jen asked.

Addy shook her head. "No, but we'll let you know when we do."

On the way to the dormitory that evening, Zeke gripped the steering wheel and glanced at Addy. "Let's set the date soon. This is torture, not being with you. I want you so much."

Addy felt that tingling sensation down in her

belly. "I need you, too. I hate it when we have to say goodbye."

He drove the auto into the driveway of the dormitory and shut the engine off. No one came to the door or windows of the building, and Zeke turned to her with longing. "Addy, may I touch you?"

She had an inner fight with herself, not knowing if she could control her urges. "Yes," came out in a hoarse whisper.

"Oh, Addy." He ran his hand over her dress and caressed her breasts. She felt her nipples tighten at his touch and her breathing became ragged. His hand moved over her stomach, sending shock waves to her innermost parts, and she quivered. She hardly cared when he slipped his fingers up her dress and felt her slit over her drawers, warm and wet. She moaned and so did he. "Addy, touch me."

He took her hand and put it on his crotch, where she felt the long hard length of him through his trousers. He made a low growl in his throat. She knew if she let this go further, she would lose control. With great difficulty, she pushed him gently away and collected herself. "Zeke, we can't do this now."

He made a fist and hit the steering wheel. "You're right, but this is the closest thing to hell on earth. Sorry about saying hell."

"That is the right word."

He exhaled a rough sigh. "Would you mind if I didn't walk you to the door?"

She felt concerned. "Why not? Are you upset with me?"

"Uh, Addy," he said, looking embarrassed, "when a man is in this condition, it's uncomfortable to walk."

She hid a smile. "Oh, sorry." Addy climbed out of the auto and took her box of gifts. She went around to the driver's side and stood on the running board.

"Goodnight, my love." She kissed him, then walked up the path, calling out, "Merry Christmas!" in her wake.

Everyone inside made over Addy's ring. "Oh, Addy, I'm so happy for you!" Roxie said as she hugged her.

"That should keep the buzzards at bay, but you never know," said Mrs. Hutton.

In the next day's mail, an invitation came from the Giovanni home. Addy took it up to her room and opened it. It read:

The pleasure of your company is requested on
December 31st at 8:00 pm
for a formal black-tie New Year's Eve party.
Hors d'oeuvres and refreshments
will be served.
You may bring a guest.
Please RSVP before December 29th.

Addy talked to Zeke at work about the invitation. "That means we will have to get formal attire to go to this thing. Can you afford it?"

Zeke thought for a minute. "I know the head of the costume department. Maybe he can lend me a tuxedo for the evening."

"I don't have time to have a formal made, but I can go to Bullocks and get one off the rack. I'm so glad you can go with me. I'll stop by shipping and tell Muriel we'll be there." Addy gave him a quick kiss and was off.

Chapter 6

The fake bridge collapsed into the rushing waters of the back lot's stream, and the handsome hero ran to save Addy from certain death, grabbing her off the bridge and leaping to the low bank. At first their footing seemed sure, but then somehow they found themselves in the water. As John Payton helped her to stand, she felt a pain in her ankle.

"Ouch, that hurts!"

Zeke ran to the bank to help them both out. "What's wrong, Addy?"

"I think I twisted my ankle."

Mr. Hanson stalked over from his station by the camera. "Well, that shot is ruined. Mr. Payton, Miss Rose, go towel off and have your clothes dried. We'll try this shot again this afternoon."

John put his arm around Addy. "Can you walk? I'll help you back to your tent."

Zeke hurried to her side. "I can attend to Miss Rose."

Hanson scowled. "Shafer, I need you to help rebuild the bridge. Get to work!"

Zeke gave Addy a look of concern. "I'll check up on you when I'm finished."

By the time Addy reached her tent, her ankle didn't seem to be hurting as much. "Thank you, John. I'll see you later." She didn't want John in her tent. Deep down, Addy didn't trust him anywhere around her.

"I'll help you to a chair and take a look at your foot before I go," he insisted, keeping his hold on her waist until they were inside, where he sat her down.

"Edwina, could you and my attendant, Lem, run down to the laundry and pick up some more towels? Our clothes need to be dry before this afternoon. You can spread them out in the sun."

Addy stood up carefully. "My ankle's fine now." Even if it wasn't, she didn't need his fingers on it or his presence annoying her any longer. She picked up a couple of towels and her robe and gave a wave of dismissal to him as she went behind the dressing screen. "Thanks for your help. See you this afternoon."

She took off her clothes right down to her skin and dried herself thoroughly before she slipped on the robe and a pair of slippers. Then, with her wet things gathered to take outside, she walked around the screen.

The sight that met her eyes was horrifying. John stood there, stark naked, leering at her. Too stunned to move, Addy felt the clothes drop from her arms as warmth flushed her face in embarrassment. "What are you doing here?" she finally choked out. "I thought you went back to your own tent." And suddenly she remembered the warning Zeke had given her about Payton having designs on her.

In one quick move, John held her and untied her sash. "I thought since everyone was busy, we could have some fun." Like an expert, he whipped the robe off her and threw it into the corner, easily holding her despite her desperate attempts to get away.

To her horror, she was completely exposed. "Stop! Don't!" she yelled.

As Addy struggled to get out of his grasp, he ruthlessly pushed her to the floor, pinning her down and trying to enter her almost immediately, while she wriggled and fought and cried out in pain.

"You're too dry down there. I can fix that." Hooking both of her legs with his own and holding her wrists on either side of her waist, he put his face between her legs and licked. Oh, God, what was he doing? What could she do? She couldn't move! Except internally, she thought, and released her bladder. He raised up, choking and spitting out her urine, but he didn't let her go. "You goddamn Mexican bitch! You think you're too good for me?" He raised her arms and held them down over her head while he hovered over her. "Take this!" and he rammed his hard erection into her.

A searing, tearing pain engulfed her. She couldn't cry out because his mouth covered hers.

Addy heard a step, then Zeke's enraged voice. "Addy! What's...Payton, get the hell off of her!" Zeke grabbed the erstwhile hero by the shoulders and pulled him up. They scuffled, then Zeke put a knee on John's stomach and held his head against the floor by his neck. "Start talking, you bastard!"

John's eyes bulged. "Take your hands off," he rasped.

"He raped me!" Addy's sobs barely allowed her to speak.

"She lies." John coughed as Zeke loosened his grip. "She invited me in here and seduced me. She told me to get rid of Edwina and Lem, and then she took off her clothes and wanted me to do the same."

Zeke stood up and finally looked at Addy, who was trying to shield herself with her hands and arms as she looked frantically through her tears for her discarded robe. "Zeke, no! Don't believe him!"

He took a deep breath. "You went back with him, even after I warned you." He turned to John, who was putting on his damp outer clothes. "Go on, get out of here."

John grabbed his shoes and underthings and went out.

Zeke located her robe and threw it over her. "Cover yourself." Giving one last disgusted glance at her, he disappeared out of the tent.

She wrapped herself in the robe and sobbed, still sitting in her blood and urine. *He doesn't believe me! Oh, God, what am I going to do?*

When Edwina finally got back with the towels, Addy was on the chaise, shaking and in pain. "Edwina, call the police. I've been raped." Edwina left the towels and hurried out.

Addy gave her story to the officer who arrived shortly, and then Edwina stayed with her while he went to investigate. Half an hour later, he was back. "Miss Garcia, I checked with several witnesses, and I seem to have conflicting stories. What I'm saying is, it comes down to what to believe, your story or his, and the only ones who know the truth are the two of you. He claims you had him come into your tent and send off your attendants for towels and that both of you then took off your clothes. Is this true?"

Addy took a deep breath. "All except that it was *his* idea to send off the attendants. And when I removed my clothes, I thought he was gone."

The officer shut his notepad. "Miss Garcia, I want to be honest with you, because I think you're telling the truth. My advice would be to drop the charges."

"But I didn't seduce him!" she retorted.

"I've never seen one of these cases go through without a messy trial. The woman is painted in the worst light and, oftentimes, her reputation is ruined for life. I've never seen something like this ever be successful for the woman." He put his hand on her shoulder. "I'm offering some fatherly advice. Drop the whole thing and never let yourself get into such a situation again."

Addy put her face in her hands. What was she supposed to do? Should she go through a trial she probably wouldn't win, just for the principle of the thing? Should she let Payton get away with this? What was the best thing to do? With a deep, shuddering breath, she looked up at the officer gazing kindly at her. "All right, I'll take your advice. Drop the charges."

"Miss Garcia, you won't regret this. I promise to keep this from the press."

"Thank you," she said as he exited the tent. "Edwina, could you tell Mr. Hanson that I'm taking the rest of the afternoon off?"

"Yes, ma'am," Edwina said softly as she went out.

****

In the lunch tent Zeke sat with Anne and Roxie, his face buried in his hands, trying to get the horrible image of John and Addy out of his mind. The investigating policeman came into the tent.

Zeke looked up at him. "Well?"

The man looked grim. "Mr. Shafer, Miss Garcia has dropped the charges."

Zeke jumped up. "What?"

He put his hand on Zeke's shoulder. "Her reputation would be on the line if she went through with this."

"Her reputation? She told me he raped her!"

"Mr. Shafer, please listen to me—"

Zeke shrugged off the policeman's hand and tore off his watch, tossing it to Anne. "Give this back to her. I don't want it anymore!"

He pushed past all of them, heading to the parking lot, not even stopping at the crew quarters. He angrily dashed the tears that started to form in his eyes. He kicked the tire of his auto before he cranked it over. *Just like Helen. She's just like Helen, in the arms of another man, just like I found Helen.* He pounded on the steering wheel as he turned onto the street. *I loved you, Addy. I was willing to give love a chance again, and you do this. My father was right. There is no rape. Women use that as an excuse when they are caught.* He felt a pain in his chest and

118

knew his heart was breaking.

****

Addy didn't see Zeke anywhere when the studio auto came to take her back to the star players building. She cleaned up, changed clothes, and went outside. When she didn't find the Model T in its usual spot, waiting to take her back to the dormitory, her vision blurred as her eyes overflowed. *What is he thinking?* She looked at the ring. *I can't lose him now! I need him more than ever!* Addy walked the mile to the dormitory with tears streaming down her face all the way, tears of both pain and shame.

Mrs. Hutton was there to greet her. "Addy, I'm so sorry. Anne and Roxie told me what happened, when they came in a few minutes ago." She hugged Addy tight.

"I haven't seen Zeke since he fought with John. He acted angry with me, as though he didn't believe me. I don't want to lose him—how could he not understand what happened?" Addy blurted out between a fresh burst of sobs.

Mrs. Hutton gave her a handkerchief. "My dear, it was probably hard on him, too. Go upstairs. Anne and Roxie are waiting for you."

The girls were sitting at the top of the stairs. "Ouch, it hurts to climb." Addy gripped the banister for a moment before painfully climbing on up to them. In her room, they all sat on Addy's bed. "What went on outside, there?" Addy asked, a rasp in her voice. She continued to mop tears from her face.

Roxie looked at her hands. "The officer had everyone that knew anything give him their statements, and then he asked a few questions. Why did you drop the charges?"

"He thought it was for the best, because rape trials never come out good for the woman, he said. I've always heard men say that women ask for it, but

I never tried to seduce John Payton. What bothers me most is, I haven't seen Zeke since he pulled John off me."

Roxie's mouth was set in a straight line. "You know, John is very handsome, and a lot of girls would do anything for attention from him."

Addy glared at her. "I have no desire for any so-called attentions from Mr. Payton. He's an arrogant, self-centered brute."

Roxie put her hands up. "Okay! I'm sorry! It's something that always seems to happen to the star players. They end up in compromising positions."

"Well, that's not going to be me. I made a promise to Zeke and I'm not going to break it."

Anne took Addy's hand. "Addy, Zeke told me to give this to you." She opened her other hand, and Addy saw the watch she had given him for Christmas. It was as though a dam had burst as she sobbed while Anne and Roxie held her. *Zeke, no, don't leave me! I need you—don't leave me!*

Later, she drew herself a warm bath. Addy watched the steam waft up and fog the mirror. She eased herself over the side of the footed bathtub and into the water, gasping as the water touched her bottom. Pain was still sharp and real in both her body and mind, and despite the soreness she kept rubbing the soap over her crotch and thighs. *I still feel so dirty. I don't think I'll ever be clean again.* Addy didn't know how long she sat weeping in the bath.

****

Zeke stared out the window of the apartment, unmoving, until Nathan came bounding in. Nathan's smile faded when he saw Zeke.

"What happened? You look like the grim reaper himself."

Zeke opened and closed his mouth a couple of times. "I found Addy with John Payton."

Nathan's face reflected shock. "Buddy, I'm sorry."

"It happened like it did with Helen. Addy told me she was raped. I warned her about Payton, and she went to her tent with him anyway."

Nathan was silent for a few moments. "Are you sure she wasn't telling the truth?"

Zeke's hand came down on the table next to the chair. "She dropped the charges!"

"Are you going to give her a chance to explain?"

"Why? So she can tell me lies? No, I'm getting a transfer tomorrow. I don't want to be around her anymore. I'll get my ring back from her first, though."

"Maybe you should sleep on it. Don't make any hasty decisions."

Zeke turned his head and gazed at nothing out the window again.

****

The next day Addy tried to be businesslike when she came on the set, but everyone knew what had happened, and the tension was thick in the air. Her bottom was still sore, but she tried to put it out of her mind. She did a few scenes where she was supposed to be relieved to see her hero, but Mr. Hanson kept stopping the filming. Finally, he drew Addy aside.

"Miss Rose, you can't be looking at your hero like you want to gut him. I know what happened yesterday, but this is where you can prove your worth as an actress. You aren't Addy and he isn't John. You are Elizabeth, who desperately needs the mortgage money or your father's farm will be taken. Your neighbor, James, finds the crook who stole the funds and gets it to you in the nick of time. You are relieved and grateful. Now show me how a great actress does it."

Addy put herself in another place and

121

concentrated on make-believe. She even managed a passionate kiss for the hero in the final scene. There was silence when Hanson called halt, then Anne stood up from the sidelines. "Bravo, Miss Rose!" And the rest of the crew gave her a standing ovation. She wasn't going to let John get to her again.

Zeke was nowhere to be found. On a break from the filming, Addy touched Anne on the arm. "Where is Zeke? Do you know?"

Anne looked sadly at her. "I saw him this morning. He said he got a transfer to work in the shipping department."

"Did he say anything else?"

Anne shook her head.

"I have to talk to him." And as if he'd heard, Addy saw Zeke standing by her tent. She didn't want to think about good or bad right now, but maybe she could ease his mind.

He watched her walk up, then put his hands behind his back and looked at his shoes. "I want to speak to you in private."

"Come into my tent." Inside, she said to Edwina, "Could you give us some privacy?"

"Yes, ma'am," Edwina said as she stepped outside.

"Addy," he began, "remember what I said about my strict upbringing?"

She nodded.

"Well, I've been having difficulty with this whole thing. My father taught that there is no such thing as rape. Girls who are raped somehow deserve it. Also, this isn't the first time I found a girl I loved in another man's arms."

"But—"

"Addy, please, let me finish. I didn't want to believe that about you. Then I started thinking. You walked back with him to your tent, even after I warned you. Then you called the police, but you dropped the charges. That's when I started to doubt your story. Until I can work this out with myself, I want my ring back."

Addy's voice shook. "Before I give it back, I need to say that, yes, I was stupid and naïve when I allowed John into my tent, but I thought he left. I was going to press charges, but the officer advised me that a trial would go badly and ruin my reputation. He said it would be better if I dropped the whole thing and never put myself in that situation again. I love you, Zeke. I would never cheat on you."

And then she took the ring off and gave it to him. *If I lose Zeke, it's all John's fault.*

He looked very sadly at the ring in his hand. "I've got to work this out," he repeated as he went out of the tent.

Addy felt her whole world crumbling away, much like her bedroom wall did in the earthquake. She felt as lost as on that long ago day, bereft of anyone who loved her.

At the star players building at the end of the day, Mr. Abrams came to see her. Addy was dressed and ready to go back to the dormitory when he came in. "Miss Rose, I must talk to you."

She turned to Edwina. "Stay in here with me, please."

Edwina nodded.

"Yes, Mr. Abrams. What do you want?"

"My dear, I know you have an invitation to the Giovannis' tomorrow night. It's a party for the studio, so I want John Payton to escort you."

Addy said angrily, "No, never! I'll work with him, since I'm under contract, but that's all. How dare you even suggest that? When did it become a studio event? When Muriel talked to me, it seemed to be a private party."

"The Giovanni family decided it would be nice to

make this a special gala for the studio. I know about your…unfortunate encounter, but two co-stars should be seen together. If you remember the clause in the contract about events for the studio, you must do as we deem necessary. This is what you must do for publicity. Now, I'll even arrange for a limo to take you both. And your girl can pick up a formal from the costume department."

Addy drew on all the courage she had. This was something she must fight. "I'll go on one condition—that I never have to be alone with him. If we go in a limo, I want a chaperone."

Abrams looked surprised at her pluck, but nodded. "I'll see what I can do for you." He turned and left.

"Edwina, please see about the formal tomorrow morning. You may go home now."

"Very well, ma'am. Goodnight." Edwina put on her sweater and picked up her pocketbook and left the room.

Oh, God, this is the worst situation I've been in here. Zeke, why did you leave me? I need you so much now. I need your strength to lean on. She gathered her things and walked out the door, only to come face to face with John Payton. She was still sore from the rape, and her anger escalated at the sight of him.

"I hear you're going to be my date tomorrow night." His smooth voice sounded oily, almost snakelike to her.

Addy filled with rage. "Yes, John, and if you dare try to touch me even once, I'll kill you with my bare hands." The slap she gave him across the face resounded loudly. "I mean it."

With a startled look, he rubbed the red mark on his cheek, as Addy strode on by him without another word.

Instead of going back to the dormitory, she

hopped the streetcar and went home to her uncle's house. She walked up the driveway, bypassing the house and going directly to the apartment. When her grandmother opened the door, Addy burst into tears.

"Child, come in. What's the matter?" The loving woman put her arms around Addy.

"Everything," she sobbed. "I hate my life! It started bad, and now it's worse."

Grandpa came out of the bedroom just then. "What happened? Do you want to talk about it?" He put his hands on her shoulders and sat her down on a chair, handing her a handkerchief.

She blurted out the terrible story of the last day and a half, while her grandparents stood listening, aghast, to a censored version of what happened, one without too many of the embarrassing details. "...and now Mr. Abrams wants me to go to the New Year's Eve party with that, that..." She banged her fist on her leg.

"Do you think it was wise to drop the charges against Mr. Payton?" Grandma asked.

"Believe me, my love," said Grandpa. "Addy would come out the worse for it." He turned to Addy. "How much of a hold does Mr. Abrams have over you?"

She wiped her eyes. "This party is considered a studio event and, according to my contract, I have to do whatever he says for publicity. I think part of this is because I wouldn't let Mr. Abrams have his way with me when I first signed."

Grandpa's eyes flashed fire. "What kind of a den of iniquity is this? Addy, can you quit?"

She sighed. "Only if I pay what they feel they will lose on me. In other words, I'm stuck."

"Good God. Does the rest of the family know you're here?"

"I don't know. Only if they saw me come up the driveway."

Grandma headed for the door. "Stay for dinner. Henry can drive you back to the dormitory. I'll tell Jen."

Grandpa embraced Addy. "My girl, now is the time for you to be brave. Life has dealt you some harsh blows, but you have to rise above it."

"I'm ruined, Grandpa. No man is going to want me now." She cried on his shoulder.

"This wasn't your fault. I know you better than that. If Zeke thinks clearly about it, he will see that, too. Now dry your eyes, and let's go to the house." He walked her inside and Aunt Jen took her in her arms.

"Your grandma told me what happened. I'm so sorry." She pulled back and put her hands on Addy's shoulders. "I don't believe you brought this on yourself, but you work in a very sinful industry, where a woman has to watch herself all the time." She cupped her hand on Addy's chin. "I wish you would quit."

Addy shook her head. "Now that I'm under contract, it's not that easy."

At dinner, all the adults avoided discussing what had happened to Addy, but even the children seemed to feel the heavy sadness in the room and were quieter than usual.

When Uncle Henry drove her back to the dormitory, neither one of them spoke. He pulled into the drive and turned off the motor. "Adeline, I know I'm very strict and hard on all of you. My father was like that, so that is what I know. I was taught from little on to suppress emotions." He turned to look at her. "But since you came to live with us, I've thought of you as a daughter. This was a horrible thing to endure, and I want you to know that your family is here whenever you need us." It seemed to take a great effort for him to say that.

"Thank you, Uncle." She kissed his cheek. He

walked her to the door and left without another word. In his own way, she thought, her uncle did care, but it was still hard to feel comfortable around him.

****

The morning sun broke through the dressing room window and over the ice-blue satin evening dress Addy would wear to the party that night. She fingered the material, then sat in the chair in front of the vanity.

"Ma'am, the jewelry goes with it. They told me to tell you to be ready by seven o'clock and the limousine will come and pick you up in front of the building," Edwina stated as she brushed Addy's hair.

"Thank you, Edwina. Are you going out tonight?"

"Yes, ma'am. The crew is going to have a party at the commissary."

Addy looked sadly into the mirror. "I'm sure I'd rather be at that one." She sighed and settled back to let Edwina work her magic to prepare her for the day's scenes.

The motion picture she was working on was a real melodrama, which seemed to fit her mood. She was required to do several scenes with tears streaming down her face. That required no effort at all. The absence of Zeke was a bigger emptiness than she felt she could take. It was as though her very breath was sucked out of her.

At the end of the day, Edwina stayed and helped her to get dressed for the party. In the full-length mirror, Addy saw a very elegant woman. The sleeveless satin flowed down her body, softly hugging it. The scooped, draped neckline was daring, but it showed off the diamond necklace that dropped in cascades over her skin. Soft white calfskin gloves covered her forearms, and a diamond bracelet was around her right wrist. Blue satin pumps with heels completed the outfit. Edwina carefully placed the diamond tiara on her head. *Now, I look like the ice queen. I should be happy, but all I can think about is Zeke. In a heartbeat, I would put on my old party dress to be with him.* The well-dressed woman in the mirror looked back at her with sad and lonely eyes.

Edwina got ready to leave. "Happy New Year to you, ma'am."

"Same to you, Edwina. Enjoy yourself tonight." *I wonder if Zeke will be at the crew's party.* Addy sighed as she put on the white fur coat with the full collar that engulfed her ears. Then, picking up her pocketbook, she went down to the entrance of the building. John Payton waited there, dressed in a crisp black tuxedo. He would have looked handsome, if she didn't hate him so much.

He glanced at her, a measure of remorse seeming evident in his eyes. "At least, let's be civil to each other tonight."

She pursed her lips. "What I said last night still goes. I'm going with you because I must, but when we get there, you're on your own."

He offered her his arm as the auto pulled up to the building. She took it, her stomach turning at the touch.

When the chauffeur opened the door for them, John helped Addy in. Already seated in the limousine were Mr. Abrams and a mature woman who hardly acknowledged her. As soon as John had settled in, as well, Mr. Abrams introduced them to his wife, Rebecca. *That bastard is even married. I wonder whether his wife cares how many women he has.* Mrs. Abrams just looked at them with disdain.

As they rode to the Giovannis' mansion, Addy gazed out the window, remembering the trip with Zeke, and she sighed. *I can't stop thinking about him. Did he go to the crew party? Who is he with?* She felt a nearly overwhelming hatred for her co-star and a growing abhorrence for Mr. Abrams because he had made her attend this party with John. *I'd love to open the door and push them both out.*

The drive was lined with autos when they came up to the house. All the outside lights were lit, giving the mansion's facade a welcoming, creamy glow. The sound of an orchestra wafted out onto the night air. It was a clear crisp night, and Addy was glad she wore the fur coat.

The chauffeur opened the door for them, and Mr. Abrams and his wife got out first. Then John helped Addy out, and she flinched at his touch. *Remember to act civil,* she kept telling herself. She refused to take his arm and walked on her own up to the door, where a servant met them and took their coats to the small room on the right side of the foyer.

Muriel and Tony came down the steps to greet her, and Muriel embraced her tightly. "Addy, I'm so sorry. But why did you come with John as your escort?"

Addy looked at her. "What do you know? I haven't seen you for a few days."

Muriel lowered her voice as she drew Addy aside, Tony right beside her. "Zeke's working at shipping now. I heard the rumors from some of the other workers, so I asked him what happened. He told me."

Addy felt a thump in her heart. "Damn! Everyone at the studio must know about it."

"Please don't swear. You know how gossip spreads. Believe me, nobody blames you."

"Did Zeke also tell you how he walked out on me?" she said angrily.

Muriel bit her lip. "He told me he didn't know if he believed you or not. He got a transfer until he could work things out in his head. You still haven't said why you came with John."

"Mr. Abrams forced me to come with John, because it was an event for the studio and co-stars are supposed to be seen together. I insisted on a chaperone, so we came with Abrams and his wife."

Tony's stormy expression emphasized his words. "Payton should pay for what he did to you."

Addy clasped his hand in silent appreciation of his support as she explained, "The police suggested that I drop the charges because my reputation would be ruined if I took him to trial."

"There are other ways of making him pay." Tony squeezed her hand, then excused himself and stalked off.

Muriel took Addy by the arm. "Come, let's go into the ballroom."

The Giovannis' ballroom was huge, made to look larger with gilded mirrors all around except by the stage, where the orchestra sat. Three crystal chandeliers were reflected and thus gave double the light. On the ceiling, cherubs flew in a painted blue sky with dramatic white cloud formations.

Joe Giovanni had been engaged in conversation, but when he spotted Addy he came up and asked her to dance. The orchestra was playing a slow tune, and they were able to talk as they danced. Joe bent down to say in her ear, "I'm happy you could come to the party tonight."

"Thank you for inviting me."

He maneuvered a turn toward a quiet hallway. "I want to talk to you about a problem that's causing me a lot of trouble. I think you can help me. Seeing that I gave you a little leverage to advance at the studio, maybe you can do something for me."

Addy felt her face burn. What did he want? Surely he couldn't be going to make advances toward her, too. It would be so awkward, with him being Muriel's father-in-law, but she would fight him just as she had Mr. Abrams and John. "What is it?"

"The master ledger for the studio has been missing for a while." He tightened his grip on her. "I think you know where it is."

Addy almost slumped to the floor. She'd forgotten about that. This could be even worse than if he'd tried something on her. She tried to make her voice steady, but it came out in a shaky squeak. "Why do you think that?"

"You were the last one to see Leman alive."

Oh, God, how does he know that? It must be the Giovanni family who had him killed. They must be the ones to keep the key away from. "He didn't say much that I could understand."

His fingers made a stabbing motion tight against her spine. "Because you're related to my daughter-in-law, I'm being very patient with you, but I'll tell you, business is business. Related or not, I know how to get what I want." The music stopped and he kissed her hand, leaving her just inside the door to the ballroom. "Thank you for the dance, Miss Garcia."

Shaking violently, Addy collapsed onto a chair on the edge of the dance floor. She had to get that key to the police as soon as she could. *I hope Inspector Cannon isn't on Joe's payroll. Should I tell Muriel what I know?* She felt nauseous and light-headed, in need of fresh air. She'd seen an exit in the hallway. Fleeing from the ballroom, she found the door at the end of the hall led to a balcony over the sunken backyard.

The night air wound around her shoulders and fluttered the satin of her dress. Vague shapes and forms outlined the shadows. She still shook but now, with the chill air, only partly because of nerves. Sitting on the corner of the balcony wall, she looked up at the stars in the sky. Addy didn't know where this path was leading her, but she had to trust someone. She couldn't deal with everything all alone.

Oh, God, if I ever needed Your wisdom, it's now. I need Zeke, too. Please don't let it be that I've lost him forever. Tears ached in her eyes.

****

Zeke had figured it was a mistake to go to the crew party, but he didn't want to be by himself for the evening he and Addy had been going to celebrate together. He sighed and stared at his glass of punch. He could tell it was spiked, but the pain was still there.

The commissary, decorated with colorful streamers and balloons, was filled with the steady drone of voices, and laughter rose all around him. Zeke gazed at the large window. The darkness made the room close in on itself, and in the window's mirror-like surface he saw himself sitting at a small table, a contrast to the gaiety going on around him. He watched in the window as a blonde woman pulled out the chair across from him and sat down.

"You look like you need a friend." Roxie raised her glass to him.

Zeke turned and looked into her deep blue eyes. "Don't let me ruin your celebration. I shouldn't have come tonight."

"Sugar, where else were you going to go?"

He snorted. "I have nowhere to go. I suppose she told you about the ring. She tells you and Anne everything." He had a bitter edge to his voice. "Did she tell you how she feels about John Payton, too?"

"Whoa, Zeke, you're starting to run before you bat the ball. John raped her, and she's going through hell about it. Did you let her tell you what the policeman told her?"

He hit the table with his fist. "I didn't want to hear any more lies."

She put her hand over his fist and squeezed it. "Listen to me. Addy admitted she was dumb to let John help her back to the tent, but she didn't know he was going to do...that. She was going to take him to trial for rape, but the policeman talked her out of it."

Zeke looked up. "What?"

"He said he never saw a case like this win and it ruins the woman's reputation. He told her nothing would get to the press, and that she needed to avoid such a situation in the future." Roxie narrowed her eyes. "You know, this was the time she needed you most, and you deserted her. Why?"

He took a drink out of his glass. "Back home, I found the girl I loved in the arms of another man. She was two-timing me. I thought it'd happened again."

"Honey, Addy hates John. It's you she loves. Think about that as you feel sorry for yourself." Roxie got up and walked away.

Zeke stared at the figure reflected in the window. *God, what did I do? Did I go and throw away the best thing that ever happened to me?* He wanted to kick himself around the building. *I wonder if Addy will give me another chance. I have to talk to her—I will the next chance I get.*

At midnight, Zeke found Roxie and gave her a kiss. "Thanks for the swift blow with a two-by-four. I needed that."

She smiled and mussed his hair. "Anytime, handsome."

****

Addy didn't know how long she was out on the balcony with her sad thoughts, listening to the orchestra and the voices from within. Suddenly, she heard a commotion and a woman's scream, and then people were running toward the front of the building. Alarmed, she followed them through the foyer and out the front door, where a group of people stood in the narrow courtyard between the guest house and the mansion, nearly surrounding a

133

crumpled heap on the concrete. The lights in the courtyard and blazing from the windows of the house showed a wide dark stream traveling from the heap to the gutters in the walkway. "We've called the police," Addy heard someone say.

Muriel, wide-eyed and shaking, came running to her. "Oh, Addy, what a terrible thing to happen." Addy put her arms around her cousin. "It looks like John Payton fell off the balcony up there."

"That's John?" Addy asked, horrified. Leaving Muriel, she shouldered through to the front of the crowd of spectators, intending to see for herself, just as Joe turned the body over. John's handsome face was covered with blood, and what looked like a broken wine bottle protruded from his chest.

Glancing over the company, Joe announced, "It looks like he got drunk and fell over the wall of the front balcony upstairs." It was a declaration of fact that was to go to the police.

Addy made her way back to Muriel and they sat together on the low wall next to the drive. They looked at each other in silence, hearing police sirens approaching from a distance.

The police investigation seemed to indicate they believed John's death was an accident, but they took the names and addresses of everyone there, nevertheless. Because obviously liquor was involved, Joe had to go with them to the station house.

Addy watched it all with a strange detachment. *Too much has happened in the last two months. I can't grasp anything else.*

As the police cars pulled out, Mr. Abrams stood on the drive and raised his hand for attention. "This is to all of Mr. Hanson's production company. We will take a few days off to find another leading man. Please report to the studio next Monday."

Muriel turned to Addy. "Looks like the party's over. Since it's past curfew, you're welcome to stay here tonight."

Addy's stomach knotted as she thought about what Joe had said to her earlier, about the ledger. "I wonder how long the police are going to keep Tony's father at the station."

"They'll probably keep him until his lawyer comes in the morning. He's been fined on illegal liquor charges before, but he seems to find a way to get off. What does that have to do with you spending the night?" She frowned at Addy.

This wasn't the right time or place to tell Muriel she suspected Joe was responsible for Mr. Leman's death, let alone about the ledger. "I'm curious about what's going to happen, that's all. Sure, I'll stay the night, but I'll need a change of clothes."

"You can borrow some of mine. It'll be just like old times." And with a hug, they went inside together.

Addy followed the maid down the long hallway on the second floor, clutching the clothes Muriel had selected for her. The yellow glass art deco wall sconces cast a strange glow onto the white marble walls. She shuddered. It was like an ice house, so cold in the midst of elegance.

The maid stopped at a large oak door and opened it. "This is your room, ma'am. Can I get you anything?"

"No, thank you. I'll be fine."

"The bath is at the end of the hall, and there are towels in your room. Pull this cord if you need me."

Addy nodded, and the maid left her to gaze at the sumptuous accommodation she'd been given. Rich decorations accented the room with its deep blue carpet and matching velvet drapes over the windows. A canopy bed with azure silk bed linens stood magnificently to one side.

Answering a quiet knock at the door, she found Muriel.

"Is the room all right?" Muriel asked. "We're putting up some of the other guests, too, and I thought I'd stop by to check on you."

Addy smiled at her. "This is such luxury. I never dreamed you would be living like this."

Muriel hugged her. "I have to pinch myself once in a while to make sure I'm not dreaming. Tony and I are in the bedroom on the floor below, second door on the left, if you need me. I left word for you to be wakened a half-hour before breakfast. It will be served in the dining room. Well, dear, goodnight."

"Goodnight to you, too." Addy watched as Muriel went out the door, giving her time to go down the hall before locking the door behind her. She felt so uncomfortable in this house—and who knew what had really happened to John?

She hung her dress in the wardrobe and put on Muriel's satin pajamas, thinking somber thoughts about the evening's events, wondering whether to go to the police about Mr. Leman's death, and missing Zeke more than ever. If only she could discuss things with him.

What puzzled her most, now that John was dead, was to feel nothing: no sorrow, no revulsion, not even a care that he was dead. *Am I in shock, or is this how it feels when you hate someone that much? I could've killed him myself without any thought.*

Addy poured some of the water from the pitcher into the washstand basin and cleaned her face and hands with the scented French soap she found there. *I want to leave before Joe gets back. That man is dangerous. I wish the police could get something that would put him away for a long time.*

She sank into the downy mattress. *What a way to start 1921. Oh, Zeke...* Addy fell into a fitful sleep, engulfed in nightmares.

Her restless sleep was interrupted by a knock on

the door. "It's eight o'clock, ma'am. Breakfast will be served in a half hour."

Addy called out sleepily, "Thank you. I'll be down."

Slipping on a robe, she went to the gold and marble guest bath at the end of the hall, her towels tucked under her arm. Then, back in her room, she left Muriel's pajamas and robe on a chair by the bed and donned the cashmere suit Muriel had lent her. It felt so soft next to her skin. She couldn't imagine such luxury as this in her own life. She took the evening dress, on its hanger, downstairs with her and let the servant hang it with the rest of her things in the little room by the foyer, while Addy went to breakfast.

She breathed a sigh of relief when she walked into the dining room and Joe wasn't there. Quite a number of other guests had stayed the night, as well, and the long table was set almost all the way down. Muriel motioned for Addy to sit next to her.

"How are you feeling?" Muriel looked at Addy with concern.

"A hard night. I didn't sleep well." Addy started on the half grapefruit set in front of her. "Could you have someone call a taxi for me?"

"I could have our driver take you home."

Addy balked at the thought of being alone with that driver. "No, that's all right. Anyway, he probably will be needed to pick up Tony's father."

Muriel shrugged. She waved at the butler, standing by the door. He walked over to her.

"Yes, ma'am?" he said with a slight nod.

"Could you call a taxi for Miss Garcia, please?"

"Very good, ma'am," he said, with a nod, and left the dining room.

Addy wanted to tell Muriel everything she suspected about the Giovanni family, but she still didn't feel the time was right. Muriel would be safe as long as she was with Tony, surely. Maybe she could talk to her at the studio.

Addy was just finishing a large breakfast of bacon, eggs and fried potatoes when the butler came to inform her that her taxi had arrived, so she laid her damask napkin neatly by her plate and went to thank Sofia Giovanni for her hospitality.

"You are welcome here anytime," was the soft reply in the lady's slight Italian accent, accompanied by a kiss on Addy's cheek.

Tony and Muriel walked with Addy to the taxi, Tony himself carrying her things out for her.

"Take care, both of you." Addy hugged them each tightly before climbing into the vehicle and waving as the taxi pulled out of the drive toward the gate.

As soon as she was back in the dormitory, Addy acted on the resolve she had made sometime during her nightmarish sleep—she called the police station and asked for Inspector Cannon. He was off and would be back tomorrow, she was informed, so she decided the next day would have to do for taking the key to him. She didn't have to be back to the studio until Monday, but now she had made up her mind what to do, she wanted to get it over and done. Maybe she could talk to Muriel about the suspicions she had about Tony's father and his hand in Mr. Leman's murder. She decided to call her.

"Are you going to be at the studio tomorrow?" Addy asked when Muriel got to the telephone.

"Yes, why?"

"Can you have lunch with me at the main commissary? I have to talk to you."

"Is there something wrong?"

"I don't want to talk over the telephone. I'll meet you outside the shipping building at eleven-thirty." Addy hung up and went upstairs. *How do I tell her I think Tony's family are killers? She won't like it if*

138

I'm too blunt, but she needs to be warned. And I need to get that key to the Inspector. I hope he isn't on their payroll, or all my planning will be for nothing.

The next morning after breakfast, Addy retreated to her room and closed the door tightly. Taking her pocketbook, she made a cut in the lining and then went to the window and removed the key from its hiding place under the block of wood. She inserted the key and its tag into the lining and sewed a basting stitch with her needle and thread to keep it secure. *After I go to lunch with Muriel, I'll take the key to Inspector Cannon.*

Addy hated doing things like this alone. She wished Zeke were going with her. She caught her breath on the quick sob that nearly escaped her at the thought of him. She missed having him to rely on, to protect her with his quiet strength. She still hated John for ruining their relationship, for breaking them up. *Oh, Zeke, am I starting to give up on you?*

She jumped, startled, at a knock on the door. Anne and Roxie stood in the hallway. "Come in, you two. I haven't seen you for a couple of days."

Anne settled herself on Addy's bed. "Is it true that John Payton was killed at the Giovannis' party?"

Addy nodded. "From what I understand, he was drunk and fell from one of the balconies." Addy, on the bed next to Anne, watched Roxie as she stood by the window.

Anne's eyes got larger. "I heard a rumor in the crew quarters that he was pushed."

"What? Who told you that?"

"Someone read in the newspaper that the police were conducting an investigation and saying the fall was no accident."

"But who would want to kill John?" Then she felt the blood drain from her face. Would they suspect her, since she was by herself on the back balcony at the time? Or Tony? She remembered his words when she first arrived at the party, about there being other ways of making him pay for raping her. Oh, God, did Tony...?

"Addy, what's wrong? You're so pale."

She gripped Anne's arm. "The Giovanni family makes me nervous. I have a feeling they had something to do with killing Mr. Leman."

"Are you sure?"

"Not completely, but I think so." Addy didn't want to reveal too much yet. "Did you two go to the crew's party?" She looked at them with the unasked questions.

Roxie studied her face. "Yes, we did. And, yes, Zeke was there. And, no, he wasn't with anyone."

Addy let out a shaky breath and stood up. "I have to go meet Muriel for lunch, but we'll talk more about this when I get back."

All the way to shipping, she pondered what she was going to say to Muriel. *Should I tell her I was threatened by Joe?*

Nerves nearly overcame her as she waited for Muriel outside the double doors, but a few deep breaths helped, and then Muriel appeared, and a cousinly hug helped, too. A quick walk brought them to the main commissary, where they got their food and sat at a small table away from the crowd.

"I've got to talk to you about something," Addy began. "And I want you to listen to all I have to tell you. At the party, I danced with Tony's father, and he asked me about the master ledger for the studio. He seemed to think I knew about it and what he said was like a veiled threat. On the night Mr. Leman was killed, the two men I saw were looking for it, and it wasn't there. But before he died, Mr. Leman told me where it is. He gave me a key to a safety deposit box."

Muriel looked shaken. "Addy, you've known where it is all this time? Why didn't you tell someone?"

"I didn't know who to trust. Mr. Leman died before he could tell me who to give it to. He did say, 'Don't let them get it.' I couldn't figure out who *they* were. I thought maybe it was someone with the studio."

"What are you going to do?"

"I'm going to give the key to the police and let them handle it."

"Where did you hide it?"

"In my room at the dormitory."

Muriel looked pensive as she finished her sandwich. "I hope you're doing the right thing."

"I just wanted to warn you that your father-in-law may be caught up in the murder. If he is, please watch out for yourself. If the Giovanni family is into racketeering, maybe you and Tony should get out of there."

Muriel smiled. "We'll be fine, Addy. Don't worry." She looked at the commissary clock. "I have to get back to work. I'm glad we had this talk. See you around."

Addy was puzzled by Muriel's lack of concern. At first Muriel had looked nervous, then pensive when she first found out about the key. But now, she acted like Addy had told her about the weather. Should Addy have revealed all that to her? Had the family swayed Muriel into thinking like they did? She needed to get this key to the Inspector, and soon. She finished her meal and hurried out.

Outside the studio gates, Addy took the streetcar downtown, where she climbed the stone steps to the entrance of the two-story police building. Nervously she approached the policeman at the front desk. "Excuse me, sir, is Inspector Cannon in?"

"Yes, he is, ma'am. Who are you?"

"Tell him Miss Adeline Garcia would like to speak to him." She sat on one of the leather-and-metal chairs in the waiting room.

The man reappeared a few minutes later. "He'll see you in his office, Miss Garcia. Come with me."

Addy took a deep, shaky breath as she walked into the plain office. There were framed certificates on the walls, a metal filing cabinet, and an old wooden desk with papers all over the top. A telephone and a typewriter were right in front of the Inspector.

He rose and indicated a wooden chair next to his desk. "Please sit down, Miss Garcia."

Addy sat and nervously shifted her pocketbook from hand to hand.

The Inspector sat back in his office chair and steepled his fingers as he watched her. "What is it you want to tell me?"

"Mr. Cannon, I was scared to tell you the whole truth about what Mr. Leman told me in his final minutes, because I know there are corrupt policemen on the force. But now I feel my life is in danger, and I need to trust you."

"Go ahead." He studied her face.

Addy opened her pocketbook and pulled out the thread she'd put in that morning. She removed the key and tag and put them on the desk. "This is a key to a safety deposit box at the Hollywood First National Bank. In the box is the master ledger. When Mr. Leman gave me the key, he said to keep it away from 'them.' But he didn't tell me who 'they' were. He was going to tell me who to give it to, but he died before he could. I've spent all this time trying to figure it out, but I'm going to trust my instincts and give it to you."

He tapped his fingers together. "Miss Garcia, do you realize I could have you arrested right now for withholding evidence?"

She felt her throat close and a tightness in her chest. "Oh, Mr. Cannon, I never meant to do anything wrong. I wanted to make sure the key got into the right hands, is all." She gripped the arms of the chair and felt a full-blown case of panic coming on.

"Well, you did voluntarily come forth with the key, so this can be our little secret. Anyway, I may need your help in capturing the ones responsible. Now, you said that you felt like you were in danger. Why?"

"I was at a New Year's Eve party at the Giovannis' house and Mr. Joe Giovanni asked me about the ledger. I told him Mr. Leman died before he could tell me anything. Mr. Giovanni said he had been very patient with me, because my cousin is his daughter-in-law, but he knows how to get what he wants. It sounded like a threat."

He leaned forward in his chair. "The Giovannis are partners in Majestic Studio. Am I right?"

"Yes, sir." Addy nodded.

He took his notepad out and a pencil. "Since you're here, may I ask you about when Mr. John Payton died? Where were you at the time?"

"I was out on the back balcony, off the ballroom. It was after Mr. Giovanni made the threat, and I went out for some air." An alarm went off in her brain. *Oh, no! He thinks I could have killed John!*

"Did anybody see you? Was anyone else there on the balcony, too?"

"I was so shocked at the time, by what Mr. Giovanni had said, I don't know if anyone saw me go out there. But, no, nobody came out while I was getting air."

"What happened then?"

"There was a lot of noise in the ballroom, people shouting. I went in to see what was going on and followed the crowd outside to the front of the mansion. I saw something on the walkway. Muriel told me it was John Payton, and we thought he had fallen off the front balcony above. It looked like he fell on a bottle and it broke under him."

The Inspector stood up and walked around the desk. He looked down at Addy. "We have reason to believe that it was no accident, Miss Garcia. We found small shards of glass on the balcony floor, and it looks like the bottle was broken and jammed into Mr. Payton's chest before he fell. We are checking on the people who may have wanted him out of the way, and your name came to the top of the list."

Addy took a deep breath. "Why do you say that?"

"He raped you, but you dropped the charges. Someone heard you at the studio, the day before the party, tell him if he touched you again you would kill him with your bare hands. Do you remember saying that?"

"Yes, I do, but I said that out of anger. I don't think I could really kill anyone."

"Even in self defense? Even if John Payton tried to rape you again on the front balcony? You said no one saw you on the balcony over the backyard. I'm sure you have enough strength to break a bottle and shove it into his chest hard enough to cause him to fall over the wall."

Addy's lower lip started to tremble. "If that were true, wouldn't there be blood on me? Ask anyone there. I wore the same thing all night." *Quick thinking. It pays to have read mysteries.*

Inspector Cannon half-smiled at her. "Very good, Miss Garcia. That's why we didn't come and arrest you right away. If you still have the dress, could you bring it in for evidence?"

Addy nodded.

"I want you to promise me you won't leave the city for a while. I'm going to get a court order to have the safety deposit box opened and the ledger removed. It will take some time to get the information out of it. I think until we can come up with some concrete evidence against the Giovannis, you shouldn't tell anyone you've given the key to us. If you need some protection, I'll get the plainclothes police to keep an eye on you."

Addy felt great relief. "Could you, please? I'd feel so much better."

He shook her hand when she stood up. "Thank you, Miss Garcia. I'll be in touch."

When she returned to the dormitory, Mrs. Hutton gave her a message to call Muriel at shipping.

"Addy, did you give the key to the police?" Muriel asked when she came on the telephone.

Addy remembered what the Inspector told her. "No, I don't know who to trust. Please don't tell anyone what I told you. Promise?"

"You know you can trust me. I won't say a word to anyone."

"Don't even tell Tony." Somewhere deep inside, Addy felt uneasy. "Thank you. I'll see you on Monday." The feeling in the pit of her stomach about Muriel just wouldn't go away.

Chapter 7

"Your new leading man is Tex Marshall. He'll be in the main assembly tent when you get there." Mr. Abrams gave Addy an information sheet as Edwina finished touching up her makeup and hair.

"Is he someone who's worked here before?"

"No, he was in town for barnstorming, and our publicity assistant, Miss Hathaway, found him." He pointed to the sheet. "You'll see here that he was an airman in the Great War, and he has his own plane. We can do some modern action stories with that. Mr. Hanson will introduce you."

The sun shone in the clear pleasant morning sky as Addy and Edwina traveled to the outdoor set, where the biplane parked on the grass in the large field had drawn a crowd near the assembly tent. Everyone was anxious to meet the new leading man.

Mr. Hanson was at the entrance of the tent. "Would you move aside for Miss Rose?" he called as she got out of the auto. He took her arm and escorted her inside. "Mr. Tex Marshall, this is your co-star, Miss Adeline Rose."

Addy looked into a strong face with beautiful reddish-brown hair and a pair of hazel eyes that looked down on her from a height. John had been close to her own five-four stature, but Tex had to be around five-ten, she figured. "Very pleased to meet you." She offered her hand.

A smile spread across his face as he took her hand and kissed it. "I'm honored to work with you. I saw the first of your motion pictures, *Escaped Convict*, with Mr. Abrams, and you're even lovelier in person. He said there's a premiere next week."

Oh, my. "Thank you. I'm honored to work with a veteran." Her voice came out a little squeakier than she wanted it. *What a gentleman!*

Mr. Hanson turned to the crowd. "Take a fifteen-minute break. We need the new scripts. Then we'll start the briefing for the new picture."

"Have you ever been in an airplane, Miss Rose?" Tex asked as they started out of the tent.

"You can call me Addy. And, no, I've never been in an airplane."

Mr. Hanson was close enough to say, "I heard that. Since the plane will be a part of future scripts, I think you should take her up to get used to it."

She felt a rush of excitement and dread. "Wouldn't that mess up my hair? Edwina went to a lot of trouble this morning."

Mr. Hanson smiled. "I'm sure any damage can be fixed."

The small two-seat plane was just a few steps away, and Tex gave her a boost over the canvas skin and into the front seat. "Put the belt around you," he called up. Then he climbed into the back.

Addy pulled the buckle as snug as she could. She could just barely see over the rim around her. He flipped her a leather helmet and goggles. "Here, put these on." While she did so, one of the men by the plane started spinning the propeller and the engine sputtered. After several tries, the plane shook to life with a roar.

Her heart went into her throat as they bounced along the field faster and faster. She heard a whoosh as she drew in and held a huge breath just as the bi-plane left the ground. In a few seconds, all she could see was sky.

"What do you think of the view up here?" Tex shouted at her.

"I can't see anything but sky," she shouted back.

"Wait a minute. I'll bank a turn."

"What? Oh!" The plane was suddenly sideways, and she could see the studio far below. A wave of vertigo washed over her and she screwed her eyes tightly shut. "I think that's enough for a first time," she yelled.

Tex laughed. "Okay, we're coming in for a landing. Hang on!"

Her stomach remained several hundred feet overhead as the plane came down, and she put her head between her knees to keep from fainting.

At the first touch of the wheels to the ground, the light machine bounced back up in the air. *Oh, my dear God in heaven!* Then they came down again and bounced to a stop. The devil engine shut off. She didn't dare move.

Addy heard Tex jump to the ground and Mr. Hanson call out, "Where's Miss Rose?" The plane jiggled as Tex climbed up on the body. She looked up and saw two Texs peering down at her. She groaned.

"Addy, undo your belt and give me your hand," one of them said, as the two reached for her.

She did as she was told, and he hauled her out of the plane, over the rough canvas side, and Mr. Hanson caught her, but her knees continued to earth until she was on her side with her hands over her eyes. "Tell the ground to stop spinning," she moaned.

Laughing, Tex removed her leather helmet and goggles and tossed them back into the plane before he helped Addy to stand. "I was like that the first time, too."

Her stomach finally came down to its correct place, but it turned over as she entered her tent, and she hurried to the back and lost her breakfast. When she staggeringly returned, Mr. Hanson stood at the entrance.

"Miss Rose, we can film some of Mr. Marshall's solo parts this morning, and then we'll have the briefing after lunch, so you can take time to recover."

She murmured her thanks and lay down on the chaise in her tent. The cool breeze came in, like a massage on her face. Before she knew it, she was fast asleep.

"Miss Rose! Miss Rose, it's time to eat." Edwina gently shook her. "Mr. Marshall set the table up himself."

Addy felt better. She ventured an open eye and saw Tex standing by the table that held sandwiches and fruits. A pot of hot tea was by her place. A wave of embarrassment caught her at the thought of him seeing her at her worst.

"Thank you, Edwina." Addy swung her legs down to the floor as Edwina exited the tent, and Tex came to help Addy up. She was still a little shaky.

"I hope this makes up for the upset I caused you." He took her by the arm and walked her to the table.

"I am getting hungry." After he held her chair for her, he seated himself across from her as she poured the tea. "Where are you from, Tex? May I call you that?"

"Yes, you may. I'm from New Jersey originally."

"Then how did you get the name Tex?"

He laughed. "From the publicity department. My real name is Chester Marcelli, but the powers didn't like it."

"I know what you mean. My real last name is Garcia, but they said that was too ethnic."

They chatted throughout the meal, finding they had a lot in common. She asked about his time in Europe, and he asked about her family. She liked this man who laughed so easily.

"Well, Addy, do you feel like you can take on the industry yet?" He smiled as he got up and went around the table to her.

"I think so." She giggled as she took the offered

arm. They walked out of the tent and came face to face with Zeke. Addy felt a flush of warmth and longing. *I miss him so much.*

A look of surprise crossed his face before he frowned. "Addy, I need to speak to you." Tension threaded his voice.

Addy glanced from one man to the other. The glow she had felt only a few seconds ago evaporated. "Tex, this is Zeke Shafer. Zeke, this is Tex Marshall, my new co-star."

He gave Tex a curt nod. "Yes, I heard. May we go inside?"

Her anger flamed. "Tex, tell Mr. Hanson I'll be there in a few minutes, please."

Tex agreed and was gone. When she and Zeke got inside, she folded her arms and tapped her foot. "Zeke, that was rude. What do you want?"

"I wanted to talk to you about getting back together, but instead I find you with another man. If you're going to be engaged to me, you can't be walking arm in arm with someone else." His voice had gotten more agitated by the time he finished speaking.

"How dare you!" Her voice quivered with angry resentment. "I agreed to marry you, and then—just at the time I needed you most—you took your ring back and walked out on me. You have no business coming in here and telling me what I should or shouldn't do."

If she had hit him in the gut he couldn't have looked more devastated. "Addy, please..."

"Get out of here, Mr. Shafer!"

He turned on his heel and left as Edwina came into the tent.

"Edwina, I need a touch-up on my makeup." Addy wiped the sudden tears off her cheeks. Why did he break their engagement and then come back and think he could tell her what to do? She didn't need more pain in her life right now. She wanted to hit it off right with Tex, since she had to be working with him. Was she too hard on Zeke? Maybe she should've listened to what he had to say. After all, that was what had hurt her most about their breakup, when he wouldn't even listen to her explanation about the rape. Deep down, Addy knew she still loved him. *What should I do? I need some good friends and some good company.*

She went to the set and put herself mentally in another place so she could work, but the pain kept nagging at her insides.

At a break in filming, Tex came over to her. "Addy, I'm sorry if I caused any trouble. I didn't know you had a boyfriend."

She felt her stomach churning again. "I'm not sure he still is. Things...haven't been going well lately."

"Then can I offer you dinner tonight? We can leave after work."

Addy mulled that around for a few moments. She needed some time to enjoy herself. "Yes, I would like that," she said aloud.

"How about I pick you up at the star players' building in my automobile?"

She smiled. "As long as it doesn't fly."

Tex laughed. "I promise."

****

Zeke pounded on the door of the shipping office. He heard Muriel ask, "Who is it?"

"It's Zeke. May I come in?"

The door opened and Muriel waved him in. "Zeke, what's wrong?"

"I want to take the rest of the day off. Would that be all right, Mrs. Giovanni?"

"Whoa, Zeke. Sit down and tell me what happened."

He hesitated, then sat on one of the chairs

across the desk from her. "It's your cousin. I tried to talk to her, to get back in her good graces, and I saw her with her new co-star, coming out of her tent arm in arm with the guy." Zeke beat the rhythm with his fist on the flat surface in front of him as he said "arm in arm."

Muriel shifted in her chair on the other side of the desk. "Well, you did break off the engagement." She looked steadily at him. "Addy shouldn't have to live like a nun until you make up your mind what you want. Getting angry every time you see her talking to a man isn't going to help, either. If you want Addy, charm her back. Apologize to her and be nice." She gave him a half-smile. "No, you may not have the rest of the day off to brood. Get back to work and think about what I've said."

"You're a hard woman, Mrs. Giovanni." Giving her a quick smile, his anger somewhat abated, Zeke slipped out the door to the warehouse.

He was stacking boxes for shipment when a slat at the bottom of a crate came loose. Carrying the crate carefully to the repair shop, he positioned it so he could hammer on the board. As he did, a bottle rolled out of the packing straw. Zeke uncorked the bottle and smelled the amber liquid. He knew what to do next.

****

Tex and Addy traveled to the Latin Quarter, a popular spot for the motion picture crowd. The lights blazed outside and the sound of a mariachi band put a bounce in Addy's step as they walked from the parking lot to the restaurant.

Inside were large white pillars holding up adobe walls, with long colorful streamers scalloped between them. The many potted plants along the sides turned the restaurant into a jungle. Around the blue-tiled fountain in the middle of the dance floor dozens of couples did the tango, which was all the rage.

As the waiter escorted Tex and Addy to a table, pungent odors of Latin food flowed through the room, and electricity seemed to pop in the air as the music made her feet move to its steady beat. Looking at Tex, she thought how handsome he was. *I would truly love to know him better.*

Tex ordered an enchilada meal for both of them, with Addy's agreement, and then they sipped their chilled ginger ale while they watched the dancers and listened to the music.

After dinner, Tex took her hand. "Would you like to dance?"

She looked down at her suit. "I'm really not dressed for dancing."

"Oh, that's all right, no one will care." And he pulled her onto the dance floor when the band started up again.

Addy loved the tango, and Tex was a very good dancer. She was caught up in the atmosphere and the music. The steady beat flowed through her veins. She twirled out and Tex pulled her back into his arms with one motion. It definitely felt good to be there. At the end, they did a breathless flourish that ended with her in his embrace.

Thirsty, they had just returned to their table for more ginger ale when an attractive woman came over to them. It was Nora Steele.

"Well, Miss Garcia, or should I say Miss Rose? I see Mr. Abrams has got a new whore."

Addy glared at her. "Just because you prostituted yourself to get to the top doesn't mean everyone does."

"I must say, you have an interesting way of getting a new leading man. Too bad you did in John. Hey, mister, I'd watch her very carefully," she sneered.

Addy took her leftovers and slung them, plate

and all, onto Nora's chest. Nora's scream, as the greasy sauce made its way down the front of her dress, was punctuated by her action: she picked up Tex's plate and hit Addy with it. In no time the two were rolling on the floor, hitting each other, until Tex and one of the waiters were able to separate them.

"Come on, let's go." Tex gripped both of Addy's arms.

When the waiter had escorted Nora away, Addy shrugged off Tex's hands and used their napkins to clean off as much of the food on her suit as she could. "I don't want this to stain the inside of your auto."

"We'd better go before they throw us out." Tex guided her through the door and to his vehicle. "Where do you live?" he asked as he got in on the driver's side.

"In Dormitory Number Three. I'll show you which one."

On the way back to the dormitory, Tex glanced at Addy. "Do you get into fights often?"

Addy felt her cheeks warm. "Mostly when I was in school. Some people didn't take kindly to Mexicans. Unfortunately, I seem to look like my father's side of the family."

As he pulled into the drive, she noticed he kept looking at his watch. "You don't have to worry, I'm still here in plenty of time."

"Oh, yes, I know." He seemed distracted.

"Umm, well, thank you for dinner. I'm sorry I got in a fight with Nora, but she deserved what she got."

"That's all right. I'll see you tomorrow." He looked at his watch again.

Addy thought his attitude was strange as she got out of the auto. He didn't even walk her to the door. As she turned, he drove out of the parking lot. *Maybe I shouldn't have got into that fight with Nora.*

Oh, why do I have such a bad temper? But no one can tell me she didn't deserve it.

Mrs. Hutton was sitting in the parlor with a couple of the girls. Addy smiled and waved as she walked by.

"Addy, what happened to you?" Mrs. Hutton looked at her in surprise.

"Oh, my suit? I ran into Nora Steele. She insulted me, and we got into a fight."

"I hope she looks worse than you do." Mrs. Hutton chuckled.

As Addy approached her room from the stairs, she saw her door partially open, the light from the hallway dimly illuminating the interior. She gasped. Everything there was turned over onto the floor! Then she heard a slight movement from behind the door, and the hairs on the back of her neck prickled.

Instead of going in, she pulled the door shut with a bang and went flying down the stairs. "Mrs. Hutton! Someone is in my room!"

Mrs. Hutton wasn't there, but Clara Stevens, one of the new girls, and Flora Norman, a slight, nervous neighbor of Clara's, were huddled on the couch by the window.

Addy heard running steps behind her and, before she could turn around, strong arms grabbed her. "Where is the key, Miss Garcia?"

Addy felt cold steel on her neck. She looked at the two girls on the couch and they were frozen with fear. She started shaking. *I'm going to die.* "What key?"

He shook her. "We know you have the key to the safety deposit box that the master ledger is in. Now, where is it?"

Who was this guy, and who told him about the key? Muriel? "If you kill me, you'll never know."

"I realize that. That's why I'm going to shoot your friends over there one at a time. You can save them by telling me."

Addy heard a gun cock behind them. "Let her go, or I'll blow your head off. I'm aiming right between your ears, mister," came Mrs. Hutton's voice.

Addy almost fainted from relief. She looked at the couch and Flora was out cold. The man slowly turned and looked down the barrel of Mrs. Hutton's shotgun, releasing Addy and dropping his gun as he raised his hands in the air.

"Addy, go call the police, while I watch him."

Addy ran to the telephone and jiggled the cradle. The front door opened and Tex stepped inside, holding a gun. Addy smiled at him. "I don't know why you're here, but we have things well in hand."

Tex leveled the gun at her. "If you know what's good for you, you'll put that down."

She suddenly went cold. Those words sounded familiar. She replaced the receiver and stared at him stupidly. His voice was all too much like one she'd heard in the shipping department the night Mr. Leman was killed.

"Now go into the parlor with the others." He waved his gun toward the door. He turned the gun on Mrs. Hutton. "Drop that shotgun."

Mrs. Hutton looked at him for a moment, then uncocked the shotgun and laid it on the floor. The first man picked it up, pointed it at her, and with a wave indicated she was to go and sit with the two girls on the couch.

Tex turned back to Addy. "Sorry, darling, I didn't think I'd need to reveal myself so soon, but I thought he would be able to find that key before now."

"How do you know there's a key?"

"Addy, now I'm asking the questions. Where is it?" He took a step toward her.

She tried not to flinch, but she did. Her mind reeled. She didn't know who to trust anymore. The inspector had told her not to tell anyone. My God, it couldn't be Muriel, could it? She and the inspector were the only ones who knew about it.

"I'm going to tell my partner to start shooting these women one at a time, if I don't get answers."

Addy heard the click of the shotgun. She took a couple of steps back. "I—I don't—let me think—I—" Suddenly, the front door opened with a bang and several policemen came in with guns drawn.

"All right, both of you, drop those weapons!" one of them barked.

Addy collapsed weakly into a chair and watched Inspector Cannon come in as Tex and the other man were being taken away.

"Are you all right, Miss Garcia?" He put his hand on Addy's shoulder.

"Yes, Inspector, but how did you know about this? I didn't get a chance to call the police."

Cannon looked at her with a half-smile. "Remember I said I would keep a plainclothes watching you?" He motioned to Clara, who was still on the couch, and she came over. "Meet Detective Stevens of our department."

Addy stared, her mouth open. "A woman detective? I've never heard of such a thing!"

"She's fully trained, and she can get into places where a man can't."

Addy turned to her. "But how did you call the police?"

Clara smiled. "We have one of the detectives out in the lot, in view of the windows on this side. I gave a signal to him from the couch, and he called the station from another building."

"Miss Garcia, I want you to come into the station tomorrow. There's been a development in the case, and I think we can set a trap with your help," Inspector Cannon said.

"But I've got to go to work tomorrow."

"Believe me, with the leading man in jail, I don't think they'll be doing any filming for a while. I want Detective Stevens to come with you. That will look like two girls out for a day. Mrs. Hutton, would you call the studio for Miss Garcia tomorrow morning, to tell them she's indisposed after tonight?"

Mrs. Hutton nodded.

Addy felt betrayed and not ready to trust anyone again. She had really started to like Tex, and now it turned out he'd been sent to get the key. Muriel must have told someone. *Why would Muriel want to put me in danger? Has she turned away from everything she believed was right?*

"Another thing. I want Stevens with you all the time because, like it or not, you are a target. I think you and she should stay at a hotel tonight. I'll have Sgt. Lamont drive you to one. Goodnight, Miss Garcia." He left with the other policemen, and Addy tried to thank Mrs. Hutton for her bravery in attempting to rescue them.

"I just wish I'd known that other one was out there," Mrs. Hutton remarked, holding a cold towel on Flora's forehead.

Clara turned to Addy. "Come on. You may get a few things from your room. I'll go with you. I don't think you should be alone."

Addy nodded. The minute she opened the door, the horrible mess in the room greeted her. The knot in her stomach grew and she swallowed hard. "I have to clean up this mess."

Clara shook her head. "Leave it for now. Just find a change of clothes for tomorrow. I'll help you when we get back."

In a few minutes Addy was ready, and they went down the hall to Clara's room for her to pick up a few things. "How did you ever get involved in police work, Miss Stevens?"

Clara smiled. "You don't have to be so formal.

Call me Clara. My father worked with the Pinkertons. I guess you could say it's in my blood. I was always fascinated with ways to catch crooks."

"That seems to be very dangerous work, Clara."

She laughed at that. "Any more dangerous than going up in an airplane? I was one of the extras this morning, and I saw what happened."

Addy sighed. "You saw that? Yes, acting does have a bad side at times."

"Detective work is a form of acting. You take on a role to get information or to protect someone, like I'm doing for you."

Addy almost said, *But you're in more danger*, but then she realized, *No, I'm in a lot of danger right now.* "Thank you for all your help."

"Just doing my job, Addy. Let's go now." The girls went downstairs and got into the police auto. A mile from the police station, Sgt. Lamont dropped them off at a small hotel where a room had been arranged for them to share. Addy and Clara figured the hotel had to be fifty years old, at least, and for all they knew the wallpaper that was starting to peel off at the corners was original. The iron bed's lumpy mattress was adorned with stained sheets, and they opted to sleep on top of the covers spread over them. The whole room smelled musty and sour, and the water in the basin had oil floating on top.

After they'd laughed about the place not being as posh as the Ritz, Clara was soon in dreamland, but Addy couldn't sleep. She felt exhausted, but she heard every little creak in the building. Her body took catnaps through the long night, and she watched the sun come up in the morning. Meanwhile, Clara slept like a baby and awoke only when her alarm clock went off.

"We should get over to the station by eight o'clock," Clara said. "I trust Mrs. Hutton called the studio to say that you're too shaken to work today.

After they read the news, they'll know why."

"I didn't sleep very well last night. I wish I hadn't got involved in this in the first place."

Clara looked at her. "Addy, it's because people do get involved that we can catch many of these criminals before they hurt someone else. The department will do everything it can to see you won't get hurt."

Addy picked up her clothes from the chair and started getting dressed. "I just wish one of that family didn't have to be my cousin."

Clara looked sad and nodded. "Let's go to breakfast at that little café down the street."

"That sounds good." Addy noticed Clara took a small Colt revolver from the drawer of the nightstand and put it into a holster under her suit jacket. "Do you carry that around with you all the time?"

Clara nodded. "We have to. I even wore it under my dress when I was an extra yesterday."

At the small eatery Clara had spotted, they ordered ham, eggs and coffee, watching the changing weather out the window by their table. Clouds were starting to gather in the normally sunny skies.

"Come on, we can catch the streetcar to the station." Clara got up, leaving a generous tip for their waitress.

Addy noticed Clara eyeing all the passengers as they put their tokens in the deposit. They chose seats close to the front, where Addy felt as though everyone was staring at her. Could she trust these strangers?

A sudden rain caught them as they ran to the steps of the police station, and she breathed in the smell of warm wet pavement. They managed to get in before they got too wet. Addy took off her hat and shook her hair.

The young policeman at the desk smiled. "Well,

Miss Stevens, I see you braved the rain to come in today. I'll tell Inspector Cannon you're here." He rose and went down the hall and was back a couple of minutes later. "You can go in now."

Addy gripped her pocketbook as she followed Clara into the office. There were three chairs in front of the desk, and one of them was occupied. Zeke.

Addy gasped as their eyes locked. She wanted to be angry and hate him for walking out on her and for telling her what to do, but her body wanted him to hold her. Her belly tingled and her throat grew tight. She could have simply melted down into his arms. Instead, they both looked away, and she took her mutinous body and was going to sit on the far side, but Clara was already there. Addy reluctantly sat next to Zeke.

"You wanted to see me, Inspector?" Addy gazed at him, avoiding a look at Zeke.

"Yes, Miss Garcia. We got a court order and removed the ledger from the bank. We're still going through it, but I have an idea to trap some of the people responsible for Mr. Leman's death. With your help, of course."

Addy felt herself shaking, but she was in it now. "What do you want me to do?"

"Did you tell anyone, besides your cousin, about the key?"

She shook her head.

"I'm sorry, but I think Mrs. Anthony Giovanni told the family what you told her."

"I know. I don't like to think about that."

The Inspector waved his hand over to Zeke. "Mr. Shafer has brought something else to my attention. Would you tell her what you told me?"

Zeke glanced at her, slid his hand over his mouth in slight hesitation, then folded his hands on his lap as he related the story of the liquor bottle he'd found in the shipping crate.

"Mr. Shafer brought that in to me for evidence," the Inspector interjected.

"I've seen people going in and out of a door that was supposed to lead to an unused part of the building, too," Zeke continued. "When no one was watching, I opened the door and could see part of a distillery down the hall."

Cannon looked back at Addy. "It looks like they're using the studio for bootleg and distributing it through the theaters they own. I need both of you to help me with a plan."

Addy looked at Zeke. He was distracting her. Why did he have to be so good-looking?

"What do you want us to do?" Zeke asked.

"Miss Garcia, since you know your cousin must have told about the key, I want you to have a change of heart and give it to her." He pushed the key across the desk.

She picked it up. "I thought you have the ledger already."

"We do, but the people concerned with it don't know that. We made arrangements with the bank security for the guard to play the part of the person in charge of the vault. When the key is brought to the bank, the guard will give a sign to one of the others to call us and, hopefully, we'll get some of those gangsters."

She looked at the key, wishing the cursed thing would just go away, and put it in her pocketbook.

The Inspector turned to Zeke. "Mr. Shafer, you told Mrs. Giovanni that you were coming to town for supplies?"

He nodded.

"I want you to tell her in the morning that you heard from a friend of yours working with the police that they are coming in the afternoon for an inspection of the shipping department. A few of the officers and I are going to dress like deliverymen, with panels on the paddy wagons. You can let us into the shipping area early in the morning, and we will wait in the back room. I imagine they'll try to get the equipment out as soon as they can." He turned to Addy. "I want you to give her the key first thing, as well, but don't you two go in there together. It would look suspicious. After you give your messages, I want both of you out of the building. That's an order. We'll take it from there."

Addy spoke up. "Will it be all right if I go to the main commissary? There's a view of the shipping department from there."

"All right, but stay out of sight. I don't want either of you hurt, and I don't want anything to tip them off that the game is up. Detective Stevens, I want you to go with Miss Garcia in the morning to shipping, but stay outside. I want you on that station."

Clara nodded. "Yes, sir."

"Any questions?"

Addy was too nervous to think clearly, much less ask an intelligent question. *I hope I'm a good enough actress to do this*, was her only clear thought. As she and Clara got up to leave, Zeke stood in front of her.

"I'll come to the commissary after I'm through at shipping." He put his hat on and tipped it to Addy and Clara, then headed out the door.

Addy really tried to say angrily not to bother, but the words refused to come out of her mouth. *He hurt me*, her brain screamed to her reluctant body that, deep inside, looked forward to time with him tomorrow.

After Zeke left, Inspector Cannon spoke up. "Miss Stevens, I think you and Miss Garcia should go back to the hotel for tonight."

Clara looked long and hard at him. "May we go to another hotel? That one is as down at the heel as they come."

He shook his head. "Funny, the other men don't seem to care."

Clara put her hands on her hips. "Well, I do."

Cannon sighed. "All right, Stevens. As long as it's not the Ritz."

Next morning at six, Addy and Clara were at the studio shipping department. "Addy, I'll stay here, since I'm the outer station for the raid. I have a clear view of the commissary from here, so if you're in trouble, just wave."

Addy went into shipping, tensing her jaw so her teeth wouldn't chatter. She saw Zeke on the far end of the building, and their eyes met. His glance seemed to send her some reassurance, and she took a deep breath and put her mind in another place. This was an acting job.

She entered Muriel's office and closed the door. "Hello, dear. Do you have time to talk?"

"Addy, how are you feeling? That was a terrible thing to go through the other night." Muriel sat back in her chair.

"I seem to have recovered. Remember, I told you about that key to the safety deposit box at the bank? Well, I've decided you should have it. I found out some of the police are corrupt, so I think giving it to you would be the best thing."

Muriel's eyes nearly popped out of her head as Addy pulled the key out of her pocketbook. "Oh, yes, yes, you did the right thing. You surely did."

"I've got to go check into the star building. See you later."

"Thank you. You won't regret this."

I already do. Addy made a beeline to the commissary and ordered a coffee. She sat at a table away from the large window but where she could still keep an eye on the shipping area. An auto pulled up about ten minutes later, and Muriel came running out and handed something to the driver.

There goes the key, I'll bet. Oh, Muriel, please don't go back into that building. Her stomach churned for her cousin, but Muriel disappeared through the double doors and there was nothing Addy could do about it.

Soon she saw two blue panel trucks, with the words 'Swift Delivery' stenciled on their sides, drive into the shipping area. Eight men got out and unloaded a few crates and barrels. One of them gave a sign to Clara, who sat on a bench, filing her nails. They disappeared through the double doors. A short time later, Zeke came to the commissary.

Addy felt that warm glow descending on her again. Why couldn't she think clearly around him?

He got a cup of coffee, then sat across from her.

"Everything set?" she asked.

"Yes." He hesitated a moment and took a sip from his cup. He looked directly at her. "Addy, I want to talk to you about the other day. We have some time now, and there are a few things I want to say."

She raised an eyebrow. "Oh? What?"

"When you reminded me I turned away when you needed me most, it was like a slap in the face—it really woke me up. I never should have deserted you, and I want to apologize for that. And for getting angry at you for coming out of your tent with another man before I even knew what was going on. I did the wrong thing all the way around."

Addy tapped her coffee cup. "And?"

"There's a reason I acted like I did. Back home, while I was still in school, I fell in love with a girl named Helen. I planned to ask her to marry me when we graduated. One evening, I walked over to her house to see her. When I came up the drive, she was in the backseat of an auto, spooning with another man. I yelled and grabbed her out of there and asked in no uncertain terms what was going on.

She laughed in my face and told me she had been courted by both of us for over two years. He was just as shocked. We neither one knew the other existed. She was just using me and had no desire to be married, especially to me." He sighed.

Addy felt a flash of anger. "Why do you think I'm like her?"

"When I saw you and John, I thought it was happening all over again. That's why I walked out. Then when I was finally convinced it wasn't your fault, I saw you with Tex, and I snapped. I'm sorry for being so stupid." He ran his fingers through his hair, his eyes pleading for her to understand.

Addy shifted her gaze to stare at her coffee. "Knowing the reason helps, but there's a lot of hurt in me right now. I can accept your apology, but you'll have to give me time. I can't describe how much pain you've caused me, inside. It's been almost as bad as the rape."

His deep brown eyes looked very sad. "I've gone through hell since then. There's not a minute I'm not thinking of you and kicking myself for ruining what we had. I can't believe I pushed you away like that. Addy, give me a chance to make it up to you," he pleaded.

She set her cup down and held out her hand. "Friends? We can start with that."

He took her hand and kissed it. "Delighted, Miss Garcia."

Addy smiled in spite of herself. *Treat me well, Mr. Shafer. You don't realize you still have my heart.*

They turned their attention to the shipping building as several trucks rumbled by.

"Looks like the inspector's plan is working," Zeke said, peering out the window.

Addy saw Clara stand up and glance toward them, motioning for them to stay back. The trucks continued around to the shipping docks.

Zeke took her arm. "Let's go to the alley between the commissary and the production building. We can watch from there."

Addy waved at Clara and pointed to the alley. Clara nodded. Once in the alley, they no sooner had gotten behind some barrels than gunfire ripped the air. People poured out of buildings to see what was going on, only to run back in. There was a loud boom that shattered windows around them. Addy was thankful they hadn't stayed in the commissary, but her main worry was for Muriel, inside the shipping building. Oh, why did she have to be in the middle of it?

"It sounds like a spark set off the alcohol," Zeke said.

They took a peek around the corner of the commissary and saw dark smoke belching out from the shipping area. Workers ran panic-stricken down the streets of the studio. Gradually, the gunfire ceased. Before they could tell who had won the battle, Addy felt someone watching her, and she turned. Muriel stood behind them, her face blank, eyes staring.

"Muriel, are you all right?" Addy asked, relieved that her cousin was still alive.

Without answering, Muriel raised a gun and pointed it directly at Zeke.

"Muriel, no!" Addy threw herself at Zeke, grabbing his arm and pulling him sideways just as the gun went off. The bullet hit him in the shoulder and he cried out, falling behind a barrel as Addy stood shielding him, facing Muriel. "Put that gun down!"

Muriel didn't move. "Addy, step away. I have to kill him."

"Then you'll have to kill me first, because I'm not moving. Give me the gun."

Suddenly tears streamed down Muriel's cheeks.

"You don't understand! Tony is dead, and I'm carrying his child. Both of you are to blame for this raid, and it's not fair that you have Zeke, so I have to kill him!"

Addy shook, but she stood her ground. "No, I'm not leaving."

Muriel leveled the gun at her, and Addy closed her eyes, waiting for the bullet to cut through her. She jumped as she heard a shot. She took a deep breath and didn't feel anything but heard Muriel cry out.

"Are you hurt?" she heard Clara call out behind her. Addy turned as Clara ran up with her gun drawn. Muriel leaned over a barrel, clutching her bleeding hand, moaning.

"No, but Zeke was hit."

"Quickly! We have two injured over here!" Clara shouted down the street.

Zeke sat with his back to the wall, putting pressure on his shoulder. Addy dropped down beside him as Clara went to Muriel. Blood soaked the white shirtsleeve down his wounded arm. Addy involuntarily sobbed.

As the ambulances pulled into the alley, Zeke looked at her. "Addy." His voice was very weak. "You were really going to take that bullet, weren't you?" He gave a tortured sigh. "You saved my life."

"Hush, now. Save your strength. Who knew my cousin was such a good shot?" she tried to joke. Hot tears ran down her cheeks as she gently put her hands on his face. Then she stood back as the medics took Muriel and Zeke into two separate ambulances and dashed off.

Clara holstered her gun and came over to her. "Good job. You made her hesitate long enough that I had time to keep her from killing you both."

Addy was shaking so badly, she had to steady herself on the wall. "I can't believe that someone who was as close as a sister would try to kill me."

"I've found those who get involved in mobster families are so taken with the loyalty between members that they get swept up in it. When Muriel comes to her senses, I think she will be horrified by what she did." Clara put her arm around Addy's shoulders and started walking out to the group of policemen just as the fire trucks came screaming in.

Muriel, how far have you gone, that you wanted to kill us? But, if she's with child and Tony is really dead, could she have just snapped? And just when Zeke and I were patching things up. Dear God, please let Zeke be all right. Please let this turn out for the best.

Inspector Cannon was just making the announcement to his team and to the reporters who were gathered that they had arrested Mr. Abrams and the studio would be shut down until further notice, by police order. He turned to Addy. "I'm sorry about Mr. Shafer. We didn't anticipate Mrs. Giovanni trying to kill you two."

Addy was worried. "What will happen to her?"

"After she is treated at the hospital, charges will be filed against her."

"She told me she was carrying Tony's child. Would they let her go to her parents, or will they make her stay in jail?"

The inspector studied her face. "I'm sure that, as soon as they come with the bail, Mrs. Giovanni would be free to go with her parents."

"Should I go to my uncle's house and tell them?"

"We already sent someone over there. Miss Garcia, I'm assigning Detective Stevens to you for a while longer, and I'm going to assign someone to watch Mr. Shafer, both in the hospital and when he's released, as well. We may not have gotten all the mobsters this time, and I imagine they will blame the two of you. The master ledger gave us the names of those who were helping them out; one of them was Mr. Abrams. We also have a bead on the government and police officials who were being paid off, thanks to you and Mr. Shafer."

But what kind of price did I pay? This seems to go on and on. "I would like to go to the hospital to see how Zeke is."

He smiled. "I think that can be arranged. Stevens, you can take one of the autos."

"Yes, sir." She started toward the nearest one, followed by Addy. Clara spoke to the driver. "Inspector Cannon told me to take one of the autos to drive Miss Garcia to the hospital."

He grinned. "Just bring it back in one piece this time, Stevens."

Addy was astonished, but Clara swung in behind the wheel as Addy climbed into the front seat. "You know how to drive an automobile? Clara, you're full of surprises."

"To get this job, I had to be able to do everything a man could. Strength-wise, of course, the men have an advantage, but the police skills I can do as well as they can, and they know it, although I do get teased. I don't mind; that means I've been accepted."

Fifteen minutes later, they were walking into the lobby of the hospital. The antiseptic smell hit Addy's nose as they entered the reception area. A severe-looking woman sat behind an Underwood typewriter at the plain wooden desk littered with files, paper, pencils, pens. Her name tag said she was Marge Taylor. Her hair was pulled back in a bun so tight her face looked like it could split down the middle. She eyed them both up and down.

"May I help you?" she asked in a voice that seemed to say, *Why are you bothering me?*

Addy approached her. "A Mr. Ezekiel Shafer was brought in here with a gunshot wound about forty-five minutes ago. I'd like to see him."

Marge Taylor's face made a smile look like a sneer. "Only family members are allowed to see the patients outside of regular visiting hours and I—ahem—don't think that you're a relative."

You bitch! Well, Addy had never told Zeke she wouldn't marry him. Politely, she said, "No, but I am his fiancée."

The sneer grew exaggerated. "Now, honey, what would a nice white boy like that be doing with a Mexican?"

Addy's hand came down hard on the desk in such a way that many of the items rained onto the floor. She wanted to see if she could fit that Underwood into Marge Taylor's mouth. Addy felt a tight grip on her shoulder.

Clara pulled Addy to a standing position. "Let me take care of this." She pulled her badge out and showed it to Miss Taylor. "I'm Detective Stevens from the police department. All that Miss Garcia said was true. Not that it's any of your business, but if it wasn't for her, that nice white boy would've had a hole in his chest instead of his shoulder." Clara put her hand on the desk and leaned in, practically nose to nose with the startled woman. "Now, where is Mr. Shafer?"

Miss Taylor's mouth went into a tight bow. She slammed down a record book and opened it. Going down a column with her finger, she stopped on a line. "Men's Ward Two, bed eight."

"Thank you, Miss Taylor. Come on, Miss Garcia." And they headed toward the men's wing of the hospital.

"Thank you, Clara, for stopping me from taking that witch apart."

Clara laughed. "You just need to be polite but firm."

They found the double doors to Ward Two and looked down a large room with beds lined up along the sea-green walls, each separated from the next by cream-colored curtains. The numbers for the beds appeared on the wall above the dividers. As the girls walked down the line of curtains, they saw that some of the men in the ward looked to be sleeping, others had company, and a few were reading. At bed number eight a doctor was talking to a nurse, while Zeke apparently slept.

The doctor turned to Addy as she came into the enclosure. "May I help you, miss?"

"Yes, I'm Mr. Shafer's fiancée, Addy Garcia, and I want to know how he is."

"You must be the Addy he was mumbling about. I'm Dr. Michaelson." He held out his hand and she shook it.

"This is Detective Stevens. She has to stay with me. How is he?"

"Mr. Shafer was very lucky. The bullet opened a gash but didn't hit bone. All I had to do was clean the wound and stitch it up. I gave him a little morphine for the pain, so he'll be out for about a half hour. I was going to tell the nurse to come get me when he wakes up, but if you're going to stay, you can do that. If there is any emergency, there's a switch by the bed that lights up a bulb by the number eight at the nurse's desk. If everything checks out, once he's awake, he can be dismissed this afternoon."

Addy smiled with relief. "Thank you, Doctor." He and the nurse left the enclosure.

Clara took one of the two chairs in the area by the bed and turned one around to face the other wall, saying, "I'll give you as much privacy as I can." She sat and pulled a dime novel out of her pocketbook and started reading.

Addy took the other chair and set it close by the side of Zeke's bed, then sat and gazed at him, overwhelmed by the thought that she had almost lost him. Sleeping there, he looked even younger than his twenty-two years. The shock of dark brown hair was over his eyes again, and she gently reached and brushed it away.

I wonder how Muriel is? Why did she think she had to kill us? Uncle Henry and Aunt Jen must be frantic.

Exhausted, she put her head down on her arms on the side of the bed, while a tear traveled its way down her nose. She wiped it away. After the restless sleeplessness of the last two nights and the drama of this morning, her eyes were heavy. Her nose pressed to the clean sheets that smelled like bleach and a slight scent of Zeke. Blissful oblivion overcame her.

She felt a hand on her arm. "Addy?" came a voice like liquid honey pouring over her.

Her head popped up and she met bleary brown eyes looking back at her. "Zeke, how long have you been awake?"

"Not long."

Clara turned around. "Stay there, Addy. I'll go get the doctor." She hurried out the door.

He smiled. "I was enjoying watching you, not quite believing that you were really here."

Her eyes filled with tears. "Where else should I be?" She interlaced her fingers through his. They stayed that way until the doctor showed up.

"Well, Mr. Shafer, let's take a look at that shoulder." He and Addy helped Zeke to sit up, and she propped a pillow behind Zeke's back as the nurse came in with some supplies. "I'm going to show you how to change the dressing on the wound, young man. This has to be done once in the morning and once in the evening." He undid the hospital gown and Addy started to back out of the enclosure.

"I'll wait outside the curtain," she said, embarrassed.

The doctor looked over at her. "No, stay, in case

you have to help him."

She slid back into the chair, and Zeke chuckled.

The doctor used hydrogen peroxide to loosen the gauze next to the wound and carefully peeled it off the stitches. Addy gave an inward gasp at the three-inch gash in Zeke's upper bicep. The edges of the torn skin puckered at the places where the sturdy black knots of thread held them together. When the doctor washed around it with soap and water, Zeke winced a little, then gave Addy a quick smile as the doctor took clean gauze and bandaged the shoulder again.

"There will be some seepage for a couple of days, but if it starts looking red and puffed, come into the hospital immediately. Do not let it get wet, just wash around it like I did. Here are a few pills for the pain. Don't take more than two in twenty-four hours. You'll have to have help getting dressed. I don't want you lifting anything or raising your arm. Otherwise, come back a week from today to have me look at it. Do you understand?"

Just as Zeke nodded, a young man rushed in with clothes bundled in his hands. "Zeke, are you all right?" He set the clothes down and ran his hands through his red-brown hair. "When the hospital called for a change of clothes for you, they said you were shot."

"Not as bad as I could have been. Addy pulled me out of the way."

The young man turned his attention to her and held out his hand. "Hello, I'm Nathan, Zeke's roommate. I've heard much about you."

She shook his hand. "I've heard about you, too. I'm pleased to meet you."

The doctor motioned Nathan over to the bed. "I'll show you how to help Mr. Shafer get dressed."

Addy stood up. "I'll wait outside the curtain." She was distracted enough by Zeke's bare chest without having to see everything. She found Clara at her post, still reading.

Clara nodded when she saw her. "How is he?"

"He's getting dressed to go."

Clara and Addy turned as they heard firm footsteps coming down the center of the ward. Inspector Cannon came up to them with a smile on his face. "We got them all, thanks to you and Mr. Shafer."

"Inspector, do you know how Muriel is?" Addy inquired.

"I stopped in before she was taken to the station from here. Her hand had only a flesh wound. Your uncle's family has been notified. How is Mr. Shafer?"

"He's being discharged. The bullet just cut a gash in his arm, which was stitched up, and he'll have to be careful for a few days, is all."

"Fine, fine. I was going to assign Lamont to him, but it looks like I won't have to now. Stevens, it looks like you're off the case. Come into the station tomorrow to write up your report." He tipped his hat to Addy. "And thank you again, Miss Garcia. I'll see you at the trials."

As the inspector was leaving, Nathan came over to Addy. "The doctor said Zeke shouldn't be left alone for twenty-four hours, and I have a dinner to go to tonight. Can you stay with him until I get back? I'll pay for the cab."

"I have to be back at the dormitory before ten."

"I'll be back long before that. Thank you, Addy."

She smiled. *No, thank you, Nathan,* she added in her head.

Chapter 8

Back at the dormitory, Clara, Roxie and Anne helped Addy clean up her room.

"What happened at the studio?" Addy asked, as she put away clothes.

Anne shook her head. "They made an announcement that the studio will be closed indefinitely, so Roxie and I are going to be looking for work. How about you?"

"I'll probably start looking, as well." Addy found Zeke's watch and slipped it into her pocketbook.

Roxie threw up her hands. "Can you believe they were making bootleg right under our noses?"

"That's what killed Majestic." Addy sighed. "My premiere was supposed to be next week. Well, I guess I wasn't cut out for this star business."

Anne collapsed onto Addy's bed. "There's some at work that blame you and Zeke for the studio closing. They don't see that making illegal liquor is a bad thing. I hope that won't hurt your search for a job."

Addy leaned against the washstand. "I don't know what else I could have done. I do feel bad for the ones who lost their jobs, but Zeke and I did, too. Doing the right thing seems to get more and more complicated."

Clara glanced at the clock. "We'd better go, Addy."

At Anne's and Roxie's questioning looks, Addy smiled. "I've got to go sit with Zeke, while his roommate, Nathan, goes to dinner."

Roxie put her hands on her hips. "Uh-huh. How

much did you pay Nathan?" They all laughed while Addy's cheeks burned, but she laughed, too.

Just then, Mrs. Hutton rapped on the door. "Addy, your uncle is on the telephone."

Addy hurried downstairs and gingerly picked it up. "Yes, Uncle Henry?"

He cleared his throat. "How are you and Mr. Shafer?"

"I'm shaken, but no injury. Zeke had his shoulder stitched up at the hospital and was released. I'm going over to take care of him while his roommate goes to dinner."

"Are you sure you—?"

"Uncle Henry, I'm not going to let him be by himself because of some outdated social mores."

"All right. We won't go into that now."

Addy bit her lower lip, then asked, "How is Muriel?"

There was a moment of silence on the other end. "Her hand will heal. I hope her soul will, as well. She still thinks she did the right thing to try to avenge her husband's death. It may be better if you and Mr. Shafer stayed away until we can talk to her."

Addy sighed. "I don't think we're ready to see her yet, anyway. Let me know how she's doing until then, if you will?"

"I will. Send along my concern to Mr. Shafer."

Clara stood holding Addy's coat and pocketbook as Addy hung up the telephone. "Ready?"

Addy nodded. "Thank you, Clara. Let's go."

Clara dropped Addy off at Zeke's apartment building, bidding her goodbye.

The bachelor building was an old clapboard with four apartments, two on the ground floor and two above. Zeke and Nathan had the second one on the ground floor. When Addy knocked on the door, Nathan was quick to open it, dressed in a black suit but with his bowtie still undone. "Come in, Addy.

Can you tie this thing?"

"Sure, I used to help my cousin James." She fixed it quickly.

"Thanks. I'm meeting the rest of my intended's family tonight, so I can't be late, and I was getting desperate about this tie." He flashed her a nervous grin and dashed out.

Zeke's passionate hello kiss greeted her as she turned from closing the door behind Nathan. "Welcome to my home. It's not the Ritz, but it has everything I need...now."

Addy smiled. "Uncle Henry called before I came over. He sends you his concern."

Zeke nodded, and Addy was unsure just what he was thinking.

She took her time to look around the apartment. It was a simple sitting room with a gas stove and an icebox in an alcove. A bathroom and a bedroom with two single beds completed the suite. It was very sparsely furnished, with a wooden table and four chairs, bookshelves and an overstuffed chair and couch. All, including the walls, were in neutral shades, with a painting of a mountain forest adding the only color.

Zeke sat on the couch and grinned at her, a book beside him.

"Does Nathan ever stay in one spot for more than two seconds?" she asked.

"No. That's what makes him the ideal roommate. Would you like some sandwiches? Mrs. Solomon, our landlady, brought them over for me. There's water on the stove for tea."

She looked in the cabinet above the sink. "Where are the cups, and the teapot?"

Zeke came over. "They should be in there." He looked on the shelf, then down at the pile of dirty dishes in the sink. "Oops, it looks like they need cleaning." He picked a cup out of the sink and wiped it off on his shirtsleeve. "Here, this one doesn't look too bad."

Addy felt a bit nauseous. "Go sit down. I'll wash the dishes. I don't want to be poisoned." Zeke sat at the table while she turned on the heat under the kettle and made short work of the dishes, giving the water just enough time to boil. Then she made tea in the freshly washed teapot and poured some into a clean cup.

"Would you like some tea?"

Zeke nodded and she poured another cup, bringing both cups to the table and settling herself on the chair next to his.

He passed the plate of sandwiches to her. "Thank you, I'm sorry about the dishes," he said with a trace of embarrassment.

They chatted and ate through the evening until, at about eight o'clock, there came a knock at the door.

Addy got up and opened it to a woman with graying black hair. "You must be Addy. Is Mr. Shafer awake?"

Zeke waved to her. "Yes, Mrs. Solomon?"

She stepped inside. "Mr. Hayes called to let you know he's been delayed but he'll be in between eight-thirty and nine."

"Thank you, Mrs. Solomon."

With a pleasant, "Well, then, good night," the landlady left, and Addy closed the door. Zeke gave her an amused look. "Well, Addy, looks like you get to change the dressing. It's supposed to be changed at eight."

She frowned as she brought the basin of water and soap into the bedroom, where he had said it would be easier to manage the procedure. He sat on the edge of his bed, the corners of his mouth twitching up, and she set the basin on the washstand and then put her hands on her hips.

"You're enjoying this too much."

"Help me with this shirt." He pulled the shirt tails out of his trousers and undid the cuffs.

Addy unbuttoned his shirt, her face burning. He shrugged his right arm out, and she carefully pulled the sleeve down his left. There was a tightness in her throat as she was confronted with his muscled arms and cotton undershirt.

"Now, Addy, pull the undershirt around my right arm first, then over my head and down my left." Did she detect some hoarseness in that voice? When she moved her hand over the taut, smooth skin of his chest, she had to close her eyes for a moment and collect herself.

Addy was all business as she used the hydrogen peroxide to help peel off the gauze so they could take a look at the wound. The cut black threads reminded her of a line of ants marching across his shoulder. "It doesn't look like there's any swelling." She tried to sound cool and professional, although she noted a swelling in the crotch of his pants. She finished washing around the wound and covered it with a clean pad of gauze, then sat next to him on the bed. "I think we've gone past the friend stage." The sight of his bare chest sent ripples through her.

He leaned in and kissed her thoroughly, and she melted. Zeke held her with his good right arm and let his mouth travel down her neck, sending hot vibrations into her stomach and between her legs. She ran her hand down the skin of his pecs, and he moaned. They both jumped when the door opened.

"Hey, Addy, I have a cab waiting outside for you." Nathan walked into the bedroom and started to laugh. "He got you to change the dressing for him?"

She was puzzled. "Why, yes. It was supposed to be changed at eight, he said."

As Zeke tried to shush him, Nathan smirked,

replying, "It could be done any time this evening." Zeke's face wore a naughty-little-boy look.

She'd been duped. What a scamp Zeke was! Addy stood up and lightly flipped the basin over on Zeke's lap. To his yelp she replied, "Goodnight, my love." She slipped on her coat, picked up her things, and waved as Nathan went into another fit of laughter.

In the cab back to the dormitory, she checked in her pocketbook and found she had forgotten to give Zeke his watch. Oh, well, there would be a next time.

Mrs. Hutton looked up as Addy came in the door. "Dear, may I see you in my office?"

"Mrs. Hutton, is something wrong?" Addy looked at the housemother's red eyes.

"I told the other girls at dinner. Because of the arrests and the financial collapse of the studio, the city is closing the dormitories as of Friday. You have three days to find a new place to live." She put her face in her hands.

Addy was plagued with guilt. "Oh, no! I'm sorry. It's my fault."

Mrs. Hutton raised her head. "No, dear, you did the right thing. I blame the studio for taking the gangsters' money and allowing them to make hooch on the premises. How is Mr. Shafer, by the way?"

"Thank goodness, he's fine. He just has a wound that needed stitches."

"I'm glad. He's a good man for you."

Addy smiled. "I think so, too. Goodnight, Mrs. Hutton."

With a kaleidoscope of feelings, she entered her room. This was her first independence, but she felt violated by the attempted robbery of the key. Her dreams of stardom had come true, then were quickly dashed. Other than Zeke, the experiences she'd had with men were not something she wanted to go through ever again. She would never forget these months for as long as she lived.

Her reverie was broken by a knock at the door. "Who is it?"

"Your neighbors," said a familiar voice.

She opened the door to Anne and Roxie. "Come in." As usual, they all sat on Addy's bed.

Addy shook her head. "This reminds me of the first night I moved in."

Roxie sighed. "It seems like a million years ago, so much has happened. How is Zeke?"

"Well enough to be a scamp. He'll be fine. What are you going to do?"

"Roxie and I are going to audition for Mack Sennett. I heard he was looking for people. Maybe you can come along."

"I might do that, later." Addy felt guilty the other girls didn't have the money she did. She could take her time looking for the right job. The girls chatted well into the night before parting with a hug and a promise that they would stay in touch.

Addy got ready for bed, thinking about what she should do, and as she lay back on her pillow it came to her. *I think I'll find a place to live first. There's enough money in the bank to rent a small house. I don't want to live in dormitories the rest of my life.*

When Addy came down for breakfast the next morning, Mrs. Hutton gave her a message. "Your uncle called this morning. He wants you to call him back. He says he'll be home all day."

Addy thanked her and, after she ate, she called.

"Adeline, as you know, we have Muriel here. She wants to talk to both you and Mr. Shafer. Is he well enough to travel?"

Addy was shocked. "Uncle Henry, she tried to kill Zeke, and she would have shot me, too, if it hadn't been for Detective Stevens."

Uncle Henry's voice got softer. "I know all this, but we have been talking with her, and I think you should both see her before the trial. She was woefully coerced by the Giovannis to fall into their 'family' ways. According to them, you and Mr. Shafer became a threat and had to be eliminated. I think now she's away from that environment she can see what is right and wrong again. Anyway, we will all be here, so I know that no harm will come to you."

Her love for Muriel won out. "When do you want us to come over?"

"How about Saturday for dinner?"

"I'll let you know after I talk to Zeke."

"Very well. Take care of yourself, Adeline."

Addy went back up to her room with the morning newspaper. *What can I do? I love my family, and I think I can forgive Muriel, but can Zeke? Maybe, if I ask him to give her a chance to explain...* Addy felt a tightening in her gut. *At least the worst part of this whole upsetting episode is over,* she thought.

Addy looked in the newspaper classifieds and circled ads for five houses for rent nearby. She started with the closest one. That was off the market. At three others, Addy had the feeling the people didn't want to rent to her. Whether it was because she was a single woman or because she was a Mexican, she didn't know. Her feet were getting sore by the time she reached the last house whose ad she'd marked. It was a bungalow, with white clapboard siding and green awnings, on a side street. The yard was a tiny patch of grass, but it had an orange tree in front. Hedges hugged the house by the porch, and at the end of the drive was a stable that had been converted into a garage.

Addy walked up the path to the door and turned the lever of the round bell. A nice-looking woman with graying hair answered.

"Hello, my name is Adeline Garcia, and I've come about renting the house."

The woman smiled pleasantly. "I'm Amelia Daily. Please come in." Addy was led into a sitting room with boxes stacked here and there. "Forgive me for how the house looks. You see, my husband passed away, and I'm moving in with my son and his family. Renting the house will give me a little extra income. The furniture will stay here. I'm just taking my personal things."

The sitting room was sunny, with white lace curtains on the beautiful diamond-paned leaded windows. The old-fashioned couch and chairs had blue velvet upholstery, and there were a few tables around the room. It just needed a few bookshelves, Addy thought.

"Come with me, and I'll show you the rest of the house." The kitchen had a dropleaf table with four chairs, a gas stove and an icebox. Addy loved to cook, and there was plenty of room to fix meals and entertain her friends. A bedroom containing a brass bed, a washstand and a chest of drawers had a window that looked out on the shaded backyard. *How beautiful this is!* A bathroom with a footed tub completed the ground floor, and there were two tiny rooms upstairs that weren't furnished. Mrs. Daily explained that these had been her children's rooms, and they'd taken all their furniture with them when they moved from home. Addy could use that for storage, if she needed. The whole house smelled fresh and clean.

They sat at the kitchen table and Mrs. Daily brought some sheets of paper. "Tell me a little about yourself. Are you engaged, dear?"

"Yes. We haven't set a date yet. I worked at Majestic Studios and lived at the dormitory. Now that it's closed, I have to find another place."

Mrs. Daily tsk-tsked. "That was a terrible thing. I read about it in the newspaper. Well, Miss Garcia, the rent is fifty a month, payable on the first. No pets are allowed. If you want to move, I need to know two weeks ahead of time. Is that satisfactory?"

"Yes. May I move in Friday?" Addy gave Mrs. Daily the first month's rent. "And could I have a telephone put in? I'll put it in my name."

"You may. I'll give you your key."

Addy put the key into her pocketbook and shook hands with Mrs. Daily. *A house! I'm going to be living in a real house,* she sang to herself as she half-skipped down the sidewalk. She hopped a streetcar to Zeke's apartment, where Nathan answered the door.

"Addy, hello. Zeke's up and around, if you want to see him."

Zeke bounced up off the chair and gave her a hug with his good arm. "Sit down, sweetheart. May I get you something?"

Addy's warm glow made her giddy. "No, thank you, but may I ask you something?"

"Sure, what do you need?"

"Are you able to drive? I just rented a house and, if you can, I need you to drive my things over for me. I have to move out of the dormitory Friday."

"I don't think driving would hurt my shoulder."

"What about cranking it over?"

"I use my right hand for that."

Nathan jumped in. "I'm off work Friday. I could give you a hand, as well."

Addy smiled. "Swell. Could you come to the dormitory about eleven in the morning? It's a furnished house, so you won't have to move any furniture." She hesitated a moment. "Oh, Zeke, we're invited to my uncle's house for dinner Saturday evening."

Zeke frowned. "Isn't Muriel staying with them?"

"Uncle Henry said they've been talking to her and she wants to see us."

Zeke and Nathan glanced at each other. Zeke

turned to Addy. "I'll go if you really want me to, but I'm not anxious to see someone who tried to kill me."

Addy's gaze dropped. "I understand. We'll leave if things go wrong, but I think we should give her a chance." She got up to go. "I've got to get all my things together. I'll see you two on Friday."

Zeke got up and gave her a kiss that set her heart racing. "I'll be looking forward to it."

When Addy got back to the dormitory, she started packing her things in the few crates Mrs. Hutton had to spare, but before long she sat down on her bed. A light breeze came in through the window and ruffled her hair. So much had happened since she'd declared her independence from Uncle Henry! She knew she had to find a job, although she had six thousand dollars in the bank. That would tide her over for a while, but she would feel better about it if she could earn her daily living expenses and save what was in the bank for a rainy day. Addy lay back on her pillow, exhausted. She fell into a blissful sleep, dreaming about a very healthy, virile Zeke.

Thursday evening, Mrs. Hutton fixed a special farewell dinner for the dormitory residents—crown roast of beef, mashed potatoes and gravy, fresh asparagus with hollandaise, and her famous fruit salad. For dessert, there was her savory apple pie with real ice cream. She had told the girls that each could invite one guest, so Zeke sat at Addy's side, across from Anne, who had just gotten engaged to Raymond, one of the extras on the former crew. Roxie was there with Herb, her high school sweetheart.

"Where are you going to live?" Addy asked Anne.

"Ray and I are going to have a civil ceremony, since our families are out East. We've got a small apartment near Sunset."

Roxie looked at Addy. "You were lucky to be able to rent a house. I'm back in a dormitory again."

Tears started in her eyes. "I'm sure going to miss both of you."

Addy's throat got tight. "Let's pledge to meet once a month for dinner somewhere, so we can stay in touch." They put their hands across the table in a three-way handshake.

Just then Gwen Meyers stood up at the end of the table and tapped her glass with her knife. "Attention, everyone! As the one who has lived the longest here at Dormitory Number Three, I have been chosen to say thank you to Mrs. Hutton for all she has done for us. Here is a card signed by everyone, with a pass to go to Avalon on Santa Catalina Island for a weekend." There were cheers from all over the room as Mrs. Hutton stood up to accept her gift.

"I—I don't know what to say," she gulped, tearing up. "You girls have been like daughters to me, and I'll never forget you. Thank you so much."

"What are you going to do now?" one of the girls asked.

"I think I'll see if one of the other studios needs a housemother. Otherwise, I might go back to Arizona. I hear it's a little more civilized now."

****

Friday, Mrs. Hutton said goodbye to the girls one by one as they moved out. She had packed a picnic hamper with food and lemonade for Addy and her moving crew, and when Addy, Zeke and Nathan finished moving clothes and boxes to the Ford, Addy handed Mrs. Hutton a piece of paper. "Here's my new address. I hope you will write to me when you can." Addy gave her a hug. "And thank you for everything."

"I will. Goodbye, Addy." Mrs. Hutton returned the hug, then gave Zeke a pat on the back. "Take good care of her."

He smiled. "You can count on it. Goodbye."

Nathan sat on the suitcases in the back, while Addy got in the front and pulled Zeke into the driver's seat by grabbing his right hand.

The day passed quickly as the trio arranged things in the house, and while the men sat recuperating from their labors, Addy walked to the grocery store a couple of blocks away to stock the kitchen. Once that was done, she joined the men in the sitting room, where they sat enjoying some of Mrs. Hutton's lemonade.

Zeke looked at the clock and commented, "It's almost suppertime. Would you like to walk down to the little diner on the side street?"

Nathan shook his head and got up to leave. "Not me. I have a few things to do tonight. I can hop the streetcar."

Addy gave him a hug. "Thank you for your help."

He patted her shoulder as he waved her off. "Anytime. You'll have to meet Babs one of these days."

"We'll get together over dinner soon."

Zeke and Addy waved as he started down the street, and then they walked in the opposite direction to the silver railroad car that had been converted into a diner with a long counter and stools bolted to the floor. They sat down and were looking at the chalkboard menu as a chubby woman in a crisp gray uniform came down the other side of the counter and set glasses full of water in front of them.

"May I help you?" she asked.

Zeke nodded. "We would each like the chicken soup and a club sandwich, with coffee, please."

She took the order on a pad of paper and put it into the window to the kitchen. In a few minutes, their order was sitting there, and she brought it over and put some Saratoga chips on the plates, as well. They topped off the meal with a dish of chocolate ice cream.

Back at the house, Zeke started rotating his left shoulder. "The gauze is bothering me."

"Maybe I should change the dressing. I have first aid supplies here." Addy went to get the hydrogen peroxide and some clean gauze. When she brought the basin of water with the soap and washcloth to the kitchen table, Zeke already had his shirt pulled out and unbuttoned. Addy's insides were shaking, but she put on her best business side while she helped him out of his shirt. She changed the dressing like a competent professional, but, just as she was adding the tape to keep the gauze in place, the desire she'd tried to suppress washed over her in a tidal wave. Her hand moved down his bare chest and caressed his stomach, and his body quivered at her touch.

Zeke looked up at her, and she could see the fire burning in those rich chocolate eyes. She leaned down to him and their lips and tongues met passionately as he gently pulled her down to sit on his knees.

As he pulled back, their eyes met, and Addy was swept away on a wave of passion. Neither one could look away. Zeke took a shaky breath. "Are you sure you want this?"

Nodding, Addy closed her eyes momentarily, and a single tear coursed down her cheek. As an answer, she unbuttoned the top of her blouse and set his hand on the row of buttons.

His eyes never leaving hers, he discarded her garments and buried his face on the side of her neck, kissing to her ear. "If you have doubts, stop me now."

Addy rose and, taking both his hands in hers and drawing him up, ran her fingers through his hair and drew him into a deep kiss. They made their way down the hall to the bedroom, dropping clothes as they went, as if leaving bread crumbs to lead them back to real life.

Dappled light of the late afternoon sun played across the walls, and the lace curtains billowed softly in the breeze at the open window. Addy's chiding moral mind was put into a deep corner, overcome by a rising awareness of a deeper, more primitive feeling. Zeke's eyes were intense, burning into hers now, and she could feel the heat radiating from his body.

They moved as one to the bed, and Zeke ran his hands softly over her skin, waking every nerve. Her whole world was this being enfolding her, loving her. Being careful of his shoulder, he gently drew her on top of him, her legs straddling him, and he raised and lowered her hips until she picked up the rhythm, letting it build, fire coursing until it consumed them both.

Then, limp, unmoving, her head on his chest, she began to cry softly. "What you must think of me. I feel like a wanton woman."

He lightly kissed her sweaty forehead. "You're not a wanton woman. You don't realize how much I love you, Adeline Rose Garcia."

"But what if I become with child?" She moved to look into his face.

He smiled. "Then we will have to get married that much sooner."

Gathering their clothing, they dressed again, with Addy helping Zeke with his undershirt and dress shirt. In the sitting room, she took the watch from her pocketbook and gave it to him. "Here, this belongs to you."

He looked at the inscription before encircling her with his good arm. "This means more to me now than it did at Christmas." He hugged her for a moment more and then put the watch on his wrist. From his shirt pocket, he took out the engagement ring. "I know now I can never be without you. I love you so, Addy." He put it on her finger and kissed it in place, then kissed her palms and her other fingers, one by one.

Addy felt the wetness of tears on her cheeks as she cradled his face with her well-kissed hands. "Promise me you'll never leave me again."

"I promise." Then he held her tight. "I'll be here at five o'clock tomorrow, and we'll go to your uncle's." She walked with him out to the Ford and helped him into the driver's seat, then waved as he started down the street.

Gazing at the ring as she sat on the porch in the cool evening air, Addy thought how much she wanted this man, how much she needed their relationship to work out this time. *Please, Zeke, keep loving me.* She thrilled at the thought of their lovemaking. What a powerful thing—she'd had no idea how wonderful it would be. Would it bond Zeke to her? Addy felt she should be ashamed of what they'd done, but she wasn't. It seemed so right. She loved him with all her heart. She watched a shooting star leave a trail across the sky, and she made a wish.

****

Addy spent the next day settling into her house, arranging everything in the kitchen, dusting the furniture again, marveling that she lived in such comfort. As the time grew close for Zeke to pick her up, she realized she dreaded seeing Muriel again. Addy loved her as a sister, but Muriel had turned on Zeke and her without any warning. Well, Addy had always preached how important family was, so this was going to be a test for her on that score, she figured. Addy's musings were broken by the sound of the Ford coming into the driveway. She gathered her things together and met Zeke at the door.

"Hello, sweetheart," he said, kissing her thoroughly. "Are you ready?"

"No, but I'll go anyway." Addy was silent most of

the way.

"I have a feeling you're not looking forward to this dinner any more than I am," Zeke ventured.

"It's hard to get out of my head the vision of Muriel with that gun." They were just pulling into the driveway, and Addy's hands were slick with perspiration.

As they walked to the house, Zeke put his arm around Addy's shoulders, and her arm was around his waist. They leaned on each other all the way up to the house, until Uncle Henry came out to meet them as they came up the steps.

"Adeline, Mr. Shafer, I know it was difficult for you to come here to see Muriel tonight, after the unfortunate happening at the studio. I think Muriel is beginning to see how she was being manipulated by the Giovannis. Her court hearing is on..." he hesitated for a moment, "February third."

"My birthday," Addy said.

Her uncle nodded. "You both will be getting a summons for it, I'm sure." He turned to the door. "Come on in."

The family was in the parlor, more subdued than Addy had ever seen them before. Muriel, looking pale and drawn, sat next to Aunt Jen. She looked at Addy, and the tears started to flow.

"I'm so sorry—I can't believe I tried to shoot you both." Muriel's voice was strained, almost unrecognizable. "I know now you were trying to warn me away, Addy, but I didn't listen to you. I loved Tony so much, I didn't see him for what he was." She rose and went to Addy, and the two embraced. "Tony killed John Peyton for you."

Addy froze. Horror flowed over her, with a trace of guilt, as though she had been the one to push John over the balcony. "John died because of me?"

Muriel looked at her. "Oh, no, dear. He died because he raped you. That's how the Giovannis take care of people who wrong them. Somehow, Tony convinced me it was the right thing to do." She turned to Zeke but couldn't look him in the eyes. "That's why I thought I had to shoot you. I blamed you for Tony's death, for bringing the police in on that raid, and in my state of mind after I found him shot to death there..." Her voice broke, and she gulped to regain it. "I didn't think it was fair that Addy still had you." Muriel's jaw tensed, as though she'd had to squeeze the words out. "I'm so, so sorry." She dissolved into tears.

Zeke put his hand on her shoulder. "It was difficult for me to come over this evening. No one ever tried to kill me before. I'll try to forgive you, but you have to understand—it's going to take time."

Muriel nodded, mopping her face with her handkerchief.

Uncle Henry glanced at Zeke. "So you and Adeline are back together again? I know you had, um, a problem between you."

"Yes, sir, that was worked out. I was a cad to have walked out on her, and I told her so. I never stopped loving her."

Uncle Henry clapped Zeke on the back. "I'm glad you've made up." He rubbed his hands together. "Let's all go into the dining room."

At dinner, Addy told them about moving into her new house and gave them her telephone number and address on a piece of paper.

Uncle Henry looked at her, puzzled. "Do you have a job yet? I didn't think you had enough money to rent a house."

"I have over six thousand in the bank, Uncle Henry. Remember, I was getting a star's wages for the last few weeks. That should be enough to get me through the trials without having to take time off from a job."

"How about you, Mr. Shafer? Are you looking for

work?"

Zeke glanced at Uncle Henry. "I guess I'll do the same as Addy. I only have a couple of thousand in the bank, but that should tide me over for a couple of months. I was working for a year and a half before Addy started at the studio. I don't think I'll have any trouble finding another job. There's plenty of studio work in this town."

His answer seemed to satisfy Uncle Henry, because he moved on to other topics.

Addy, helping to clean up after dinner, was taken aside by her grandmother. "I noticed looks going between you and Mr. Shafer. Those were the looks of a man and woman who have been intimate with one another."

Addy felt her cheeks burn. She should have known Grandma would know the truth.

"It's not my business what you do, my dear, but be very careful of your reputation."

Addy smiled. "I never could get anything past you. I do understand what you're saying. I already talked to Zeke about this. We'll deal with any consequences."

"I know how hard it is to be chaste when you're young."

Addy almost asked, but she realized she really didn't want to know how Grandma knew. For one thing, that would be prying. For another, well, it was her grandparents.

When Zeke dropped her off at her house, she turned to him at the door. "Grandma knew."

He looked at her, puzzled. "Knew what?"

"That we were intimate with each other. She said she could see it in the way looks passed between us."

"Hmm, well, we're going to have to be careful." He grinned, then kissed her. When he pulled back, he looked at her with that fire in his eyes. "Come to think of it, I wouldn't mind trying it again. May I come in?"

"I don't think we should've done that in the first place." Addy saw disappointment on his face. "Not that you weren't magnificent, but I do worry about becoming with child too soon." She put her hand on his chest and pushed back a little. "Goodnight, my love."

He kissed her on the lips. " You've wounded me, but goodnight, sweetheart."

Addy didn't care if Grandma knew. She watched Zeke drive away. Someday, the whole world was going to know. She turned to go inside, but felt a chill go down her spine. She knew the inspector had said they got everyone, but she still looked over her shoulder all the time. Maybe she should have taken Zeke up on his offer. But, no, she had to get used to living alone, for a while, anyway.

Chapter 9

Three weeks passed in uneventful quiet. Addy and Zeke enjoyed the quiet to relax and to make plans for their future. A few days before Muriel's hearing, Addy heard the Ford in the driveway.

"Addy!" Zeke called as he jumped out of the driver's seat. "You've got to see this!"

She ran out the front door. "What is it?"

He gave her a hug and swung her around on the porch. "I got a letter from my brother!"

"It was a while ago when you wrote to your mother, wasn't it?" They sat on the porch steps, and Addy looked at the letter, waiting expectantly for Zeke to explain further.

"Listen! My father has disowned me—which I expected—and he was treating my next brother, Joshua, like he did me. Josh ran off to the Alaskan Territory, but he took with him the letter I sent, and now he's written to me. He bought an old opera house in Juneau, and he wants to know if we would be interested in running productions in it!"

Addy clapped her hands. "Oh, that sounds like a real adventure!" She grew serious. "But that will take us so far away from here. What about my family?"

"I thought about that. Addy, I don't think this thing with the mob is ever going to end. Someone somewhere is going to try to cut us down for ruining the bootlegging. This may be a way to avoid them. We shouldn't tell anyone about this."

Addy put the letter on her lap and leaned her head against his shoulder. "Of course, you're right.

I've wondered about that myself. I remember in school I read about the Hydra, a creature that if the head was cut off, it grew seven more. The mob seems to be like that. One gang gets cut down, and another takes its place." Tears came to her eyes. "Zeke, I'm so tired of this. We do what we think is the right thing, and now it seems like we have a price on our heads."

"I think that's what they call a contract. Let's set a date in May to get married. The trials will be over by then, and we can leave on a train on the pretence of going on a honeymoon, but we'll never return." He put his arm around her and buried his face in her hair. "Maybe someday, if things change, we can come back."

Addy was devastated, but she knew he was right. One earthquake had taken her parents and brother; now this manmade upheaval seemed to be separating her from more people she loved. She clung to Zeke for a long time, grieving how with each episode of her life she lost something. But she also gained something, she reminded herself. Zeke was her life now, and she was happy he loved her.

He drew back and kissed her tenderly. "We can tell your uncle about our plan and the reason behind it. We can trust him, and I'm sure he'll understand. You can keep in touch with them—I know how important your family is to you. There's always a chance someone might find out where we are, but I think we can take the risk."

She looked into the face she loved. "Thank you. For the last couple of weeks, you have been my rock. You've changed since the raid on the studio. I trust you with my life."

His smile crinkled the corners of his eyes. "I will never stop loving and protecting you, darling, I promise."

They sat on the steps for a long time, just

delighting in the nearness of the other. He leaned to kiss her gently, yet passionately. She felt the fire of desire spread over her. As if with one mind, they stood up and went inside the house.

Zeke swept her into his arms and carried her to the bedroom. "I know what you said before about becoming with child, but I've got to have you again, my darling. I can't help myself."

Addy's body outvoted her. She wanted him again, too, but a sudden concern surfaced. "Is your shoulder strong enough to lift me?"

He grinned. "The stitches came out the other day. I'm fine."

Addy felt his heart pounding through his shirt, and her body responded. As he set her down, they locked together in a deep kiss before she pulled back enough to whisper, "Yes, my love. I want you, too." She looked deep into his eyes. This was not sin, when you loved someone this much.

Their clothes fell like orange blossoms on a breezy day. Addy loved the intense burning in his eyes. It seemed to transform him even further into her ideal man. The bed enfolded them in their hideaway from the world. She felt his soft lips and warm hands urging her on to the heights of her senses.

For a moment, Zeke ran his fingers through her hair and seemed to look into her soul through her eyes, and then she felt him enter her and start to move. Addy couldn't remember a feeling so strong as this one of being loved and cherished in a way that left her breathless. After the last ripples had floated away, they kissed again, deeply, and then lay together, the sweet and salty smell of sex all around them. Addy caressed his sweaty forehead and kissed him again.

"Zeke, you make all the bad thoughts go away. I love you so much."

"My Mexican Rose, all I want is you." He nuzzled her neck.

Her moral mind tried to resurface and chide her. She pushed it back into a dark corner. How could something so beautiful be wrong? Well, it wouldn't be long before they could legally do this as much as they pleased. They spent the rest of the morning exploring and delighting in each other.

The day of the court hearing came, and Zeke picked her up at the house. "We'll celebrate your birthday later on." He smiled as he kissed her.

Addy was in a state of turmoil as she got into the Ford. She hadn't been able to sleep most of the night, and when she did, she had the worst, most foreboding dreams. "I don't know what it is, but I feel something horrible will happen today."

He squeezed her hand. "That's just nerves. I've never testified in court, either. We'll both be fine."

She tried to believe him, but she couldn't shake the feeling of doom.

When they got to the Federal Court House, he took a firm hold of her hand and they went into court together. Addy saw her family behind the defendant's side and she sat beside Aunt Jen. Uncle Henry, James, and Grandpa were on the other side of her aunt. Zeke took the seat next to Addy. Her aunt took her hand and smiled.

"Where's Grandma?" Addy whispered to her.

"She's watching the boys and Maggie."

Waiting for the hearing to begin, Addy looked around the courtroom. It was the first time she'd ever seen anything like this. In theaters, they had stage scenery, and she'd seen pictures in books and magazines, but the impact of the real thing had never come through to her as it did now.

The gray marble walls with the dark wood paneling and raised benches looked like a medieval throne room in a castle. Over the judge's bench were the words *Justice will serve* in raised gold letters.

The actors in this real play started to take their places. The court recorder and the bailiff arrived first. The Federal prosecutors, with their black bags full of papers, sat at the right-hand desk facing the bench. They whispered to each other constantly. Next came the defense attorney, with an equally impressive black bag. Muriel was escorted in behind him. She was in her best suit, looking very pale and lost under the smart hat.

Addy felt a surge of sympathy for her. The room was well lit by the shafts of sunlight coming in the arched windows on one wall, and the gallery seemed to be full with reporters and the curious. The warm smell of a room full of people came to her nose.

She noticed Inspector Cannon, Clara, and a few of the policemen who had been at the studio the day of the raid. She and Clara exchanged a slight smile of recognition.

The bailiff stepped to the front of the bench and the room hummed in expectation. "All rise. The Federal Court in the State of California for the City and County of Los Angeles is now in session, the Honorable Judge Samuel T. Hardy presiding."

The judge came in like a king in a flowing black robe from stage right and ascended the throne. He was a very hard-looking man, with graying black hair and bushy eyebrows that nearly hide his eyes. He pounded his gavel. "Please be seated. The Hearing in the case of the United States versus Muriel Agnes Carter Giovanni will now come to order."

Zeke put his arm around Addy as the prosecution laid out its case against Muriel. She glanced at Muriel and saw her nervously twisting her handkerchief after dabbing at her eyes. One by one, all the players in the drama were called up to perform on the stage in front of the judge.

Addy's name was called, and it took her a moment to recognize it. Zeke kissed her cheek and her aunt squeezed her hand. She nervously walked to the box that reminded her of a small prison cell from which she couldn't escape. The bailiff came up with the Bible, and she put her sweaty palm on it, swearing to God she would speak the truth. But what was the truth?

The prosecutor stood up. "Miss Garcia, where were you on the morning of January the fifth?"

"I was at Majestic Studios, sir."

"Tell us what happened that morning."

"I went to the shipping department to give a safety deposit key to Muriel."

"Let the record state, she means Mrs. Giovanni. Why did you give the said key to Mrs. Giovanni?"

Addy took a deep breath. "It was part of a trap set up by Inspector Cannon to catch the people involved in an illegal distillery in the shipping department."

"Did they believe Mrs. Giovanni had knowledge of this distillery?"

Addy bit her lip. "Yes, sir."

"What was in the safety deposit box that the key opened?"

"The police had already removed the contents, but originally it was the master ledger for the studios."

"For the court's information, Inspector Cannon revealed the contents of the ledger in his testimony. Now, what did you do after you gave Mrs. Giovanni the key?"

"I went to the commissary."

"Did you see Mrs. Giovanni while you were there?"

"Yes, a man got out of an automobile and she came out of Shipping to talk to him."

He handed her a photograph. "Is this the man

you saw?"

Addy looked at the sinister face. "It seems to be the one I saw."

The prosecutor gave the photograph to the judge. "This is the man who was picked up at the bank with the safety deposit key that Miss Garcia gave Mrs. Giovanni." He turned back to Addy. "Did you see Mrs. Giovanni give him the key?"

Addy shook her head. "I was too far away to see that."

Next, Addy had to relive that horrible moment when Muriel shot Zeke, as she answered more questions. When the defense attorney stood up, his questions came fast, but Addy answered simply what she remembered. She glanced at Muriel several times, trying to read what she was feeling. It felt like a million years before she was finally dismissed by the judge. She went back to her seat, walking on rubber legs that she prayed would hold her up.

Zeke was called up next, and he looked like he was in his own private hell, recalling his part in the trap.

The prosecutor came up to the bench. "Mr. Shafer, when did you see Mrs. Giovanni again?"

Addy could see Zeke's jaw tense up, and her heart went out to him.

Zeke took a quick breath. "She came from the back of the alley between the commissary and the next building, just as the raid was ending at the shipping department."

"What happened?"

"She pointed a gun at me, and I froze. Addy, um, Miss Garcia pulled me out of the way just before Mrs. Giovanni fired. The bullet hit me in the shoulder."

"Do you think Mrs. Giovanni was trying to kill you?"

The defense attorney jumped up from his seat. "I object! He's asked the witness to speculate."

The prosecutor shot an angry glance at the defense. "Were you afraid for your life?"

"Yes." Zeke's voice shook.

Muriel's face was in her hands during most of Zeke's testimony. Zeke came back to his seat looking drained. He took Addy's hand and held it tightly. Addy didn't know which of them needed to draw strength from the other, at this point.

Muriel took the stand and, between bursts of tears, recalled being carefully taught in the ways of the family into which she had married. "I heard so many times from them that it isn't a crime to defend your family. I was led to believe that if the police won't help you, you have to get justice on your own, even if it means eliminating someone who has wronged you."

"And you believed Mr. Shafer had wronged you?"

Muriel sobbed. "I blamed him for Tony's death."

"You are immune from prosecution in the matter of John Payton's death, so would you state to this court what happened on January first of this year? That will give an example of how the Giovanni family executes justice."

Muriel took a deep breath. "Mr. Payton attacked my cousin, Addy, um, Miss Garcia, and Tony told me that since the police didn't do anything, we should make him pay for the crime. He didn't tell me what he was going to do. After the police had left, Tony told me about it. He said Mr. Payton was drunk, and Tony led him to one of the balconies in the building. There was an empty wine bottle that Tony took with him. When they went outside, onto the balcony, Tony broke the bottom of the bottle and jammed the jagged edge into Mr. Payton's chest, and then Tony threw him over the railing onto the walk below."

Addy's stomach turned over, and she clung to Zeke's arm.

After Muriel's testimony, the judge listened patiently as the prosecutor and defense attorney each laid out their arguments for whether Muriel should be held for trial. When all had been said, Judge Hardy took a recess and went to his chambers to study the case.

Addy wanted to get out of the suffocating courtroom atmosphere for a few moments, so she and Zeke went out to the hallway. They were both crushed by reporters clamoring for information.

One reporter called out, "How does it feel to be the ones who brought down Majestic Studios?"

Zeke turned on him. "We didn't bring it down. The ones doing business with the gangsters did."

Another asked, "Do you fear for your lives for being snitches?" The crowd pushed in around them.

Zeke grabbed Addy's arm. "Let's go back inside." They fought their way back to their seats.

Addy was shaking as she sat down again. *Oh, dear, the reporters are making it sound like we were to blame for the studio's fall.* She squeezed Zeke's hand. "What are we going to do?"

He looked serious. "We'll have to go through this until things calm down. Don't worry, I'll take the brunt of it."

A few minutes later, the bailiff took the floor again. "All rise. The court is now back in session." The judge ascended his throne again and Addy held her breath as he looked at Muriel with a hard stare. "Please be seated. Mrs. Giovanni, remain standing. I've looked over all the facts and testimony in this case and have come to a decision. Whereas you were young and naïve when you eloped with Mr. Anthony Giovanni, I believe you were easily coerced into the family business. As for the attempted murder of Mr. Ezekiel Shafer, I added the factor of the shock of seeing your husband killed, and your condition, as a situation of temporary insanity. I'm dismissing this case. Mrs. Giovanni, you are free to go."

Aunt Jen nearly flew over the railing to hug her daughter, who dissolved into tears. Addy sent up prayers of thanks. She glanced at Zeke, but it was impossible to tell what he was thinking. Inspector Cannon came up to Zeke and Addy.

"I'm glad this turned out the way you wanted it, Miss Garcia, but I have to tell you, the trials of the Giovanni mob and Mr. Abrams won't be quite so easy."

Addy shook his hand. "I know, but I'm glad Muriel won't be going to prison."

Uncle Henry greeted the Inspector. "We're having a celebration at our house this evening. You're welcome to stop by, if you wish."

"Thank you, but no. I'm on duty tonight. I appreciate the invitation, Mr. Carter." The men clasped hands and the Inspector departed.

Uncle Henry turned to Zeke and Addy. "Both of you can come over to the house from here. We'll make a day of your birthday and Muriel's freedom."

Addy nodded. "We'll be there."

Most of the way, neither spoke. She knew by the twitch in his jaw that Zeke was having a problem forgiving Muriel. *I wish I could convince him that's not the way Muriel really is.* Looking down at her hands, Addy said, "You know, we have to set a date tonight for our wedding. How about May seventh? That's the first Saturday. We could have a backyard wedding, since I have a small family and you don't have any relatives here."

"Addy, do we really have to have it at your uncle's house? You know, we can elope."

She pursed her lips. "I know how you feel, Zeke, but if there's anything I learned from the earthquake, it's to hang on to the family I have. I know it's Muriel you have a problem with, but please listen to me. I hate what she did to you, but I also know she feels an enormous amount of remorse about it. The judge let her off today because of what the Giovannis did to her. Could you give her some mercy for my sake? She's still my blood."

Zeke stared straight ahead. "My father was my blood, and he disowned me."

"Just think about what I'm saying?"

He sighed. "Anyway, that will give us three months to plan our getaway. I'll write to Josh this week."

Addy felt a pang. Suddenly, three months didn't seem like a long time before she must leave those she loved. In her mind, she wanted to curse every member of the Giovanni family. They were the ones responsible for ruining her life. *Oh, God, did you desert me, too?* Then she felt ashamed, for she still had Zeke and her family. And now Muriel, too.

The Ford pulled into the driveway; they were the first ones back from the courthouse. The boys and Maggie had been playing in the backyard, and now the boys ran around Zeke, while Addy picked up Maggie and gave her a kiss.

"What happened to our sister?" Casey asked.

"The judge dismissed her case," Addy answered.

"Does that mean she's coming home?" Maggie wanted to know.

Addy spun her around, and Maggie's brown curls bounced. "Yes, she's free to go."

"Hooray!" the boys shouted.

Grandma came out the back door. "I thought I heard someone out here. Did I hear you right, child? Muriel is free?"

Addy put Maggie down and embraced her grandmother. "Isn't that wonderful news? The others should be home soon. Can I help you in the kitchen?"

In mock horror, Grandma looked at her. "You know better than to work on your birthday. Now you and Mr. Shafer can either take some sun out here or wait in the parlor."

Addy glanced at Zeke. "We'll stay out here until the others come home."

Zeke and the boys played at marbles in the dirt, and Addy and Maggie played jacks on the back porch. A few minutes later, they heard the Packard drive up to the garage. The children darted over, and Zeke and Addy followed. The back door slammed as Grandma joined them.

Muriel looked very pale as she got out of the car, and Grandma embraced her. Uncle Henry came around the auto, looking like fury itself. "We were besieged by those reporters when we came out of the courthouse. I have never seen such a belligerent bunch of fools. It made me regret working for the *Times*."

Muriel turned to Uncle Henry. "Please, may I go up to my room and lie down?"

"But we have company."

Addy waved her hand. "We're not company. After what she's been through, let her go."

Addy wasn't allowed to help in the kitchen, so she and Zeke went into the parlor with Uncle Henry and Grandpa.

Almost immediately Zeke spoke up. "Mr. Carter, Addy and I have set a date to get married. We were wondering if we could have our wedding in the backyard here on May seventh." Addy was proud of him for his straightforward request, when she knew he could hardly keep from clenching his teeth at the idea.

Uncle Henry almost smiled. "I think that would be all right."

Grandpa got up from the chair and shook Zeke's hand. "I'm glad you decided to join the family, son."

Uncle Henry went to get Aunt Jen and Grandma, so they could hear the happy news. After many hugs and kisses, the women went back to the kitchen. Addy felt a sad pang, knowing this might be the last birthday she celebrated here. Her optimistic side added, *For a while.*

At dinner, Uncle Henry gave a toast. "Today, we celebrate our Muriel's freedom from the clutches of the Giovanni family. Also, we celebrate this very happy occasion of Adeline's twenty-first birthday and news of her wedding. We welcome Mr. Shafer into our family. May all three have long lives." Everyone cheered, but Addy noticed Zeke's smile was forced.

During the meal, Addy contemplated asking Muriel to be in the wedding. *Maybe I should ask Zeke first, but he has to realize that he's marrying my family, not just me. Muriel is the only one I could ask—she means so much to me. I can't hate her for a one-second misstep after fifteen years of love and companionship. He has to realize there is such a thing as forgiveness.*

When dinner was finished, Addy sought out Muriel. "Dear, would you be my matron of honor?"

Muriel almost dropped the dish she was carrying. "Me? I nearly killed your intended. I didn't think I would even be invited."

Addy took the dish and put it on the table. She held Muriel's hand. "You are my family, my blood. I think of you like a sister. The Giovannis might be a family, but they lie, cheat, steal and even murder to get what they want. You may have loved Tony, but he thought like they did. Instead of revenge for what you did, I'm offering forgiveness and love."

Tears streamed down Muriel's face and she embraced Addy. "I love you, Addy. Yes, I'll stand up with you."

Grandpa got out the gramophone and cranked it

up. It was a long time since they'd danced in the parlor. Strains of the old waltzes drifted in the air.

Addy and Zeke were dancing when she told him she had asked Muriel to be her matron of honor.

Zeke frowned and stopped dancing. "Couldn't you ask someone else?"

She led him into the hall before she replied, "She's as close as a sister to me. I told her I believe in love instead of revenge. She's not bad; she was just misled."

He sighed. "I wish I had your spirit of forgiveness. Damn it, Addy, she tried to kill me!"

"Don't you realize you're not just marrying me, but becoming a member of my family, as well? They disowned my mother when she married my father, and they never saw her again. They didn't have to take me into their home. I probably would have been brought up in an orphanage somewhere. But Uncle Henry and Grandpa found me, because I was part of the family and needed help. Grandpa said his biggest regret was never seeing his daughter alive again." Addy stamped her foot to emphasize the point.

Zeke looked exasperated. "Let me—"

Suddenly, there was a banging on the front door, and Uncle Henry came to open it.

Inspector Cannon stepped in quickly. "We've got to get Mrs. Giovanni, Mr. Shafer and Miss Garcia into hiding now!"

Uncle Henry was taken aback by this abruptly threatening announcement. "What's wrong?"

"Joseph Giovanni and a couple of his henchmen have escaped. It would be best if the three people they'll be after are each taken to a different place, undisclosed locations, because they are prime targets. Of course, a police detail will be left here to guard your house. I'll stay here until the teams call in."

Addy felt faint. Zeke held her elbow, but he had gone pale himself. Everyone was in the hall by now, and Muriel and Aunt Jen clung to each other, crying.

Addy's voice shook, and tears streamed down her cheeks. "What do you want us to do?" she ventured.

"I've sent for three police autos, and they will escort each of you away from the city to a separate hideout. There you will stay until he is caught. You'll be under guard."

Clara ran up the steps to the front door. "The patrol autos are here, Inspector." There was a policeman and a policewoman right behind her.

"Good. Go now! Don't stop for anything."

Addy and Zeke stared at each other awkwardly as they were hustled to the waiting autos. Addy squeezed Muriel's hand. Clara led Addy to the third auto. Clara slid into the front passenger side and Addy hopped in the back behind the driver. There was another uniformed man next to her, his hat pulled down low over his forehead.

When they were in, the driver set the auto in motion. Addy didn't breathe for the next few seconds. Clara turned to look at her.

"Addy, this is Patrolman Peterson..." She stopped for a moment as a horrified look crossed her face, and then Addy saw a slight movement of her hand reaching under her coat. Without a word, the driver fired his gun. Addy screamed as what was left of Clara's head slumped against the blood and brains splattered on the passenger window. The driver stopped the auto, got out, and went around to pull the lifeless body from the front seat and dump it at the side of the road.

As soon as she realized they were not moving, Addy grabbed the inside door handle, ready to make a run for it, but a large hand clamped on her arm. The man next to her said, "Going somewhere, Miss

Garcia?" and Addy stared into the coldly glittering eye of Joe Giovanni, looking all the more sinister with that eye patch on the other side of his face. All of her senses left her, like a rabbit mesmerized by a snake. He hit her hard with the back of his hand and she felt a trickle of blood on her chin.

The driver got back into the auto. "Here's the rope, Mr. Giovanni." He flipped it over the seat. "Do you want me to help you tie her up?"

I know that voice. "Tex?"

Joe grabbed Addy's arms. "No, just drive. I can take care of this."

The driver turned around and grinned. "At your service, Miss Rose." He started the engine and took off down the street.

Joe struggled with Addy and got her hands and feet tied. He took out his handkerchief and gagged her. And to think she had actually liked Tex—a cold-blooded killer! She started shaking uncontrollably. *I'm dead. Oh, God, help me!*

Addy felt like a sack of meal, trussed up, leaning against the door. Joe pushed her down so she wouldn't be visible to passing traffic, and she stayed like that for what seemed like hours, hardly able to breathe. She wondered if all the police in the autos were part of the plan. *Oh, no! That means Zeke and Muriel will be going through this, as well.* Finally, she heard what sounded like gravel under the tires, and they came to a stop.

"Okay, Chester, leave the headlights on so we can get to the cabin." Joe got out of the auto and dragged Addy out, then heaved her over his shoulder and carried her.

Chester? Oh, yes, that's Tex's real name. Addy smelled clean, crisp, pine-scented air. *We must be up in the mountains. I don't know if anyone will think to look for me here.* She started to shake again, but this time not just from fright, but because it was cold;

there was snow on the ground.

Joe went up a few wooden steps and into what looked like a hunting cabin, from what she could see in her upside-down position. It was lit by kerosene lamps, and there was a wood fire going in the large stone fireplace. The man she saw in the shadows she remembered as Tex's partner the night her room had been ransacked, when they were looking for the safety deposit key. Joe called out to him, "Frank, bring that chair over here by the fire."

Frank took one of the plain wooden chairs at the table and set it by the fireplace, where Joe dumped Addy onto it. She almost fell over.

"Would you like something to eat, boss?" Frank asked.

"Yeah, let's have a bite, it's almost midnight." The three men sat around the table and ate silently, except for a few small comments, while Addy tried to think of how she could get out of this perilous situation.

She tried moving her hands and feet around, to see if the rope could be loosened, but Joe was apparently an expert at this. Could she roll off the chair and somehow make it to the door? But where would she go? Screaming was out of the question— they were probably miles from anyone else. Could she fight them? Three of them and one of her. She didn't think she would get very far.

Addy closed her eyes. It was almost like being in a motion picture. The damsel is in danger from three thugs who want to kill her. Suddenly, the handsome hero comes riding up on a pure white stallion and rescues her from the dastardly trio. The hero is Zeke, and he cuts her bonds, pulling her up in a passionate kiss. Fade out. Mr. Hanson yells, "Cut!"

She opened her eyes again, hoping the whole thing was just a horrible dream. No, she seemed to be trapped in this nightmare.

****

Zeke was hustled into the small hotel room by two of the policemen while the third stood on guard downstairs. The one named Darby went out into the hall to call the inspector at the Carters'.

He came back in and said to Patrolman Jenkins, "We were the second ones to call in. He's still waiting for the third call."

Zeke addressed them both. "Where did they take Addy and Muriel?"

Jenkins turned to him. "For security reasons, we weren't told where the others went."

Zeke nodded and sat down on the old couch on the far side of the room, staring out the window into the night sky. *I wish I hadn't been forced to leave Addy in the middle of an argument. Now I'm hoping I'll see her alive again.* He brooded while the patrolmen paced the room.

A half hour later, they heard a pounding on the door. Darby went over with his gun drawn. "Who is it?"

"It's Mason. We have to go back to the Carters'. Something's happened."

Darby threw open the door. "What's going on?" He closed it quickly as Mason came in.

"Peterson's team never called in, and the caretaker of the garage found Peterson's and Jones' bodies behind the building. The inspector wants us all back, in case the destinations were leaked out."

Jenkins slapped his forehead. "Oh, God, no."

Zeke jumped off the couch. "What does that mean?"

Jenkins started, "I don't want to alarm you—"

Zeke grabbed Jenkins' coat. "I'm already alarmed. What?"

Jenkins took a deep breath. "It looks like the Giovannis took one of the women."

"Who?"

"We'll find out when we get back there."

Zeke grabbed his hat and coat and the four of them flew down the stairs to the patrol auto parked on the street. His thoughts were dark as he climbed into the back seat. *Somehow, I know Addy's in danger. Hang on, sweetheart, until I can find you.* Tears spilled onto his cheeks.

****

Joe Giovanni brought his chair over and sat in front of Addy. "Chester, take the gag off her. There's no one around who can hear her anyway."

The handkerchief was removed. Her jaw hurt from being tied back like that.

Joe stared at her, looking like the devil himself. "Well, Miss Garcia, I have to congratulate you on the damage you've done to our business. Nobody has ever come that close to ruining the Giovannis before. You were one of the people who took Mr. Rudd out. I regretted that, because he was one of our most loyal operators. Not many can run a successful speakeasy and cat house. Too bad you're not on our side. I could've used a conniver like you." He ran his fingers down her cheek. "But now, you have to die."

Addy trembled, but she refused to cry in front of this monster.

Joe walked over to the fireplace and picked up one of the logs stacked on one side. He came back over to her. "Since you're a motion picture actress, if it had been a small infraction, I would've just ruined your face—like this." He swung the log and hit her squarely across the face.

Addy screamed as she felt the cartilage of her nose collapse, followed by a river of blood rushing down onto her clothes. Blood and mucus gathered in her throat and she had trouble breathing.

"But since you are going to die in an accident off a cliff, I don't have to do that." He turned to the two men. "Take her away!" He put his face close to hers.

"Goodbye, Miss Garcia."

Addy gathered up as much saliva, blood and mucus as she could and spat it into his face.

Joe backhanded her again. "Take this bitch out of here!"

Chester lifted her up and slung her over his shoulder. "Frank, you take the other auto, and I'll take the patrol with Miss Garcia."

He piled her into the back seat and started out. She saw the reflection of lights from the other auto behind them. They went through the dark mountain forest for a while, until they came to a lookout point with a parking area off the road. Chester stopped the auto.

Frank left the headlights on behind them and he came walking up to the patrol. "Hey, Chester, why don't we use her first, before we kill her? It seems a waste of good pussy."

Addy recoiled in horror as he opened the back door and undid his trousers. "No, please!" She started to cry.

Chester grabbed Frank and pushed him back. "No! She has to die, but let her die with some dignity."

Would Tex save me? Maybe he'll let me go. She started to tremble again.

Frank swung at him angrily. "You son of a bitch! You're getting soft."

Chester drew his gun and pointed it at Frank's head. "I can as easily kill you, too. Now, go back and wait in the auto, but give me the keys first." He cocked the hammer on the gun with an audible click. "Now, Frank."

Frank threw the keys on the ground next to Chester's feet and stalked back to the other auto.

Chester pocketed them, then pulled Addy out of the back and put her in the driver's seat of the patrol auto. Making sure Addy's arms were securely tied behind her, he tied her feet to the gas pedal. The auto was on an incline, facing down toward the outer edge of the mountain lookout, only a few hundred feet away. "This slope ought to give you enough speed to go over the edge. You'll die fast, but we'll be gone before then. Goodbye, Miss Rose." Chester released the brake and gave the patrol a shove from the back. Then he ran to the other auto.

Addy watched as the other car's headlights faded into the forest and she rolled toward the lookout. She struggled to get free of her bonds so she could reach the brake, but they were too tight. The auto was picking up speed, and she squeezed out a prayer for a miracle as her life flashed before her. She thought of Zeke and started to cry. *Oh, why did we have to have an argument tonight? That will be his last memory of me. Zeke, I love you so much. Please remember me with love. How ironic to be spared in the earthquake, only to die this horrible way. God, this must be part of a plan I don't understand.*

The patrol auto bounced over the edge of the lookout and down the mountainside. Addy was jostled as it went over rocks and plants. A tree branch hit the passenger side and the windshield shattered. Shards of glass pierced her skin like Lilliputian swords. Then there was a violent jolt and Addy's head hit the steering wheel. Darkness washed over her.

Chapter 10

When they arrived at the Carters' house and Zeke saw Muriel on the porch, he gave a great cry of anguish and practically flew out of the back seat. He rushed past her and found Inspector Cannon in the hallway, where he grabbed the man's lapels and jammed the large man against the wall. "Where is Addy? What have you done?"

Addy's Uncle Henry and Grandpa Applegate gently removed Zeke from the inspector, and Mr. Applegate put his arm around Zeke. "Calm down, son. Give the inspector a chance to talk."

Cannon adjusted his suit. "I could have you arrested for that, but under the circumstances, I'll give you a warning. Seems like the Giovannis commandeered one of the patrol autos after they took out the men I assigned to that vehicle. I don't think they knew which one of the three of you they'd get, but that's enough to start their revenge. We've asked Mrs. Giovanni to think of a secluded place they could have taken Miss Garcia."

Zeke was shaking, and Mr. Applegate helped him to a chair, while Aunt Jen brought him a glass of water. "Do you know what direction they took?" Zeke asked.

"From here, they went north."

The gray of dawn was sending streaks into the sky as Muriel tiptoed in to stand by her mother. The phone rang and Mr. Carter answered. "Inspector, it's for you."

Cannon talked for a few minutes, then hung up. "The body of Detective Stevens was found near

Vermont Avenue. Mrs. Giovanni, can you think of a place they could be going from that direction?"

Muriel had tears on her face as she nodded at the inspector. "The Giovannis have a cabin in the mountains. It's where Tony and I spent our honeymoon. I can show you how to get there."

Cannon sprang into action. "Since it's getting light, Mrs. Giovanni, you come with us and show the way. Jenkins, you drive the lead car with me and Mrs. Giovanni. The rest of the officers will follow us."

Zeke jumped from his chair. "I'm coming, too."

"No, Mr. Shafer, that wouldn't be wise."

Zeke stood blocking the inspector's way. "I insist. You owe me that. If I can't ride with you, I'll follow in my auto. Whichever, I'm going."

Cannon hesitated, then he clapped Zeke's shoulder. "All right, but you'll ride with me. Let's go!"

They stopped by the station to pick up one of the paddy wagons that could serve as an ambulance, if needed, and then the four vehicles raced toward the mountains.

Muriel sat in the front of the first auto, driven by Jenkins, and guided them through the twists and turns of the mountain dirt roads. In between giving directions, she glanced back sadly at Zeke where he sat next to the inspector in the back seat.

Zeke watched the forest awaking to a new morning. The sunlight streamed through the trees in shafts of light. It would have been beautiful, if he weren't so sick at heart. Deep down, he felt Addy was still alive, but he wondered if it was just hope run amok. He squeezed off a prayer to God—something he hadn't done since he left Indiana.

Finally Muriel showed them the drive to the cabin, and the inspector had the vehicles pull to the side of the road.

"I want both of you to stay here, in the auto." Cannon waved to Jenkins. "Guard these two while we go in."

Jenkins stood by the driver's door. "Yes, sir."

Zeke fought the impulse to follow the inspector. It was so hard to wait, not knowing what was going on. He glanced at Muriel, and she was rocking back and forth in her seat, her hands covering her face. Something in him wanted to comfort her, and he lightly put his hand on her shoulder.

Muriel looked at him and sobbed. "I want her to be alive. This is all my fault. I take responsibility for all that's happened to both of you."

Zeke had no response to that. He still was unable to forgive her, but the fact was, she was doing all she could to find Addy. That was something.

****

Addy felt puffs of light air around her. It went up her nostrils, cool and moist. She had a sensation of floating on that breeze, and she could feel her hair moving slowly with it. Her eyes opened and she found her head was against the steering wheel. She thought at first something must be wrong with her eyes, but then she realized there was a thick gray mist surrounding the auto. The dark shadows she could see out the driver's side window must be trees and rocks, she decided. She raised her head and was surprised to feel no pain. The top of the auto had been bent back and that odd mist made swirls above her.

Addy looked to her right and gasped in surprise. Where the windshield was broken away, a man sat on the hood with his feet dangling over the dashboard. And a woman with a child in her lap was in the passenger seat. She recognized these people! "Am I dead, Papa?"

He smiled at her. "No, my dear little Rosa, but

we're here to support you until you're rescued." Tomas Garcia was as handsome as she remembered, and his dark wavy hair and black eyes were so much like her own. With her woman's eyes, she could see why her mother had defied her family to marry him.

"Didn't I go off the mountainside?"

"The rear axle was snagged by a tree root sticking out of the ground."

Her mother looked a lot like Aunt Jen. "We are watching out for you as best we can. We can't prevent bad things, but I want you to know we're there with you through your trials." She put her hand lightly on Addy's arm. Her silky brown hair was done up in a bun high on her head, with wisps moving in the mist.

Little Joey looked just as he had before the earthquake, except he was quieter. He grinned. "We help Sissie."

Addy glanced back at her father. "How will they ever find me? Even if I am alive now, I may not be, in a day or so."

"There are ways of giving hints to the right people. The police and Zeke are looking for you right now. Muriel helped them find the mountain cabin."

"How do you know about Zeke?"

"Like I said, we have been with you, supporting you. And I do approve of the boy. He loves you very much. If I were still alive, I would have given my blessing to you both."

Addy felt ashamed. "Even though I did sin with him. I must be weak—I just couldn't help myself."

Her mother patted her shoulder. "Love is a complicated thing. We all are weak sometimes. Will it help to tell you that you were born five months after Tomas and I married? That's part of the reason both of our families were so angry with us."

How much am I injured? Will I become a burden for the man I love? Or maybe he won't want a cripple for a wife, and he'll leave me. Would it be better for everyone if I died? Addy contemplated this for a few moments, then looked at her father. "I want to stay with you. Just let me die."

Her father shook his head. "You have so much more to do. You represent us. You're the only one left of our family, and I know you care about family very much. We're proud of our brave girl."

Addy was getting tired, and she put her head back down on the steering wheel. Her father's voice came through to her. "We have a message for Henry. Tell him Hubert is safe and happy."

"Yes, Papa," she murmured and fell down into the hole of unconsciousness again.

****

Cannon and the other policemen came back to the autos some time later. As the others searched the drive, the inspector leaned into the open window of the patrol.

"The cabin is deserted. I won't tell you what we found there, but it isn't pretty. The patrol autos have special tires with thicker treads, and we found their tracks on the drive. I have a hunch if we follow those tracks, we'll find Miss Garcia."

One of the men came running up. "Sir, we found which way the autos went."

Cannon stood up. "Good. Tell everyone to follow slowly and study every inch of land along the way for *anything.*"

"Yes, sir." He ran back to the others, and the caravan was formed.

To Zeke, it seemed as though they were crawling at a snail's pace, but he realized if they missed the smallest clue, they might not find her. About a half-hour from the cabin, at that slow pace, Zeke spotted a lookout ahead, on one of the turns of the dirt road. When he noticed one of the barrier boards on the edge was broken, he pointed it out to Cannon.

The inspector turned to Jenkins. "Stop here!"

Jenkins pulled to the side of the road and the rest of the vehicles followed suit.

Zeke was out of the back seat before Cannon could stop him. As he ran to the broken board, he saw tire tracks leading right up to it.

Cannon ran up behind him. "Get back to the auto. We'll check this out."

Zeke set his jaw. "You don't understand. If Addy's down there, I have to be there when you find her."

Cannon studied his face briefly. "All right, but stay behind us."

One of the policemen tied a long rope to one of the trees by the road. The slope going down was steep but manageable. Cannon and two of his men inched along the rope through the torn brush, with Zeke behind them.

Cannon shouted up the line. "I see the patrol auto!"

The vehicle's back wheels were raised and Zeke could see the axle caught on a large tree root. Just a few feet away was a cliff, and beyond it a deep ravine. He trembled as the four of them made their way slowly down to the auto. When he saw a form slumped over the steering wheel—in the dress Addy had been wearing—he let out a cry.

Cannon called up the line, "We found her. Send down the stretcher from the wagon."

Zeke hurried ahead to the auto and opened the door.

"Don't move her yet," the inspector cautioned. "Wait for the board."

Zeke felt his tears start when he looked at her face. It was a bloody, bruised pulp. He touched her arm, and she moved slightly. "She's still alive," his voice rasped.

Cannon cut away at the ties holding her to the

auto, while two of the men from the wagon worked down the rope with the stretcher. Carefully, Cannon and Zeke eased Addy out of the auto and placed her between the three straps and buckles of the stretcher, and Cannon tightened them over her chest, hips and feet.

The two men from the wagon brought down two ropes, secured from the road, with hooks on the end of them. These they hooked onto the stretcher end, so it could be hauled up while the men on the other side guided it.

Muriel stood by the road as the rescue party made it to the top. After one look at Addy, she vomited into the bushes and then, still leaning against a tree, burst into tears. Zeke put his arm around her.

"She's still alive. You may very well have saved her life. Thank you." He gave her his handkerchief and gently walked her back to the patrol auto. He turned to the inspector. "I want to ride to the hospital with Addy."

Cannon nodded and ordered the men to let him into the back of the wagon. Addy lay on the shelf along one side of the rear cabin of the paddy wagon. Zeke sat on the bench on the other side and gently took her hand for the long ride back.

****

Somewhere, far away, Addy heard voices shouting at one another. Were they at a distance or was she? There were disjointed things she heard and felt. Sounds of loose rocks making clacking noises. Being touched by many hands. Then a feeling of being strapped to something and moving roughly somewhere. All the while hearing the talk around her, yet not recognizing any words.

At times, she drifted into nothingness where dreams didn't even find her. Her body didn't respond to any commands: *eyes open!* and there was only darkness; *mouth speak!* and it was frozen shut; *body move!* and from the top of her head to the tips of her toes there was a crushing weight on her.

She was on a soft cloud surrounded by many different voices, and she felt warm pressure on her hands. It seemed that love and strength were traveling up her arm and into her very soul from that warm pressure. She was sad when it went away.

She saw a gray light and decided she must follow it, even though she was so far down and the light was so small. Her mind struggled up the rocky sides of her psyche but hesitated when the thin ribbon of pain hit her. It felt so much better in the nothingness, she reasoned. You have to live, you have so much to do, her brain insisted. She moved into the shell and started slowly to stretch her hands. Her body groaned and her eyes fluttered open. The light was blinding.

A voice called out, "She's coming to! Get the doctor!"

Her face was enveloped in bandages and the smell of tape and gauze entered her senses. It was hard to breathe. A firm grip came onto her hand and a handsome face came into focus. It had tears on its cheeks. *That's silly—men don't cry,* she thought.

An older man's face came into view. "Miss Garcia, can you hear me?"

Oh, yes, that sounds like my name. She didn't move for a few moments, trying to remember how to talk. She was aware of the air on her vocal cords and activated her jaw. Her "Yes," sounded like a whoosh of air, but seemed to be understood.

"Tell me, Miss Garcia, do you know who he is?"

The handsome face came back into view, and she felt the warm glow riding through her veins to her brain. *I know him.* "Zeke?"

The doctor nodded. "Good, good. There doesn't

seem to be any amnesia."

She was very tired after traveling so far. Her body went back to sleep. It had been such an ordeal. She opened her eyes again and felt rested. Sighing, she looked around the room. It must be a hospital room, with a table by the bed. The window on one wall let in shafts of sunlight through blinds. On a chair next to the bed, a young man was reading.

"Zeke? Where am I?"

He bolted up. "Addy, you're awake! Oh, my dear love, you're in the Hollywood Hospital. You've been here five days. Inspector Cannon put you up in one of the private rooms, and I'm sleeping in an empty one next door, so he could guard us. I've been sitting with you during the day."

"You've been with me all this time?"

"He arranged it with the hospital. They have two guards outside the door. I refused to go anywhere else." He took her hand and kissed it. Then he went to the door. "Tell the doctor she's awake again." He walked back. "One of the guards will get him."

"How on earth did they find me? I thought no one would think of looking in the mountains."

"You can thank Muriel for that. She had a hunch they would take you to that mountain cabin of theirs." He went on to tell her of the search.

Addy suddenly asked, "Was the rear axle caught on a tree root?"

Zeke stared at her, astonished. "How did you know?"

She shook her head and winced at the pain it caused. "A strange dream. I'll tell you later." Just then the doctor came in.

"Miss Garcia, I see you've come out of the coma well. I'm Dr. Richards. Let's see how you're doing." He motioned to a young nurse who came in with him, carrying a tray. "Mr. Shafer, could you wait in the hall?"

Zeke gave Addy's hand a kiss and left the room.

The nurse took Addy's blood pressure and temperature while the doctor wrote on the chart at the foot of her bed.

"Now, my dear, let's see how you're healing." He took scissors off the tray and started cutting the gauze bandages off her face. "Your nose was broken, so we set it, with a support. You sustained a concussion where your forehead hit the steering wheel, and there were shards of glass all over your face. Luckily, none of them pierced your eyes." He gently worked the bandages off with the hydrogen peroxide. "Healing nicely. It's a good thing you were out for a while; it gave your body a chance to repair itself. Your nose is going to take about three weeks, so we'll leave that bandaged."

The air hitting her face caused a little stinging, but it wasn't bad. *How terrible do I look?* She couldn't bring herself to look in a mirror yet.

He pulled the sheet and blanket down. "You have some bruised ribs, so we have them taped. There are various cuts and bruises on the rest of your body." He checked everywhere and replaced the bedclothes. "I believe you'll be ready to go home in a couple of days. Are you hungry, dear?"

The minute he mentioned that, her stomach growled. "Starving."

"Nurse, bring in some food for her." The doctor finished up and called Zeke back in.

Zeke brought in some company. Aunt Jen rushed to the bed and took both of Addy's hands in her own, while Muriel came in behind her, and Uncle Henry and Grandpa stood at the foot of the bed with Zeke.

"Oh, sweetheart, it's good to see you awake. Your poor face! Does it hurt much?" Aunt Jen squeezed Addy's hands with concern.

"It hurts, but I can bear it. At least, I'm alive." Addy actually felt glad of that. "What happened after I was captured? I thought the Inspector was going to send Muriel and Zeke away."

Uncle Henry took the chair by the bed and gravely told her what had happened at the house that night.

Addy looked at Muriel. "How did you figure out they took me to the mountain cabin?"

She sighed. "It's so secluded, I knew no one would think to look there. I remembered the road to take to the mountains, and I knew for sure when they found poor Detective Stevens' body in a ditch on the way."

Addy was sad, thinking of Clara's death. She'd died in the line of duty, but that didn't excuse it. The hate Addy felt for the Giovannis kept growing. Just then, the nurse brought in a food tray for her. "I feel funny, eating in front of everyone."

Aunt Jen squeezed her hand. "You need to eat, darling."

Addy ate ravenously of the vegetable soup, rolls and a plate of cherry gelatin, although she did as little chewing as possible; it was somewhat painful.

Inspector Cannon came in as she was finishing. Giving him a glaring look, Zeke went to stand by the window with his arms folded across his chest. Addy wondered what was wrong.

The inspector tipped his hat. "It's good to see you alive, Miss Garcia. What did the doctor have to say about when you could leave?"

"He said I could leave in a couple of days."

"No thanks to you, Inspector," Zeke added angrily.

"Mr. Shafer, sometimes things happen that make plans go wrong. I hope I can have your cooperation to try to keep all of you safe."

"You just about got Addy killed!" He hit his

hand on the wall.

Grandpa went over and put his arm around Zeke's shoulders. "Now, boy, why don't we give the inspector another chance?"

Zeke quieted down, but he remained like a thundercloud.

"All right. Splitting the three of you up didn't work, so may I impose on your hospitality, Mr. and Mrs. Carter? I would like to use your house as a lure for the gangsters. We'll use some of our policemen to give the impression that all of you are home, with the use of mannequins and the men walking around the downstairs area."

Uncle Henry frowned. "Where would we stay?"

"The city can put all of you up in a hotel until we capture them."

Uncle Henry nodded. "Yes, that sounds acceptable. What did you have in mind?"

"An ambush. With all of you seemingly in one place, that will bring the Giovannis out, for sure. We won't have visible guards. We can post them in unmarked autos on the street away from the house, in the garage to watch the back yard, and in the house. The ones inside can call the station when there's a strike, and I don't think it will be long."

Uncle Henry rubbed his chin. "I don't think we can rest easy as long as the Giovannis are still on the loose. I guess this would be the best way."

"Fine. I'll start on the plan. Good day to you all." He tipped his hat again and left.

Aunt Jen looked at Addy. "Do you remember anything after the auto took you down the mountain?"

"Only impressions, like a dream. It's starting to fade in my mind now, but I did have a vivid dream that my parents and Joey were there with me." Addy shuddered. "But from what Zeke told me, the dream had truth in it. Papa told me the rear axle caught on a tree root."

Aunt Jen glanced at Zeke and he shrugged. "I didn't tell her that; she asked me if it was."

"Did they say why they were there?"

Addy felt a warm glow as she remembered it. "They said they were there to support me and that they always watch over me."

Aunt Jen had tears in her eyes. "I wish we'd gotten to know Tomas. I fear we judged him too harshly. Abigail loved him with all her heart. Well, it was a good dream, anyway."

Addy heard a reminding voice in her head. "I don't know if it means anything, but Papa gave me a message for you, Uncle." It seemed to be burned into her brain. "I'm to tell you that Hubert is safe and happy. Does that mean anything?"

Uncle Henry rose abruptly and left the room.

She looked at her aunt. "Have I said something wrong?"

Her aunt was gazing at her in amazement. "How do you know about Hubert?"

"I don't. Who is he?"

"Hubert was your Uncle Henry's twin brother. He was stillborn. The family contended that because he wasn't baptized, he was a lost soul, and they never spoke of him. Henry found out about it by accident when he was sixteen, and he told me, but no one else knows."

Grandpa spoke up. "Perchance, that wasn't a dream you had, child. Blessed be."

Addy felt love all around her. Maybe they were watching over her, after all.

Later, after her family had gone, she looked at Zeke. "I don't think you should get angry with the inspector. He's just trying to help us. He didn't know that Joe and his men would take the policemen's places."

"Addy, he miscalculated that Muriel would try

to shoot us, and now this. We both have been hurt because we alerted them about the activities at the studio. I only hope the Giovannis don't find out where we really are and kill us there." He sat on the bed and took her hand.

She looked at him steadily. "I don't think we have a whole lot of choices." They sat holding hands as the waning sunlight filtered through the blinds.

****

As Addy continued improving, the doctor was ready to release her on the promised day. Uncle Henry and Aunt Jen stopped at Addy's house to pick up some clothes for her, since she would be staying with them at the hotel, and after leaving those with Addy they let the inspector, who had dropped in on her, know they had found footprints around the house and unknown tire tracks on the drive. Someone had been looking for Addy.

After the midday meal on the day she was released from the hospital, Addy took her first look in the mirror, where a strange being gazed back. Her nose was still bandaged, with the gauze spread into a triangle in the middle of her face. Black-and-blue bruises were around her eyes and forehead. Yellow patches were starting to appear where the lesser of the bruises were already healing. There were tiny cuts all over her face and neck. *Well, there goes my career. No one will want to film a face like this. And what does my nose look like?* She felt a touch of vanity, and a tear soaked into the bandage.

Zeke came up behind her and put his hands on her shoulders. "You're still my Addy, and I love you dearly. The cuts and bruises will heal in time."

She turned, putting her arms around him, and he held her gently, because of her bruised ribs. Addy sighed. "If we're going to work in a theater, grease paint will cover the scars. I'll be all right. After all, I could be dead, although we're not out of the woods yet. I sincerely hope the inspector's plan works."

Zeke drove with Addy to her uncle's house and parked the auto next to the garage, just in case the house was being observed from the street. Together they crossed through the neighbor's backyard and were picked up by an unmarked police auto on the next street over. Zeke held her hand as they were ferried to the hotel only a couple of blocks away from the house.

The city had reserved four rooms for them under assumed names. Uncle Henry and Aunt Jen were in the first one on the second floor; next to them was where Grandma would be with Grandpa. Directly across, James and Zeke would stay with the boys, and Addy and Muriel would look after Maggie in the fourth room. The inspector would come for them after the ambush.

Zeke and Addy were shown to their rooms and Muriel embraced Addy as she went inside. "It's so good to see you up and around again. Look, we can see the house from here."

Maggie went next door and brought Aunt Jen, Grandma and the boys over. The women each gently hugged Addy, and the boys danced around the group.

Grandma turned to the children. "Why don't you boys take Maggie next door and play some Picture Lotto with her?"

Once the brood was out of the room, Aunt Jen asked Addy, "Is everything quiet at the house?"

Addy nodded. "So far. Did you all come here the way we did?"

"Yes, one or two at a time, so things wouldn't look suspicious. I moved all the valuable things out of the parlor and dining room. I hope they don't tear up the house too badly."

Grandma looked at Addy. "You still look rather pale, child. Perhaps you should lie down on the bed."

She was feeling tired, so she slipped out of her shoes and put her feet up. Grandma went to check on the children and brought back her crocheting and Aunt Jen's sewing. Muriel was knitting some baby clothes.

The afternoon passed slowly, and they truly tried to keep some normalcy in their conversations with each other, but tension crackled in the air. Addy went through a dozen what ifs and knew she never wanted to be face to face with Joe Giovanni ever again.

They had left their door open to the hall, but Uncle Henry rapped on the door jamb before he came in. "It's five-thirty, and I've ordered room service for all of us. It should be up here in a few minutes. It will all be on...trays," he said distastefully.

"Henry?" Grandpa came up behind him. "Since the girls have the best view of the house from their window, I suggest we bring chairs in here and eat as a family should."

Uncle Henry looked at Aunt Jen. "Is that satisfactory?"

"By all means," she replied, glancing up from her sewing.

Uncle Henry left word with the hotel staff where they would take dinner. Addy stayed on the bed and Zeke brought a chair in to sit beside her. He'd been with the men, she knew, but she felt so much better with him beside her. She sighed. They reached out their hands to each other, and she felt his strength flow into her.

The dark settled in on the street and the lights along the sidewalks winked on with a soft creamy glow. Before long, the room service staff brought the free-standing trays and set them up all together in one room, as requested. Addy looked at the meatloaf, the mashed potatoes with gravy, and the buttered peas on her plate and knew this was probably better than the hospital fare she had been eating, but she hardly felt hungry for it, with the anxiety of what would happen at the house soon.

When all were served, Uncle Henry offered grace. "We are grateful, Lord, for this food, and we ask that we may be home soon, by Your power. Protect the policemen who guard our house this night. Amen."

They all answered with an "Amen," even Zeke.

Toward the end of the meal, they heard what sounded like firecrackers and small explosions. The family quickly turned off lamps, in order to see outside better, and crowded around the window to watch the police lights and hear the sirens down the street. Grandma and Aunt Jen started to cry, while everyone else looked on in horrified fascination. Maggie and the two younger boys looked confused and scared, unsure just what was going on, but unsettled by the tears and anxiety of their elders.

Uncle Henry looked at his watch. "It's six-fifteen. We would have all been eating supper in the dining room," he said quietly.

Grandpa nodded. "He wanted to make sure he got all of us."

Addy picked up Maggie, and the child buried her face on Addy's neck. "There, there, now. We're safe, honey," she soothed the little girl with reassurances that she herself didn't feel.

Aunt Jen and Grandma did their best to distract the boys, but Addy could tell by their faces that the children knew something important was going on. Finally, the noise died down. People were gathering outside their homes to see what had happened. Addy gave Maggie to James and leaned against the wall next to the window, thinking.

Zeke stood next to Addy with his arm around her, and she looked up at him. "I have to go down there."

He gave her a concerned glance. "We shouldn't get in the middle of that."

She swallowed. "I have to make sure he's dead, myself. Otherwise, I'll be looking over my shoulder for the rest of my life."

He hesitated, then squeezed her, carefully. "I'll go with you."

The family protested, but Addy was determined. With Zeke's strong arm around her, they walked the three blocks together. Addy shook inside as they neared the scene. They spotted Inspector Cannon directing the chaos a couple of doors down from the house. He stood blocking their path. "You can't go down there."

Addy looked at him. "Please, sir, I have to know that they're dead and they won't come for me anymore."

He stared at her for a moment. Then he motioned to a policeman. "Lamont, take Miss Garcia and Mr. Shafer to the scene."

"But, sir..."

"They have clearance." He turned to Addy and Zeke. "Just don't touch anything."

They both nodded.

The section of street was blocked off at either end. As they neared her uncle's house, she could see what looked like a pile of junk metal in the middle of the road. Her shoes were already crunching on broken glass and metal parts. Zeke held her firmly, his arm around her, and the policeman on her other side held her elbow. They stopped walking when they were twenty feet away. With one glance at the house, Addy gave a violent shudder. The plate glass window to the dining room was blown away and the siding underneath it looked like it was blown to bits, riddled by bullets.

"That's how they hit, sweetheart," Zeke said.

"They fire a shot about mid-room, and then when everyone drops to the floor, they open up low. We all would have been dead in there, or at least badly wounded."

Firemen finished spraying water on the smoking remains of a vehicle in the street, and the police searched the wreck with flashlights. Addy turned to Officer Lamont. "What happened?"

"I was in the auto parked across the street. The guards inside had just put the mannequins in the dining room when this auto turned onto the street. It slowed down in front of the house, and one of these thugs fired a shotgun into the dining room window. Then another hit along the floor line with a machine gun. By that time, we'd blocked their path. They tried to turn the car around, but the guards from the garage and the house came out with machine guns and blew the engine and tires. The Giovanni gang jumped out of the auto with their guns, but we got them." There was almost no emotion on his face except resignation at the horror of what he'd had to do. For a young man, he looked very old at that moment. "Can you identify the bodies?"

Addy nodded. "I'm sure I can."

He took out his flashlight and they moved toward three shapeless forms under a tarp on the side of the road. The coroner's truck had just pulled up. Officer Lamont waved his flashlight at the coroner as he got out of the truck. "We have someone who can identify the bodies," he called out.

The coroner came over to the trio. "I'm Dr. Simonson. Which one of you knows who they are?"

Addy stepped forward, swaying a little, and Zeke held her. "I'm Miss Garcia, and I'm sure I know."

He nodded. "Ah, yes, the one who was taken last week. Bring her over here."

She clung to Zeke as the coroner removed the

tarp from the first body. She looked at the bullet-riddled body and ghastly gray face in the light. Addy felt almost sad. "That's Chester Marcelli." He may have been a cold-blooded killer, but she'd almost thought he cared for her.

They moved to the next body. "That's Frank. I'm sorry I don't know his last name. He was never called anything else in my presence."

With the last one, Addy started to tremble violently, and Zeke held her tighter. She was looking at the devil's face that had haunted her for so long. "Joe. That's Joe Giovanni." In an insane moment, she expected him to rise up and reach for her, taking her to the bowels of hell with him, but he lay there with his horrible eye clouded over. He could never hurt them again.

The coroner said quietly, "Thank you, Miss Garcia."

Addy felt weak and tired. She stumbled several times as the officer and Zeke guided her back to the roadblock, where Inspector Cannon held out his hand to her. "We appreciate all you did, Miss Garcia. All your bills will be handled by the city. That includes the damage to your uncle's house."

Addy nodded as she took his hand.

He turned to Zeke. "As will yours. We need more people like you to bring down these gangsters. I hope we can part on friendly terms."

Zeke held out his hand. "I'm glad it's over."

"Miss Garcia looks tired. You can ride with me to the hotel and I'll explain what happens next for all of you." Officer Lamont brought a patrol auto around, and Addy and Zeke climbed into the back, with the Inspector in the front passenger seat. Addy was trembling again. It was too soon after that horrible night to sit in a police auto, but she rested in Zeke's comforting arms.

The boys and Maggie were tucked in bed, so all

the adults met with Inspector Cannon in Uncle Henry's room. "Well," the inspector said, clearing his throat, "it looks like there won't be so many trials after all. The only one you might get a summons for is Mr. Abrams' trial, and that is in April. We won't have the guards posted at your house any longer, but we will keep an eye on it."

Uncle Henry knit his brows together. "Why? Do you think there are more out there?"

"You never know, with the syndicate. This may have affected workings all the way back east, but the chances are good that they already have a new distillery in place. This is too good a market for illegal hooch to let it go."

The room was silent. *There's no end to this,* Addy thought, and she could see by the concerned faces that the others must be thinking the same thing.

The inspector got up to leave. "I think you're safe for the time being. I want to thank you all for your cooperation. The city should have your home ready to move back into in a couple of days. Until then, we'll pay for your hotel stay."

Uncle Henry rose, also, and held out his hand. "Thank you for all the protection. I'm glad you were able to get Joe Giovanni." They shook hands, and the inspector left.

Everyone said their goodnights and Zeke told James he wanted to talk to Addy for a bit, but then he would be in. *What did he want,* Addy wondered. As Muriel headed to the bath at one end of the hall, Zeke led Addy to the other end, where he opened the window leading to the fire escape, and they climbed out and sat on the sill watching the lights of the city.

He took her hand. "Addy, I think we should leave soon. I don't know if we'll still be alive by May, the way things are going."

"We could have a civil ceremony. I'm sorry, but I

237

couldn't elope and exclude my family. After all they've been through with this, I can't just shut them out."

He put his arm around her. "Why don't we think about it? We don't have to make a decision yet."

"Yes, but you heard the inspector, we may have to testify in April."

They heard Muriel scream, "Watch out!"

Addy and Zeke jumped off the sill onto the iron grid of the fire escape, turning as they did so to see a young dark-haired woman coming at them with a knife.

Zeke was on his way back through the window to fend her off when Addy saw the woman turn to look at Muriel, who was close behind her.

Muriel grabbed the woman's hand and twisted it, but the woman shifted the knife to her other hand, slicing Muriel's forearm. By now, Zeke was behind the woman and grabbed both of her arms, holding them back, and Addy ran for the hall telephone.

The ruckus brought the other adults into the hall. Grandma ran back into her room and brought out a towel to put pressure on Muriel's wound, while Zeke managed to shake the knife loose from the woman's grip, and Uncle Henry scooped it up.

"Who are you?" Uncle Henry demanded.

The woman just spit at his feet.

"That's Gina Giovanni, my sister-in-law," Muriel said.

"Sister-in-law, bah! You are no longer a member of the family. You betrayed all of us! At least we knew your cousin and her intended were our enemies, but you were even worse!" She glared at Muriel with a hatred that oozed from every pore. "My father cursed when he found out Miss Garcia still lived. He was going to make sure all of you were dead tonight!"

Addy watched all this as she called the desk to report the attack. Hotel security came up and took the woman away. All of them knew the police would be back to ask questions soon.

Zeke went over to Muriel. "How's your arm?"

She looked at him a little hesitantly. "It's a small cut. I don't think I'll have to go to the doctor with it."

He put his hand on her cheek. "Thank you for warning us."

Muriel was quiet for a moment. "I do care about both you and Addy very much. I want to make up for any hurt I've caused."

Zeke gave Addy a small smile, then turned back to Muriel. "Then take care of yourself. I wouldn't want anything to happen to Addy's matron of honor."

Addy felt a warm glow as Zeke came over and put his arm around her shoulders. "Addy, let's sit on the sill and wait for the police."

She put her head on his shoulder and felt that old feeling again. Just being with him made all the bad things go away.

Before long, the police had returned and the family had all given their statements.

"Inspector Cannon," Uncle Henry said, "how much longer should we expect things like this to happen?"

The inspector rubbed his chin. "Usually the women of the family don't do this sort of thing. I think this was a one-time attack."

"But you can't guarantee that, can you?"

He was silent for a moment. "We'll have to watch the rest of the Giovannis very carefully, and we'll step up keeping an eye on your house. I'm sorry, but that's all I can do. If nothing else happens in the next month, you should consider yourself safe. For now, I have to go back to the station, but I asked hotel security to keep a monitor on this floor."

Uncle Henry nodded.

Addy leaned against Zeke's chest as he put his arms around her. Now she worried about the rest of them. Would they ever be safe?

Chapter 11

Two days later, Addy stood on the lawn in front of Uncle Henry's house with the rest of the family. Her uncle and her grandfather were inspecting the repairs after the attack. The large dining room window had been replaced, as had the wood siding damaged by the machine gun bullets.

Inside the house, they still had problems.

Aunt Jen had sobbed as she inspected the dining room. The table and chairs were in splinters, and the glass doors on the china cabinet had been shot out. "Well, I'm glad I moved the dishes out of the room." She sniffed.

Grandma was checking the walls. "We can paper over the holes, and you can get a new dining room set. Just be happy we weren't here."

Aunt Jen nodded. "I am."

After the first night in the hotel, Zeke had gone back to his apartment. There didn't seem to be any more attacks after Joe's daughter had tried to kill them.

Addy called Mrs. Daily and gave her the necessary two-week notice that she would be leaving her little house. She couldn't bring herself to live alone again just yet. She was constantly looking over her shoulder, anticipating another attack. Until Addy was married, she would be living at home in her old room with Muriel.

Under Aunt Jen's and Grandma's care, Addy was able to recover her strength and health. Zeke took her over to the hospital, after the end of the three weeks, for the doctor to see how her nose had healed.

She sat on the examining table, deep breathing while he cut and pulled off the gauze. It was an immense relief to get the prop removed from her nose. There was a soreness where it had been all that time, but she could breathe more easily. Dr. Richards looked at her critically. "Well, the cartilage knitted together, but you will always have a bump midway down your nose." He handed her a mirror.

Addy gazed at what had been a straight, shapely nose. She knew she was making more of this than she should, but a tear made its way down her cheek. A lot of small scars and now a bent nose. She'd never work in motion pictures again.

The doctor watched her carefully. "The scars will fade in time, and the swelling on your nose will go down, as well."

"Thank you for your help. I just have to get used to this."

When Dr. Richards got up and called Zeke to come in, Addy put her hands over her face.

"Addy, let me see your face." Zeke gently removed her hands and held them tight. "It's not so bad, sweetheart. You're still beautiful."

"No studio will want to film me. I'm ruined." And a rush of tears ran down her face.

Zeke pulled her up and took her in his arms. "There's still theater, remember. You will be our A-one star on the stage."

Dr. Richards opened the door. "When you're ready, you can go, Miss Garcia. Just check out at the desk."

She smiled. "Thank you, Doctor." But it was Zeke she was most grateful to. *What would I do without Zeke. My rock, my love.*

On the way to Uncle Henry's house, Zeke took out a letter and handed it to her. "I received this from Josh this morning. He's fixing up the apartment in the back of the theater for us, and he's living in a room upstairs. He said there's a lot to do on the building, but we should be able to open in a year, if not sooner. There seem to be plenty of jobs up there, so we can earn money while we work on the theater."

Addy finished reading. "Josh is a dear to fix the place for us. Be sure to thank him when you write back." She put the letter back in the envelope and sighed. "I want to thank you for changing your mind about Muriel. My heart was sick when I thought I would die and your last memory of me would be that argument."

Zeke was silent for a moment. "I thought the same thing when I was looking for you. I couldn't bear it that we had quarreled and not yet made up. We started out from your uncle's house at dawn..."

"Was that after they found Clara?"

"Yes, one of the officers spotted the body in the ditch while we were still at the house. After that, I was so very afraid of what they would do to you." He choked up a little, and then went on to tell Addy how they'd found her. "I told Muriel then that I was grateful she was able to give the search team a lead, and she said she could never forgive herself if you died because of her. Then when she saved us from her sister-in-law, I knew it really was time to forgive her."

Addy was crying. "Thank you," was all she could say, against the rough fabric of his coat sleeve.

Zeke stayed to dinner with Addy's family that night and told them of their plan to go to Alaska. "We can't take the constant feeling that someone might still be out there wanting us dead. I think it would be better if Addy and I start a new life in a new place."

The family was quiet until Aunt Jen spoke up. "Of course, we understand your reason, but I hate to think of you two so far away from us."

"I agree," Uncle Henry put in. "Your presence will be missed."

"That doesn't mean we can't come down to visit," Zeke added. "Or you can come up to visit us."

"Let's just enjoy the time we're together," said Grandma. "Zeke and Addy deserve happiness, after the trials they've been through."

Everyone nodded.

Addy had promised her friends Anne and Roxie to meet them for lunch the next day. With Zeke's permission, she told them of their plans.

"Oh, Addy, how exciting!" said Roxie. "But do they even have electricity up there?"

Addy nodded. "They've had it since 1914. Josh says the theater should be ready to open in a year's time. We'll have motion pictures, plays and vaudeville. What was the old bar, we'll turn into a dining room."

Anne sighed. "Keep in touch. I hate to see the three of us get broken up, but after what you and Zeke have been through, I understand you wanting to leave here."

"I can't stand not being able to walk down a street without looking behind me. I never know if someone is waiting to kill me. I can't live like this anymore."

Though their conversation went on to other topics, the sadness in the air because of their separation lingered. Part of Addy wished she didn't have to leave her friends and loved ones, but she didn't want to give up safety and peace of mind, either.

The weeks passed all too quickly. Preparations were almost complete when Addy's uncle took her aside one night.

"Adeline, come out with me on the porch," Uncle Henry said. He moved to the front door and opened it. The night was cool, and Addy sat on the swing while her uncle leaned against the railing. He had a cigar in hand and puffed on it. "There are a few things I must say to you before you leave us. I know you think of me as very strict, but that is the only way I know. I do care for you like a daughter."

"Uncle, I—"

"Wait. Listen to what I have to say. I know that I always told you that you were too plain. That problem with your school beau's family rejecting you as a wife for him made me realize that you would come up against prejudice, simply because you looked so much like your father's family. I thought telling you that you were plain would harden you a bit, so you could handle it when you were rejected because of your background. I think you're beautiful, but I see you through biased eyes." He paused for a minute, looking out at the stars. "I'm sorry if it was the wrong thing to do."

She swallowed a lump in her throat, not knowing what to make of what her uncle said. "It was harsh, but I do see why you did it."

"Also, I regret the judgment on your father because he was Mexican. With what you told me from your vision, he was the one who put my mind at ease about Hubert. Now, come back inside—I want to give you something." At the desk in the parlor, he opened the bottom drawer and took out a brown envelope, its flap fastened with string looped between two cardboard buttons.

Uncle Henry stood a moment with the envelope in his hand, gazing at it almost as though he were saying goodbye to it, and then he handed it to Addy, who took it from him and opened it. She caught her breath and her eyes misted. She was holding the family picture her mother had sent the Christmas before the earthquake. They had gone to a formal photographer because her mother insisted. Her father sat on a fancy wooden chair in the center, holding Joey on his lap. Addy stood by the arm of the chair and her mother was next to her. A fancy backdrop of a classic garden with ivy walls was behind them. She remembered the crisp linen dress she wore, with the lace around the collar, and the big white bow in her hair. Her mother had worked all morning on Addy's long curls of hair. This was the first brand-new dress she had ever known, and she had felt like a fairy tale princess. They didn't have much money, but her mother thought this would be an important memory in the future. None of them had realized what a horrible change would come only a few months later. Now she was glad her mother had argued for the expense.

Her uncle, behind her, laid his hand on her shoulder. "Your mother sent this to us for Christmas in ought-five." He was silent for a moment. "We took this with us when we went up to San Francisco to see if any of you were alive. I want you to have it."

"All the pictures we had were lost. Oh, thank you, Uncle." She started to cry and felt his arm go around her shoulders. She seemed closer to him than she'd ever been before in her life.

****

The night before the wedding found Addy and Muriel engaged in last-minute fixing and packing. The round swell of Muriel's sixth month was a source of joy and pain to her.

"Addy, what on earth am I going to tell this child if it asks about its father? I loved Tony, but he was a criminal." She looked up from sewing the sequins on Addy's veil.

Addy stopped her packing and sat down by Muriel. "Do what your heart tells you. He was good to you, he loved you, and he would have loved this child. Tell the good things about him, the things you loved in him. Yes, he was raised in the ways of his family—I'm sure that seemed normal to him—but that is not the most important thing about him. His child doesn't need to be affected by that."

Muriel got a faraway look in her eyes. "Remember when we were children, we pledged to each other that when we both got married we would live next door to each other forever? How I wish that could happen. Now I think I'll never see you again." There were tears on her cheeks.

Addy put her arms around Muriel. "Don't say that. There's a good chance we may be able to come back someday. I don't feel safe here anymore, and that's no way to start a marriage—afraid you might get killed any minute."

"And I feel I'm to blame for that, too." Muriel sniffed.

"Please don't dwell on that. I didn't have to get involved in the intrigue, but I felt someone had to. I couldn't let poor Mr. Leman down, and somehow I knew many more would be killed if nobody stopped the Giovannis."

Muriel kissed Addy's cheek. "Thank you for still loving me." The girls sat there silently for a few moments, each contemplating her own dreams. Then they went back to what they were doing, until it was time for bed.

****

Zeke closed his suitcase and turned to Nathan, who stood by the bedroom door. "Thank you for getting the rest of the crates shipped off to Josh. All we have to take is our clothes."

"Sure thing, pal. I'm going to miss you. We practically grew up together. I wish you could have held on long enough to be my best man."

Zeke ran his hand through his hair. "You know I wanted to, but it's too dangerous for Addy and me. Thank you for being mine."

They had moved to the sitting room, where Zeke

sat on the overstuffed chair. "You know, you and Babs could come up and help get the theater going. She and Addy are talented performers."

"I'll talk to her about it. It'll be a while before we have the funds to move up there."

Zeke smiled. "Yes, but if we can look forward to it, that's great. It would be easier to have people we know there. I think I'm already getting a little homesick."

Nathan clapped him on the shoulder. "That's just nerves, buddy. You're getting your ball and chain a little earlier than I am."

"There was never a more willing prisoner." Zeke laughed along with Nathan. Deep down, he prayed they would be able to get out of Los Angeles alive.

****

Addy barely slept that night. The excitement over her wedding, and the sadness she felt over leaving everything she knew behind, kept marching through her head. She and Zeke were going to get on a train on Monday and go off into the sunset. Just like a motion picture ending. Finally, she was able to get a few winks of sleep in before Muriel shook her.

Aunt Jen brought a breakfast tray up, because it was a tradition in the family, on a wedding day, so the bride wouldn't be seen downstairs until the ceremony. If that ceremony was to be in a church, the bride would be hustled to the dressing room there early in the morning. Addy was thankful she'd chosen to stay home.

She looked at the clock. Eight a.m. Addy sighed. She still had hours left until the one o'clock ceremony.

Setting the tray on the bed before her, Aunt Jen admonished, "Eat up. You won't have any more until this afternoon."

Addy inhaled the fragrance of warm maple syrup, and her stomach growled. "Thank you, Aunt

Jen."

Her aunt and Muriel went down to breakfast with the family and left her with her thoughts. She looked at her tray. There was a huge stack of Grandma's cakes, with bacon rashers on the side, a half of grapefruit, two poached eggs and a cup of coffee. She dug into it like a prisoner going for her last meal. The thought of the analogy made her laugh.

After she finished eating, Addy drew a bath for herself. She borrowed some of her aunt's lavender bath salts and soaked in the fragrant water. Her body, so bruised and battered such a short time ago, felt healthy again. *I'm not going to think any bad thoughts today. This is one of my best days.*

She rose out of the tub and wrapped herself in the towel she'd laid on the nearby stool. After drying herself off, she put the towel turban style around her hair. The water gurgled down the drain as she slipped into her robe and went back to her room, where Muriel and Aunt Jen waited to help her get dressed.

"Here, I've brought some oil so your skin won't dry out." Aunt Jen set the bottle on the vanity.

Addy laughed. "I really feel like a pampered princess today. I haven't had such a leisurely bath for a long time." She opened the bottle and rubbed some of the liquid on her arms and legs.

Muriel put on her new blue drop-waist dress with the blue silk rose on the right-hand side of the sash. Addy's dress was the same, except it was white. "My stomach shows too much." Muriel turned in front of the mirror.

Addy smiled. "You look beautiful like that, dear. Motherhood becomes you."

Muriel put her hand on her belly. "It's wonderful to feel the baby move." And then her arms were around Addy. "It's too bad you won't be here when it's born. I'll miss you so."

"We all will," said Aunt Jen sadly.

Addy waved off the tears. "I refuse to be sad today." She put on her underwear, including the long silk stockings secured with garters, and pulled her slip over her head before she could resist temptation no longer. She went to the window facing the backyard and looked out from behind the lace curtain. Zeke sat on one of the wooden folding chairs down there, in a deep discussion with Nathan. Her love for Zeke filled her up to the brim and her eyes misted over. He was the reason for her happiness and this day. She couldn't even think about what it would be like without him. She sighed contentedly. *In less than an hour, I'll be Mrs. Ezekiel Shafer.*

"Addy." She felt Aunt Jen's hand on her shoulder. "You'd better get dressed. He'll still be there."

Addy's face warmed. "I'm sorry." Then she laughed. "I just love him so much."

Aunt Jen and Muriel dusted her with talc and her aunt brushed her hair.

"You know, I do like your hair this length," Aunt Jen remarked. "It curls so beautifully, and it takes only seconds to do. I may get mine cut."

Muriel giggled. "I can picture Father's face if you do. I don't think he'd like it a bit."

Addy grew sober. "More than ever, I wish my mother could be here."

Aunt Jen's hand dropped onto Addy's shoulder. "Abigail would be in her element here. She always loved special occasions, and I know she would fuss over every detail. When we were young ladies, we celebrated many times with our friends. Abigail was only two years older than I, but she took charge of everything." She was quiet for a moment. "I still miss her."

Addy put her hand over her aunt's. "If Mother is

watching now I hope she likes the honor I gave her and Papa."

She smiled. "I'm sure she will."

They helped Addy with her dress and Muriel put the cap of the veil carefully over Addy's hair. The veil was two feet longer than Addy was tall, so she carried the excess over her arm. She slipped on her shoes and then sat so her aunt could apply a light glaze of rouge to Addy's cheeks and lips, just enough to add a bit of color. They were ready right on time, just as Uncle Henry called them from downstairs.

Addy was a shaking bundle of nerves on her way to the back door. The upright piano had been moved outside, and Grandma was playing it while the guests took their seats in the garden.

"Here are your gloves." Aunt Jen handed Addy her white kids.

"And your bouquet." Muriel gave her the fragrant orange blossoms.

Aunt Jen went outside first, as a signal that the ceremony was ready to begin. She sat on the third seat from the aisle. At Addy's request, the first two seats had been kept empty for her parents. There was a corsage on the first and a boutonnière on the other.

Muriel put on her wide-brimmed blue hat and picked up her nosegay from the kitchen table. When Grandma started playing the Bridal March, Muriel walked out the back door into the garden.

Grandpa smiled and offered Addy his arm. "You are beautiful today, Granddaughter. I'm proud you chose me to stand in for your father."

"You and Uncle Henry are as much my fathers, too." Addy pulled his arm, and he leaned down for her kiss on his cheek.

Uncle Henry held the door for them, then walked on Addy's left side to the makeshift altar by the rosebushes.

Addy saw a look of sheer joy in Zeke's eyes, and she couldn't look away. The lovelight seemed to radiate between them. Both of her escorts shook Zeke's hand, and then Grandpa planted Addy's hand firmly in Zeke's. Zeke kissed it as they turned to face the minister.

Muriel straightened Addy's veil, and it billowed in the gentle spring breeze. Throughout the ceremony, Addy couldn't take her eyes off Zeke, she loved him so much, and at the end, when the minister pronounced them man and wife, she melted into his loving kiss.

Grandpa stood up. "Now, let's go to the GAR Hall. There's a band to play for us and a banquet for everyone."

They decided to walk the three blocks to the hall. Addy smiled the whole way, hearing automobile horns honk at them and seeing people wave at the festive group. In addition to her family, there was Nathan and his Babs, a bubbly redhead. Anne and her husband, Ray, Roxie and her boyfriend, Dan, and Mrs. Hutton and her son, Richard, made the rest of the lively bunch.

I wonder what kind of band Grandpa hired? Well, I can put up with anything today. She smiled to herself. Then they walked in and she saw the sign announcing Paul Dime and the Ragtimes. She flew into her grandpa's arms. "Oh, thank you! The members of the GAR won't turn the cannon on you for this, will they?"

He laughed and kissed her forehead. "This will be our little secret."

The day's festivities proved to be bittersweet for Addy. It might be the last time for a long while that she would be with family and friends. Everyone put their wedding presents into the large steamer trunk that would be shipped to Alaska, while she made sure she wrote down everyone's addresses. And then it was time to say goodbye.

Nathan and Babs were the first to leave. Addy had found herself quite taken with Babs, who could sing and dance. "I'm sorry we can't stay for your wedding next month, but you know we'll be there in spirit." Addy hugged Babs and Nathan.

"I hope you give what we talked about some consideration." Zeke shook his old friend's hand and gave Babs a kiss.

"We sure will, pal." Nathan slapped Zeke's shoulder.

Babs hugged Addy. "Nothing but good luck for both of you." And then Nathan and Babs were gone.

Mrs. Hutton came up to the newly married couple. "I'm so happy for you both. You deserve all the happiness you can get. I'm sure going to miss you." She kissed Addy on the cheek and patted Zeke's shoulder.

"Keep in touch," Addy said. "I owe my life to you."

It was even more difficult to say goodbye to Anne and Roxie. She had known them less than a year, but they had a bond as tight as family. They huddled in a three-way hug and vowed to stay close forever.

Addy and Zeke stood there, watching their friends go, one by one, not knowing if they would ever see them again. He held her close and nuzzled her neck, which awakened every nerve in her body.

"Shall we go?" she said huskily.

"I want one last dance first," came a voice behind her.

She turned, and her grandpa stood there with his hand outstretched. "Of course," she said.

Her grandpa gave a signal to the band and they started playing "Sweet Adeline." She danced this special number with her grandpa holding her tight, and neither could stop the tears. She looked up at the aged face of her grandpa and realized that his history was in it: the horrors of the War Between the States when he was younger than she was now, the joy of his marriage to Grandma for over fifty years—and they still held hands; the sorrow of losing most of his children—three had died in childhood, a son died in the Spanish-American War, and her mother—Aunt Jen was the only one left.

Grandpa put his hand on Addy's cheek. "Thank you, Adeline. I missed this dance with your mother. I was honored to do this in place of your father. I hope in some way it makes up for the mistakes I made."

Addy gently put her hand over his and kissed it. "No one could be a better grandfather than you've been to me. Thank you."

Zeke came over to them just then, and Grandpa put his arm around Zeke's shoulders. "Take good care of my granddaughter, boy, or you'll have me to answer to."

Zeke smiled. "Yes, sir."

Then Uncle Henry arrived with Zeke's and Addy's suitcases. "I walked home to get the Packard and called for a taxi to take you to the hotel."

The rest of the family came to say their goodbyes. Grandma gave Addy and Zeke each a hug. "Can't even give you a good old-fashioned shivaree."

Addy felt puzzled. "What is that?"

Grandma laughed. "That's where we stand under your window all night and make noise."

Addy grinned. "That's a strange sort of custom. I'm glad it's out of fashion."

Zeke shook Uncle Henry's hand. "Thanks to all of you for everything."

Grandpa leaned over to Zeke. "Just make sure you're back at the house Monday morning to catch your train. Don't make me come looking for the both of you." He poked Zeke in the ribs and Zeke blushed.

When Aunt Jen announced that the taxi was

there, the new couple picked up their cases and headed for the door, the family close behind as far as the curb to see them off to the Biltmore Hotel, where the Honeymoon Suite was rented for two nights.

The Biltmore was one of the popular hotels in the Los Angeles area, and their clientele were some of the most important people to stay in the city. Its large triple towers of stone loomed several stories over its domain, and the lighted rooms gave a checkerboard effect against the dark sky.

Addy looked at Zeke as the taxi pulled up to the main doors. "Can we really afford a two-night stay here? We need all the money we have."

He cupped his hands on her face and gave her a kiss. "Sweetheart, this was a gift from your uncle."

She stared at him, amazed. "Why, that lovely man! I don't think I even know him anymore."

The taxi driver opened the door for them, and Addy saw their cases already sitting next to the auto. Zeke gave the man a tip and picked up their luggage. Together he and Addy went through the glass doors into the richly dark-paneled lobby with its elegant chandeliers. Everything was so polished that Addy could see herself in the wood and in the floor as though they were mirrors. She watched Zeke register them as Mr. and Mrs. Shafer, and a thrill went through her. She was now in truth a wife.

The desk clerk handed Zeke the key to their suite, called for a bellboy, and a young man in a crisp blue uniform with a pillbox hat picked up their cases and led them to an iron-gated elevator. Zeke nuzzled her neck on the way up and she felt a tingling through her body, but she pointed to the bellboy and mouthed, "Not yet." Zeke just gave her a leer.

When the iron gate on the elevator opened, the bellboy led them to Suite Two. He opened the door for them, and Addy gasped as she walked through it.

The suite was huge, and she floated on thick pile carpeting. The walls and the furnishings were Wedgwood blue, trimmed in white. In one corner was a couch with a coffee table in front of it, and in the other, a table with two chairs. In the center of the back wall, and up two steps, was the largest bed she'd ever seen. It had draped net curtains attached to the wall above the headboard, just like the ones she'd seen in pictures of castles in Europe. And they had their own bathroom!

Zeke tipped the bellboy, after he'd finished setting up the cases on the stands next to the wardrobes, and closed the door behind the young man, turning toward Addy as he did so. She had gone to the window next to the couch and had just opened it for some fresh air when there was a loud bang from the street. She jumped and grabbed the arm of the couch, crying out.

Zeke flew to her. He held her tight as she started to weep. "Addy, that was just an auto backfiring."

She trembled. "I can't help it. Every night, I dream that someone is trying to kill me."

He rocked her back and forth in almost a dance-like move. "I'm with you now, my love. We'll face anything together." He cupped her face and kissed her tears away.

That gentle move stirred her. Slowly, the fear was replaced by her desire for this man. She kissed him passionately and felt him respond warmly. He put his arms around her and unbuttoned the back of her dress, and the fire in her awoke at the touch of his fingers on her back. He slid the dress off her arms and down to the floor, kissing down her neck. Addy trembled with the lightning streaks going through her. The world contained only the two of them.

Zeke had never looked more handsome.

Somehow, as his passion radiated, he became her fantasy hero.

They shed their clothing naturally, as if coming out of a cocoon in transformation. At the foot of the bed, Addy was caught up in his embrace and she felt the warm skin of his back. A hot hardness was forming between them, but he was in no hurry.

"Since we've done this before, love, we can take it slow," Zeke said, lifting her up onto the bed. He lay down beside her, and she gave a long intake of breath as he traced his fingers over her hard nipples. Then he began kissing her and gently nipping at her breasts.

Addy felt spasm after spasm going through her body, and the tingling drove her mad. She drew him up for a kiss and ran her fingers down his chest to his stomach. She smiled as she felt a deep tremor go through him. "What's good for the goose, you know," she teased.

They spent time exploring each other and finding new pleasures and sensations along the way. There was a satiny slick of sweat on their bodies and their breath was coming in gasps.

Zeke moved over her, and Addy instinctively opened for him. She was in a haze of passion and abandon that she wanted never to come out of. She felt the long length of him enter her and they both moaned together. They traveled up that high plateau in a building frenzy. For Addy, it had never been this intense before, and when the release came, she felt like every part of her being was flying apart in sparkling ecstasy. They lay together until their breathing became normal again, her legs around him and his head on her breast.

He raised up a little and she put her legs on the bed. Zeke stroked her hair from her face. "I must be getting heavy."

She shook her head. "I don't want you to ever

move."

He smiled and pulled out of her. "That would be awkward." He turned out the lights in the room and crawled back into bed, molding his naked body next to her. The intimate warmth of his skin comforted her more than anything she'd ever known.

In the morning, Addy experienced unbelievable joy at waking up with Zeke beside her. The sunrays were coming in through the window, casting patterns on the bed as the curtains moved with the breeze. Since Zeke had put up the Do Not Disturb sign on the room door, they were able to spend the time before lunch consummating their marriage again.

Finally, their empty stomachs got the better of them, so they dressed and went downstairs. The restaurant was buzzing with the Sunday lunch crowd, and they got a table near the wall, for which Addy was grateful. Since all of this with the mob, she felt uncomfortable with her back to any door. She needed to see anyone who came in.

Zeke looked at her over the menu. "What would you like to eat, sweetheart? Their special is Eggs Benedict with Hollandaise Sauce and fruit."

"That sounds good. We can get that with coffee."

Zeke gave the order to the waiter when he came to them. "Is something wrong?" He looked at Addy with concern after the waiter left.

"I guess I'm still nervous, being out in public like this. I keep seeing enemies around corners. I'll be glad when we go tomorrow. Maybe I can relax then." She was twisting her napkin into a knot.

Zeke smiled. "They probably don't even know where we are, and it's a big city. I wouldn't worry." He reached out and kissed her hand.

She set the abused piece of linen on her lap and sighed. "You're right. I'm not going to think about that now. But I do feel strange not going to church this morning."

Zeke gave her a wide grin. "Well, we had a religious ceremony yesterday and, if I do say so myself, we praised the Lord in our own way this morning."

She felt her cheeks burn and threw her spoon at him just as their order came.

They attended the Sunday afternoon tea dance and had dinner under the stars. "This must be what it feels like to be rich," Addy said. "I guess if things had gone well at the studio, I might have been."

Zeke took her hand. "I don't know if we'll ever be rich, but I do know that whatever happens, we can face anything together."

Her love for this man knew no bounds. She felt strength in what he said, and she wasn't afraid of anything anymore.

They had brought Addy's alarm clock with them to the hotel, and it went off at eight o'clock Monday morning. She was sad, because this was her last day in the city that had been her home for fifteen years. Her life was full of big and uncertain steps, but everything had turned out so far. She smiled. *I'm with Zeke now, and we'll take care of each other.*

They had a quick breakfast in the restaurant and then went out into the bustling Monday morning city to wait for their taxi. The warm sun greeted them and the smell of exhaust from countless autos going by filled their senses. After being in an ivory tower for a couple of days, it was time to come back to earth.

Their taxi took them back to her uncle's house, where they were warmly greeted by the whole family. Before long, Zeke took James aside and walked him over to where Zeke's beloved Model T was parked.

As the rest of the family watched, Zeke put his arm across James' shoulders. "I can't take the auto with me, and I wondered if you would like to have it. I'm sure your father would be willing to teach you how to drive it."

James stood there, mouth agape. He looked back at his father. "May I?"

Uncle Henry cleared his throat. "I think you're coming of age, but you must take care of it."

Zeke gave James' back a slap. "She's all yours."

James shook his hand. "Thank you. This means a lot to me." And he immediately began inspection of his new auto.

Addy was moved that Zeke treated her family so well. Zeke's father was such a cruel man; he didn't realize what a wonderful son he had. Now he'd also chased off Zeke's brother, to Alaska. *I hope Josh is like Zeke.*

The Packard held their trunks. There was just room in the auto for four people, so Uncle Henry and Grandpa were going to the station with the young couple, to help unload the trunks and luggage.

"I guess we'll have to say our goodbyes here." Aunt Jen sniffed.

Addy and Zeke in turn hugged Aunt Jen and Grandma. Grandma smoothed the windblown hair from Addy's face. "I always thought you were a beautiful girl. You two take care of yourselves and write." There were tears in Grandma's eyes.

The boys jumped around Zeke, and Addy picked up Maggie. Zeke put his arms around both boys' shoulders and gave Maggie a kiss on the cheek. "All of you be good, you hear?" Zeke tousled Buster's hair.

"Are you coming back, ever?" Maggie asked, clutching her doll.

"We'll be back, you'll see." Addy gave her a squeeze and hoped they could. *I miss them already.* She put Maggie down and went to say goodbye to James, who was on his way back over from his auto.

Muriel stood by the Packard, crying. The girls hugged each other tight. "You're the hardest to leave." Addy drew back and held Muriel by the shoulders. "You have been my dear sister for a long time. Remember to write to me. And be sure to let me know when the little one is born."

When Zeke hugged Muriel, she whispered in his ear, "Thank you for forgiving me. Take care of Addy and yourself."

He touched her cheek. "You take care, too."

Addy got into the auto, not wanting to let go of their hands. These people had been so dear to her, she felt her insides were being ripped out. She trembled in Zeke's arms as they went down the street, still waving to the family she could barely see through the tears in her eyes.

Soon they were at the station, where Uncle Henry pulled up to the entrance. One of the waiting redcaps wheeled a metal cart over and put the trunks and suitcases on it, with the men's help. They all went inside and Zeke gave the tickets to the balding agent behind the counter. The round little man came out from behind his counter and tagged their luggage for Seattle, and then Zeke tipped the redcap and the man took the cart out the doors to the train.

The small party went out the passenger gate to where the train waited, its engine huffing and snorting like an impatient stallion. The smell of burning coal and sweat filled the area. A conductor came bustling along, looked at their tickets, and directed them to their car.

Uncle Henry cleared his throat, looking uncomfortable. "Adeline, Zeke, goodbye. I wish you both all the best." He stiffly leaned in and kissed Addy on the cheek, then shook Zeke's hand.

Addy stood there for a moment, then with a cry she threw her arms around her uncle and gave him a resounding kiss, much to his dismay.

Grandpa was less formal. He gave both of them a hug. "Addy, I'm so sorry you have to leave us. Don't forget to write."

She hugged him back. "I'll write as much as I can. I love you."

He made a swipe over his eyes and nose with his handkerchief and he turned to Zeke. "Take good care of her, son."

"I will, sir. I promise." Zeke gripped Grandpa's shoulder as they shook hands once again.

The noise from the engine got louder and the conductor shouted, "All aboard!"

Addy and Zeke climbed up the steps and the conductor shut the half-door. Uncle Henry pulled a white envelope out of his coat. "Here, take this!"

Zeke leaned down and took it from him, just as the engine started tugging on the train cars. "Mr. Carter, you didn't have to do this!"

"It's payment for your auto!"

The noise from the moving train drowned out anything further that Uncle Henry said. They both waved to Uncle Henry and Grandpa as the mighty engine shook and groaned, gathering speed.

When the station was so small they could no longer see anything of the people left behind, Addy and Zeke found their seats in the car. Zeke opened the envelope and gasped.

"What's wrong?" Addy asked. Zeke handed her the envelope. There were ten crisp one-hundred-dollar bills.

She gave the envelope back, and he put it in his inside coat pocket. "That auto wasn't worth that much new."

Addy shook her head. "Uncle Henry must have known…"

Zeke put his arm around her shoulders. She looked at him, and he nodded.

What a way to be generous without it seeming like charity.

They both watched the moving scenery as they took the first small step to the rest of their lives.

About the author...

Ilona Fridl was born in West Hollywood, California, where she developed an interest in the movie industry. *Silver Screen Heroes* came to be from her love of silent movies. When she was in her twenties, she moved to Wisconsin, where she lives now.

She always had a love of writing, but a hatred of typewriters, so she started writing when she got her first computer. She sold short stories to magazines, but always dreamed of selling a novel. She credits her family and friends as her biggest cheerleaders.

Other Vintage titles to enjoy...

BAD BETTIE by Layne Blacque: In 1948 Los Angeles, a handsome cop's world is turned upside down when his squad raids a nightclub and he rescues the sultry blues singer.

DON'T CALL ME DARLIN' by F. Cunningham: In Texas, 1957, Carole the librarian faces censorship. Will the County Judge who's dating her protect or accuse her?

SCHERESADE by Ronit Lèvy: Erika's life is full of promise with her new life in America. So why have nightmares returned? With a passionate young neurologist and an embittered Holocaust survivor, she follows the clues to unravel the mystery of her past and discover true love.

SHE'S ME by Mimi Barbour: A spoilt model pricks her finger on a rose thorn and is transported back to 1963 and into a chubby librarian's body. As "roomies" they learn a lot from each other and each finds the man of her dreams!

HE'S HER by Mimi Barbour: Same rosebush, different victims!

SOURDOUGH RED by Pinkie Paranya: At the end of the Klondike gold rush, Jen and her younger brother search for her twin, lost and threatened in Alaskan wilderness.

SHATTERED DREAMS by Margaret Tanner: Three World War I soldiers leave a shattering legacy as they pass through Lauren's life. Which is killed? Which one's child does she carry? Which one does she marry?

A TRAIN THROUGH TIME by Bess McBride: On a sleek modern train heading to Seattle, Ellie awakens in the midst of a Victorian-era re-enactment. The leader of the group, handsome, green-eyed Robert Chamberlain, finally convinces her the date is 1901...